Mattie

**Center Point
Large Print**

**This Large Print Book carries the
Seal of Approval of N.A.V.H.**

ॐ श्री गणेशाय नमः

Mattie

Judy Alter

Center Point Publishing

Thorndike, Maine

For my daughters, Megan and Jordan

Author's Note

Readers familiar with Nebraska history and the story of pioneer doctor Georgia Arbuckle-Fix will recognize some elements of her story in this novel. Dr. Arbuckle-Fix's life and dedication did indeed inspire me to explore the personality of a woman who stayed on the prairie when easier ways of life offered themselves, but Mattie Armstrong is wholly imaginary and is intended in no way to reflect particular actions or beliefs of Dr. Arbuckle-Fix. All other characters are purely imaginary, and any resemblance to real individuals, living or dead, is purely coincidental.

This Center Point Large Print edition
is published in the year 2002 by arrangement with
Ray Peeker Literary Agency.

The text of this Large Print edition is unabridged. In other aspects, this book may vary from the original edition. Printed in Thailand. Set in 16-point Times New Roman type by Bill Coskrey and Gary Socquet.

ISBN 1-58547-228-X

Library of Congress Cataloging-in-Publication Data.

Alter, Judy, 1938-
    Mattie / Judy Alter.--Center Point large print ed.
        p. cm.
    ISBN 1-58547-228-X (lib. bdg. : alk. paper)
    1. Women physicians--Fiction. 2. Nebraska--Fiction. 3. Large type books. I. Title.

PS3551.L765 M38 2002
813'.54--dc21

                                                                    2002024732

MY MOTHER was an unmarried mother, fallen woman, they called her back in Princeton, Missouri. They called her that and a lot worse names, most of which I didn't understand at the time, thank goodness. It wasn't just that Mama made one mistake—me—but I had a little brother, Will Henry, and neither of us had a father that we knew about. Will Henry was seven years younger than me, and you'd think I'd remember a man being around the house about that time to account for my brother's appearance, but I didn't. I used to wonder if Mama had somehow gotten caught in the great war just passed or if my father had fought in that war. For much of my growing-up years, Mama never told us if we had the same father or not. When either of us asked, Mama became flustered and impatient and usually just said, "I don't want to talk about it." There would be tears in her eyes that made me feel guilty and cruel, so I would abandon the subject.

But Mama's status caused both of us a lot of grief. I can still remember trips to the store for whatever small bit of staples Mama could afford. Other kids would tease, "Where's your father?" "Ain't you heard? She ain't got none." "You know what that makes her mama." I never did learn to ignore those taunts. I'd turn bright red and feel myself tense up as I headed for home instead of completing my errand. Sometimes Mama sent me to collect ironing. Taking in ironing was one way she made a little money for us, and I can still see her heating that sad iron over the stove, then struggling to press its weight down just right on some sheer and wonderful dress that belonged to a rich lady in town.

We lived in a two-room wooden shack, two rooms only because Mama hung a frayed blanket kind of in the middle to separate the cooking area from the sleeping area, and we three slept in the same bed, all the time until I left home at the age of fourteen. But that's getting ahead of my story.

Mama also took in sewing, and that's how I met the Canary family. One day I had to go with Mama to fit a dress on Mary Jane, the daughter, who was just about my age. Will Henry was a toddler then, and Mama left him with someone else; heaven only knows at this point who it might have been. But she dressed me up the best she could, even ironing my patched cotton dress, and taking great care with her own appearance, wearing a worn flannel dress in subdued gray. She had cleverly redone it to hide the worst spots and had even added a small white ruffle at the neck. If you didn't look too closely, she seemed as well dressed as the next grand lady.

"Least the patches are neat, Mattie. We want them to know that I sew a fine seam and that I have some taste in clothes, don't we?"

"Yes, Mama." I was always ready to agree with her when Mama was happy, like she was that day.

"La, child, this may be the beginning of a better life for us. The Canarys may take a liking to my work and maybe to you, and that would . . . well, it might make things easier." She laughed and tied her bonnet in a flourishing bow. Being less than ten, I believed Mama that it could all be true. I hadn't yet learned to be skeptical about Mama's new beginnings and search for my own.

We were both in high spirits as we set out. Mama was

still a beautiful woman, with pale brown hair and high cheekbones that maybe came from a not too remote Indian ancestor, but she was beginning already to look tired and worn out. I guess she must have been near thirty then. Still, tired or not, she drew looks as we walked down the dirt road and crossed the tracks to the "right" side of town.

On the other hand, I must have resembled my unknown father, or at the least that Indian ancestor, for I had none of Mama's prettiness. Tall for my age and skinny, I was an awkward, angular child with coarse dark hair which I wore pulled back so that it emphasized my high cheekbones and dark eyes. I used to dream about that unknown Indian in the family background and imagine that my Indian looks were mysterious.

Little kids didn't tease me when I was with Mama, but they were only slightly more discreet about their curiosity. I saw them pointing and staring, but there was no way I could run and hide, so I marched right along beside Mama, wishing the earth would open and swallow me.

"Isn't it a grand day, Mattie?"

"Yes, Mama, it sure is."

"What would you most like to do today?"

"Well, maybe mend that doll of mine . . ."

"Oh, fiddle, Mattie, let your imagination go. Choose something that we probably can't do."

I didn't hesitate at all. "I'd like to hitch up a horse and buggy and leave here . . . forever!"

Mama looked alarmed. "Mattie, why? This is our home now."

"Now? Wasn't it always?"

"Ever since you can remember, baby. But not always for me." She had a wistful look on her face, and I wondered again about Mama, where she had come from, who her own mama was and all those questions she never would answer. In a way, I was cut off from my own roots, for we had no relatives in Princeton, Missouri, not even any friends. Somewhere, I guessed, Mama had a family, but there was no contact between them, and if it bothered Mama, she rarely let on.

Because of the lilt in her voice and her genteel ways, I thought Mama came from the South, and that made me think of the war again. "Mama," I asked hesitantly, "where are . . . well, where did you come from?"

"Not here, child," she said, laughing, "certainly not here. But it was a long way away and a long time ago. I don't want to talk about it."

I could guess that Mama's family must have been pretty rich, because my own piddling amount of schooling by then had shown me that Mama had had a lot of education. She had one or two books—a copy of Shakespeare and some books of poems that she read aloud to me some-times. Mostly then, I didn't understand them, but I lis-tened because it seemed important to Mama and seemed somehow to calm and soothe her to read those big words about things that were beyond me. I was, you might say, a tractable child.

And somewhere Mama surely had learned to sew a fine seam. Her handwork was as neat and tiny as any I've seen to this day, and she had an eye for good lace, fine materials and well-cut dresses.

That, of course, was what had brought us out that day.

We arrived at the Canary home, which looked like a mansion to me, big and white and neat and clean, with blooming flowers in the front and a white picket fence, freshly painted all the way around. It was a two-story house with a gabled roof, lots of windows and even a balcony with a railing below and gingerbread decoration at the top. From outside, you could see heavy drapes pulled back for the day at every window.

"Golly gee Ned!" I exclaimed as we started up the brick walk to the dark wood front door with its huge brass knocker.

"Mattie, hush. Try to act like you go in houses every day that are just like this or maybe even grander."

"But I don't," I protested. "I've never seen anything like this." Of course, I had seen big houses, this very one, on my one or two ventures into the other side of town. But I didn't take exploratory trips very often because of all the teasing. And I never, ever thought I would go into a house like that. I remember today, clear as ever, that awestruck feeling, like my stomach was going to fall right down to my toes or else come up through my throat.

Mama acted like she'd been in houses like this all her life, and maybe she had. "Mrs. Canary? I've come to fit dresses for Mary Jane."

The Canary family may have felt they were the grandest folk in Princeton, but nobody there had a maid, and Mrs. Canary opened the door herself. Years later I wished, nastily, that the lady could have known how far from being grand she really was. Somehow, living in places like Missouri and Nebraska, some of us got notions of grandness that were out of kilter with the rest of the world. We accepted as grand things that were really mighty small, like fine furniture and big houses. Yet there's another kind of grand out here . . . But back to Mary Jane.

Mrs. Canary let us into a fair-sized entry hall, with a straight staircase carpeted in red. By peeking, I could see a parlor to one side of the hall and a dining room to the other. The furniture all looked new—velvet, I suppose—and everything was very neat, like nobody lived there. The tabletops were marble and bare, except for one gilt-framed photograph, presumably Mr. and Mrs. Canary as newlyweds. The sofas and chairs had wood trim and looked awfully uncomfortable. There were antimacassars everywhere and a flowered carpet on the floor. I thought a minute about our crowded shack, with Mama's sewing flung here and there, and my pitiful doll, with which I was now too big to play but which still sat on the bed each day. The Canary house made me cold inside.

Mary Jane hung over the railing at the top of the stairs, smiling like a cherub and wearing a blue satin dress with a huge white collar, her blond hair done in sausage curls. I was acutely aware of my patched cotton and tried to avoid looking at her, but as soon as Mama turned her back, Mary Jane stuck her tongue out at me. I would never have been brave enough to do that.

Mama saw the tongue, though, and reached out for my hand, holding it tight and smiling at Mrs. Canary, who led us upstairs to what she called the sewing room. I couldn't see that anybody did much sewing there, except maybe for the pincushion with a few needles in it and some spools of thread next to it.

Mama got right to work, measuring Mary Jane, who

stood like she thought she was some kind of princess, smiling down at her servants from the footstool on which she stood. I longed to kick the stool out from under her, but I pretended to busy myself looking out the window.

"I wouldn't want the dress too long, Mrs. . . ."

"Armstrong," Mama supplied calmly. "Of course not. A girl her age doesn't need a long dress, do you, Mary Jane?"

Mary Jane disagreed. "I won't dress like a baby. I need my dresses lots longer than this one you made me wear today."

"Mary Jane . . ."

"I will not!"

"Very well, dear. Mrs. Armstrong . . ." She hesitated again, as though it stuck in her throat to call Mama "Mrs." "We'll let her have her way."

I had a sneaking suspicion Mary Jane always got her way, and years later I remembered that scene and thought probably all her troubles started right there.

Mama finished measuring and helped Mary Jane down from the stool, then asked Mrs. Canary for the fabric she wanted used, and they busied themselves in a corner, looking at material and discussing the best way to cut it. Mary Jane sidled over to me to whisper, "I don't like having a bastard in my house."

Fortunately, I didn't know what the word meant, but I knew well enough that I had been insulted, and pretty royally, too. If it were today, there are lots of things I would have done, but I just stood there, studying the flower in the carpet at my toes, and muttered, "I don't like being here either." I really think Mary Jane considered kicking me—she turned to see if her mother was looking—but I moved away before she could turn back.

I told Mama what she'd said on the way home, and Mama was indignant. "Why, that awful girl! I'll never sew another stitch for her, not ever!"

"What does bastard mean, Mama?"

"Never you mind. It's just not a nice thing to call a person."

I had guessed by then. It had something to do with all those questions about where my father was, questions Mama wouldn't answer. And now she wouldn't explain the word to me.

Of course, Mama did sew for Mary Jane, made her a bunch of dresses, but it never turned out to be the new beginning she expected. The Canarys were miserly about paying and picky about the work she did, not that Mama's work was imperfect. But they would change their minds about a sleeve or a collar after Mama got a dress made, and then they'd claim it was all her fault. Mama never said anything, for we needed the little money they paid, but I felt sorry for her that the relationship didn't turn out like she envisioned. We were never invited to tea.

Things went on without any big change for quite a while after Mama started sewing for the Canarys. Will Henry grew bigger all the time, and pretty soon he had to endure school with me. Teasing never did seem to bother him like it did me, and I often thought he just wasn't bright enough to understand what other kids were saying. He seemed to take it all as a compliment.

"They like me at school, Mattie, they really do."

"That's good, Will Henry. How do you know?"

"Oh, they laugh with me all the time and call things to me."

I loved that little boy, and it made me sad to hear his story. At least, I guessed it was better if it didn't make him sad. But every time something like that happened, either to him or to me, I resolved that I would get even when I grew up. Course, I never did, but timid child that I was, revenge burned pure in my heart, and I hated.

I never did know if Mama got teased or anything because she never talked about it and always acted like she was the grandest lady in town. Some days Mama didn't feel too good and spent the day in bed. Those were the days I would run errands for people, fetching a bag of sugar from the store or taking a notice to the weekly journal office, all to earn a little money for us. Some days I had to skip school between trying to grab a few pennies and taking care of Mama, but I usually kept up in my schoolwork.

You see, Mama's next new beginning was a real bad one. By the time I was twelve or so, I was aware that she was tired a lot. She not only had to rest much of the time, but she looked tired, with great dark circles under her eyes. And her cheeks were the brightest pink I'd ever seen. Sometimes she'd be burning up with fever, and I'd sit and wipe her forehead with a wet cloth.

Once when I was sitting with her, I remember asking quite clearly, "Mama, tell me about my father."

She was tired and the question made her cross. "Why, Mattie? He's no one you'll ever know."

"But can't I know about him?"

"It wouldn't make you proud," she said, turning away

with a tear. To this day, I wonder if maybe she married a Northern sympathizer who moved her to Missouri, left to find his fortune out West and only came back long enough to father Will Henry. It was another of my fantasies, but a less appealing one than some others. I never asked Mama about it again.

I was getting a little tougher. I didn't run for home anymore when I was teased, and I didn't turn red in the face. But I hadn't yet gotten to the point of talking back, which, in my ignorance, I thought would be the pinnacle of growth. There was one boy, Tommy Hawkes, who was particularly mean and even threw a rotten apple at me one day. I used to think it would be the greatest satisfaction in the world to rub his face in the mud. I don't know, maybe it would have been, but I never did get the chance. And I was still vaguely ashamed of something about Mama that I didn't completely understand but that I knew had to do with me and Will Henry and that Northern soldier of my fantasy.

Mr. Reeves came into our lives about that time. He was a big, handsome, happy man, the first man I had ever had a chance to be around or know well, mind you, and it was a new experience for me. I was tongue-tied most of the time.

"Well, Mattie, what's new today?"

"Nothing."

"Come on, now. Did you go to school?"

"No, sir."

"Why not? Every girl your age needs to be in school." His huge hands clasped together, he announced this solemnly.

"Mama didn't feel too well, and I had to do some errands."

His face was real serious. "I know your mama's not feeling well. We're going to have to do something about that."

I don't know where Mama found Mr. Reeves. He was a drummer, as they called salesmen back then, and he sold all kinds of kitchen products to every small town in northern Missouri. But he had been a farmer and a river boatman and all kinds of things, and I began to suspect there wasn't anything he couldn't do. He was a big man, and from those days, I remember most his wide grin. When his sales brought him to Princeton, which seemed to be more and more often, he spent his time with us, and under his hand our little shack began to be sturdier and to look a little better. He nailed up loose boards, chinked in spaces where the cold wind whistled in winter, and nearly rebuilt the tiny front stoop, part of which was rotting away. He brought fabric for Mama to make new and bright curtains, and he filled our kitchen with more pots and pans than we could ever have food to fill.

But we ate better, too, and I began to feel Mr. Reeves must be rich. He brought all kinds of things we rarely if ever had, like beefsteak, which he must have bartered from someone, and fresh vegetables that he bought from someone else's garden, and lots of staples from the store—coffee and tea, which usually were too dear for Mama to buy, and pieces of horehound, which were an unheard-of luxury for Will Henry and me. Life was sweet, and for a while Mama began to get better.

And the brightest thing in my life was that I had a job. I

was to baby-sit every afternoon for the doctor and his wife, so the wife could have a rest. The Dinsmores lived in a comfortable, clean house, not as grand and frightening as the Canarys but more like what I thought a home should be—great, comfortable chairs, books to read and window seats where you could sit and watch the rain. They had only one child, three-year-old Sara, and she was nice as babies go, about as nice as Will Henry had been, so I had no trouble with her. She played, and I like as not spent the afternoon with only one eye on her and the other on a book I had found in the shelves. Dr. Dinsmore liked that, and next to Mr. Reeves, I thought he was the grandest man ever. The schoolmaster, a Mr. West, who rapped people's knuckles with a ruler and made us memorize long, dull passages of poetry, went rapidly downhill in my mind.

"Reading again, Mattie?" Dr. Dinsmore stood there, thumbs hooked under his suspenders, looking, I thought, very grand with his mustache and dark suit. He was not a tall man but so thin and wiry that he gave the impression of height and strength.

"Oh, yes, sir, but I was watching Sara real carefully."

"I'm sure you were. It's all right. I was just glad to see someone using the books. What are you reading?"

I showed him a copy of *Pamela* and asked if he knew the story.

"Yes, Mattie, I know the story." Was there laughter hidden in his voice? "I'm not sure your schoolmaster would approve of you reading novels, but you go right ahead." He walked over to the shelves and appeared to study for a moment, then said, "When you're through with that, you might want to try this." He handed me a copy of *Five Weeks in a Balloon*, by Jules Verne. "You're free to take it home as long as you're sure to return it."

I was astounded. Not only did he not think I was lazy for reading when I should have been playing with little Sara, but he gave me another book to read. And he would let me take it home.

I fairly flew home, ignoring the darkening and dingy streets of our part of Princeton. "Mama"—I burst in the door—"Dr. Dinsmore let me borrow a book." Caution came to me too late, and I hastened to add, "Of course, I won't read when you need me."

I never knew how Mama would react, though lately since Mr. Reeves had been around, she was more predictable. Still, there was always the chance she'd start on about how I could do more errands, try to earn another nickel or two or help out with Will Henry, who was really big enough to take care of himself, or so I thought. But she surprised me this time.

"Let me see it, Mattie. Oh, Jules Verne. I read that, a long time ago." She got that faraway look in her eyes. "It's a good book. You'll like it."

Later, when Mr. Reeves came, she said brightly, "Mattie's reading Jules Verne's book about his balloon trip. Dr. Dinsmore let her bring it home."

"Well, now, isn't that fine! Course, I don't know next to nothing about books, never could read much, and I ain't heard of that one, but I know it's important for a young person to get all the education they can. You go right on and read, Mattie, and I'll help your ma." He patted me on the head, and as I looked up, I saw Mama give him a long sideways look. I wasn't sure what it meant, but I read a little hurt and disappointment in her face.

Dr. Dinsmore continued to be my unofficial tutor. He and Mrs. Dinsmore got so they liked each other less and less; at least that's how it appeared to me. They never argued. I'd even heard Mama and Mr. Reeves raise their voices some, but the Dinsmores were always coldly polite. I knew he wasn't that way by nature, for he would get down on the floor and play with Sara, laughing and tossing her in the air until she giggled almost out of control. Whenever Mrs. Dinsmore saw this happen, she'd say, "Arthur, you'll damage the child." And he'd say, "Stuff and nonsense. Little roughhousing never hurt anyone."

Mrs. Dinsmore was blond and pretty like Mama, only her eyes were kind of an ice-cold blue, and her lips were tight, even when they smiled. She never had the laughter that sometimes welled up from Mama, and she looked worse in her fine clothes than Mama did in her patched and worn dresses.

Big as I was then, almost thirteen years old, I was only beginning to know the facts of life, as they are called. I had an inkling, though, that it took a great liking, even love, between two people to make a baby. I wasn't really sure about love—heaven knows, have any of us ever learned?—and I wondered a lot about that mysterious man Mama liked or loved well enough to have two babies with, but I also wondered about the Dinsmores. They didn't seem to like each other well enough to make a baby.

Mrs. Dinsmore was nice to me, though not as friendly

as he was, and I sensed she didn't approve of my reading program. She'd say, "Reading again, Mattie? Don't ruin your eyes with all that study," or "Why don't you take Sara outside? Too much indoors is never good for young-sters, even as big as you are." But she continued to pay me regularly, and sometimes they asked me to stay to supper, which was a treat, because there was much more food and better kinds of it than Mama could afford, less greens and cornbread and red beans and more meat and potatoes. I ate heartily on those nights.

"Mattie, child, are you hungry?"

"Not really," I would lie. I didn't want to say that I was kind of storing up, like a squirrel putting away nuts for the winter. "It's just that it tastes so good."

"Well, here, have another helping of meat loaf."

And I would eat away. It's a wonder I didn't get fat as a piglet in those days, but I suspect all that food made up for what had been a sparseness in my diet. Lots of times, I'd sneak extra pieces of meat in my napkin to take home to Will Henry, especially during the times Mr. Reeves was out of town and there was less food on our table. I suspect the Dinsmores would gladly have given me food for Will Henry, but I was too proud to ask.

I overheard them talking one night after I had stayed for supper and, as a way of thanks, had volunteered to bathe Sara and get her ready for bed. She was running around her room, stitch-stark naked, giggling up a storm, and I stepped out to get a towel to wrap her in. They were at the foot of the stairs, and I could hear them talk without having to go anywhere nearer the banister.

"I suppose she doesn't eat right at home," Mrs. Dinsmore said in that slightly disapproving tone.

"Probably not. It's a marvelous thing if we can feed both her body and her mind."

"We're not running a charity house, you know."

"Come now, Emma, that child doesn't take one thing from us. She gives us laughter and love for Sara, which the child sorely needs, and she brings me happiness." It was one of the few times I heard him criticize his wife, even obliquely.

There was no answer from Mrs. Dinsmore, and I didn't know enough to realize how significant that was. Poor woman. I never could figure out why she was so stiff and cool and how Dr. Dinsmore ended up with her.

But the fact that they had such an armed truce gave him lots of extra time to spend with Sara, and he spent some of it with me. We were both glad for his company, even though he seemed preoccupied a lot of the time. Dr. Dinsmore had unusual ideas for a physician, even back in those days when medicine wasn't regulated much. He hadn't gone to medical school, of course—few men did, and medical schools were so unregulated that you might learn more harmful things there than good. He had simply read medicine by following an old country physician around somewhere in northeast Missouri. There was a doctor over there in a small town named Kirksville who had announced that he had a new approach to medicine. Name was Still, and it seemed that he felt medical practice as he knew it wasn't helping people; matter of fact, he thought it killed two of his children. So he went about it in a new way, saying that the body was naturally healthy and the physician's job was to aid that process, not hinder it. One thing he advocated was very little medicine. Well, Dr. Dinsmore believed in that, and he'd sit and talk to me about it at night. Of course, at that age I didn't understand much, but I was flattered he wanted to talk, and I listened.

"God wouldn't have invented a faulty machine, Mattie. We were meant to be healthy and not to be taking a draught to sleep and another to straighten our bowels and another to ward off colds. We need to get all that out of our systems and keep our bodies in good shape, like good machines."

I didn't know much about machinery, so the comparison was a little odd to me, but I went along with Dr. Dinsmore's idea that we should keep our bodies healthy. Of course, all the walking I did back and forth to the Dinsmores', to school and on Mama's errands kept me pretty well exercised. But I thought about Mama, cooped up in that little shack all day.

By that time, Mama's health was really poor again. The last time she had gone to the store herself, instead of sending me, she had come home exhausted, out of breath and nearly faint. Seems she had only gone because I was at Dinsmore's, and my heart lurched in fear at the possibility that I would have to quit Dinsmore's and stay home to be more help to Mama.

"Mama, I would have gone to the store for you."

"You weren't here." She sounded a little like a spoiled child.

"But I'd have come back. You mustn't tire yourself out."

"I'll just rest awhile and you fix the supper, Mattie.

Then I'll be all right. I don't know what's the matter with me."

I didn't know either, but I did know that her cheeks were feverish red again, her skin pale, and pretty often she had a bad cough. I guess Mr. Reeves knew only too well what was wrong, because he made some startling announcements the next time he visited.

He arrived late one night, after Will Henry and I were asleep, and we didn't see him till we sat sleepily at the breakfast table, with Mama stirring a big pot of oatmeal with much more vigor than usual.

"Your ma and I are going to get married," he announced. "Today."

I looked quick at Mama, but she was still busy with the oatmeal, and I couldn't tell if she was happy about this or not. After a minute's thought, I decided I was happy. It would, I thought, make life easier for her, and that in turn would make things easier for me. I guess kids always have a way of relating everything to themselves. I should have known better, for his next words tore my world apart.

"We'll all be leaving for the West soon as we can get going. I used to farm once back a long time ago, and I'm gonna do it again, because your mama's got to get out of this Missouri climate before it kills her."

Mama stirred harder, and I bit my lip. Move? Not that I was so fond of Princeton—there was a time when my dream was to leave—but now I had the Dinsmores, and I didn't want to leave them and all the opportunity they represented to me. Will Henry, meanwhile, was jumping with joy, and I could have crowned him.

22

"West!" he shouted. "Where West? Will there be Indians? Cowboys?"

"Whoa," Mr. Reeves laughed. "We'll go someplace civilized, or at least as close as we can get."

I suppose Mama had the same vision of a white cottage with a picket fence and a great sweeping field of wheat or corn that I did. It turned out things were to be very different, and Mama might as well have stayed in Princeton, but none of us knew that. Mr. Reeves loved her, he really did, and he was doing what he thought was best. He really wanted to settle Mama in a comfortable home instead of a shack and give her the kind of life she apparently had known as a child. I think he thought he could restore her health by improving her life, but he was too late. Who knows? Maybe if he had come earlier, she never would have gotten sick.

Meanwhile, I was fighting my conscience. If it was good for Mama, I should be glad to go, but I was feeling mighty selfish, wanting to stay in Princeton so I could read the rest of the books in Dr. Dinsmore's library. I suspected that we would leave pretty quickly—and I was right—and I never could read fast enough to make any progress at all.

Will Henry and I went to school, with him talking nonstop about our big move and telling every kid in the schoolyard. They all snickered and said things like, "He's gonna marry your mother?" in incredulous tones. I could have kicked Will Henry but I kept my silence, lost in my own problems. That afternoon I was slow walking to the Dinsmores and late getting there.

"Mattie, whatever is the matter with you? Looks like

you've lost your best friend."

"I don't have a best friend," I muttered unpleasantly, even though I knew he was trying to be helpful.

"All right, Mattie, I know that." Dr. Dinsmore turned serious. "What's the matter?"

"We're leaving Princeton," I blurted out, the whole story then tumbling from my lips in a rush.

"Leaving Princeton?" He asked it as though he was not at all surprised. "Has your mother . . . I mean, can she . . . well, Mattie, what I'm trying to say is, how will your mother take care of you and Will Henry somewhere else? And where are you going?"

Dr. Dinsmore had never been critical of Mama, like the rest of Princeton, and I was grateful. I knew what he said now was simply straightforward truth.

"We're going out West. I don't know where, but Mama is going to marry Mr. Reeves, and he says for her health we have to take her out West."

"He's right, of course. I told her she needed to go two years ago, but she said there was no way."

"I don't guess there was until Mr. Reeves came along."

"Well, Mattie, I think this is good news, but you still look like you've lost your best friend."

"Oh no, I'm real pleased." I had to bite my lip to keep from crying, and I sank down into one of the great big, comfortable chairs in the library. Why didn't he, one of the few people I trusted and cared about, see how bad this was? Right then Dr. Dinsmore taught me a lesson: If you don't take matters into your own hands, nothing good happens.

"I don't think you want to go," he said slowly, as though

refusing to do all the work for me. He stood before me, straight and unbending, looking just a little stern.

"I don't."

"What are you going to do about it?"

"What can I do? I'm only fourteen."

He almost laughed aloud, and I could have hit him. "Self-pity, is it? That won't get you very far. Have you tried to do anything about it?"

"Like what?"

"I don't know. You tell me. What would you like to do?"

I took a deep breath and rushed into boldness that I could hardly believe I dared. "Stay here and live with you and take care of Sara."

"Oh, would you now?" He turned a little, as though pacing, but I thought I saw a slight twitch of the corners of his mouth. Embarrassed by my own forwardness, I said nothing.

"Have you told your mother that?" he asked.

"No."

"Should you?"

"How can I? I don't know if you'd let me stay."

"Why don't you ask?" He was not going to make this easy for me.

My face turning deep red, I stared at the floor and muttered, "Will you?"

"Why do you want to stay?"

"Because, mostly because . . . of the books. I mean, I really love Sara, and you're both good to me, but if I go to a farm somewhere out West, I'll never . . . probably never read a book, never get education."

"And education is important to you?"

"Yes," I said fiercely. "I don't ever want to live like Mama has." The very thought brought me upright in the chair, and I looked directly at him.

"Maybe . . ." He stopped, and I knew he had been about to tease me again and then thought better of it. "You're right, Mattie. Education is important, as much so for girls as men. I'll talk to Mrs. Dinsmore tonight, but I think such an arrangement might work out." He was the one who stared silently off into space for a moment then. "I know this isn't exactly a happy house to be in, and I worry about that, for Sara and now for you. Mrs. Dinsmore isn't always as well as might be, and frankly, I could benefit from your presence."

Thoughts tumbled together in my mind. I had no idea at that time about depression and what it can do to a person's life, so I didn't know what he meant by his wife not being well, but I knew there was something serious there. And I didn't understand how complicated our lives could become, with my being a "benefit" to him. I don't think he understood then either. Dr. Dinsmore was a wonderful and kind man, but he was lonely. It was all too much for a fourteen-year-old, fairly naive mind, but I sailed into my future as though certain it would all work out.

Mrs. Dinsmore, anxious to have all the care of Sara taken from her shoulders, agreed readily to the plan, and Dr. Dinsmore relieved me of the burden of talking to Mama. It was uncharacteristic of him, since he had insisted on making me work out my future myself, but I think he did it because he wanted me to stay as much as I did.

Mama was waiting for me one day when I came home

from school. She looked tired and frail, and I was worried about her. "Mattie, I want to talk to you."

"Yes, Mama."

"Come here in the bedroom." She pulled the blanket across its wire as though that made the bedroom a separate, soundproof room in the little house. "Dr. Dinsmore was here today."

"Yes, Mama, I knew he was coming to talk to you."

"Why didn't you tell me yourself?"

"I don't know. I guess I thought, well, you wouldn't like the idea, wouldn't let me stay."

"Oh, Mattie!" She grabbed my face in both her hands and looked deep in my eyes, an occasional tear trickling down her face. "How could I not let you stay? It's an opportunity for you, a chance for a better life. You know how things have been for me in this dingy, gossipy little town. But being here was something beyond my control. I had no choice. I had, uh, promised to wait here for someone, and by the time I knew that was hopeless, well, there was no place else to go. But now you have a chance to, well, to do whatever you want. If you stay here now, then you won't have to stay here always." It was a long speech for Mama, and it left her out of breath because of her bad lungs. She sat a minute, just staring at me.

"I'll miss you . . . you and Will Henry something awful," I said. But inside I was thinking that now I knew a little more about the mysterious man who had fathered us. He left Mama in Missouri and never came back for her. One thing seemed certain to me: I was descended from a cad.

"We'll miss you, too, but it isn't like we'll never see you

again," she said brightly. I guess she didn't believe it even then, but I didn't know any better.

The next couple of weeks were a nightmare. Mr. Reeves was most efficiently getting my family ready to leave, and I was torn with guilt for not going with them. How could I abandon my own mother?

One day I sat and watched Will Henry and Mr. Reeves pore over a map. "Now, right about here, I think, Will Henry, is some good farmland. Nice and rich soil. We could raise wheat . . . But maybe that's a little north for your mama. If we went south some—"

Will Henry was enthusiasm come to life. "We could raise cattle, couldn't we? Right there on the prairie."

"Maybe so. Do you know much about cattle?"

"I'll learn," he said with eight-year-old confidence.

"I'm gonna need you some to take care of your mama, you know. She can't do any hard work."

"But nursin's girl's work."

"Will Henry, we will each do what we have to do." That was delivered in the sternest tones I'd ever heard from Mr. Reeves.

"I'm going, too," I announced suddenly. "It's my place to care for Mama."

"Now, Mattie, your plans are all made, and your mother agrees with them. We'll get by."

Maybe that was what bothered me. They would get by without me, but would I be all right without them? Much as I had railed against our life, this was my family, and I loved them. I wanted to watch Will Henry grow up and see Mama grow strong and happy again.

When Mama heard about it, though, she took one of her

firm stands. "No, Mattie, you'll stay here. It's best."

"Here?" I cried, suddenly in a rage. "Here, where everybody teases about my mother and knows I have no father? Here, where I haven't a friend my age in the whole world? Here, where I hate to go to the store or run errands because of what other kids say to me? Where I watch Mary Jane Canary look at me like I'm scum?"

Mama was stunned, but Mr. Reeves recovered after just a minute. He raised his hand as though to hit me and was stopped only by Mama's scream.

"Don't hit her!"

"I won't have her talking to you that way."

"No, she's right. Life in Princeton has been pretty bad for her . . . for all of us . . . but it's all she's known. Mattie, come into the bedroom with me."

We sat together on the bed in silence for a moment, and then she put her arm around me. "I didn't know, Mattie, I didn't know how awful it was for you."

"You couldn't have done anything about it anyway. And for a long time I didn't know what I was missing. I guess until the day I went with you to the Canarys' house and saw that awful brat."

"You may come with us, of course. We won't leave you here."

"I don't know what I want," I said, biting my lip. "I hate Princeton, but I want to stay with the Dinsmores and read those books and somehow make things better."

"Mattie, how do you know that the problems you have here, your feelings about me, your questions about your father, won't follow you to a new town? Will Henry can go easily. He has none of those feelings, but I really doubt that geography is going to change much for you."

I thought about what she said. "Couldn't . . . wouldn't things be different if you arrived someplace married to Mr. Reeves?"

"Ah, Mattie, marriage for me isn't going to make the difference for you. What I've done, or what you think I've done, isn't so terrible, you know. What is terrible is the way others have treated you because of it. And something you won't realize for years is that you're at fault, too, for the way you have responded to the teasing. No, all those mixed-up feelings inside you will just go right with us West."

I lay down on the pillow and began to sob, knowing she was probably right. I wasn't an attractive child, and at that point it didn't appear to me that I had much personality to balance my physical deficits. Even though I knew Mama was right and suspected she had much more sense than I had ever given her credit for, I began to wonder if maybe she didn't want me to go, if my sour attitude and my resentments were unpleasant enough that the family would be happier if I stayed behind. I had no way of knowing how hurt Mama must have been and how hard it was for her to leave one of her own children behind, especially when deep down she must have known that she'd never see me again. Lord, I was stuck with self-pity and not a spark of life. As I look back on it, I can't believe all the good things that have happened to that colorless girl from Missouri.

"Mattie, I want you to come with us, you know, more than anything. I will miss you terribly. But I think your future, your chance at what you want, starts here in

Princeton, not on a journey west without a destination."
She put an arm around me to hug but had to turn away as
a coughing fit struck her.

And so, that was how I stayed behind when they left to
go West. I watched them pack up our meager belongings
and the new things that Mr. Reeves had added. Sometimes
I helped, but mostly I just stood and watched.

And then one day I stood and watched as they drove
away in a great huge cart loaded down with everything
they owned. My own things, which were pretty few, had
already been taken to the Dinsmores', and Dr. Dinsmore
had offered to come with me to see them off, but I
declined. I guess I thought standing there watching them
go was something I had to do alone. And I did it, with a
great knot in my stomach.

We made a great fuss, of course, about how soon we
would see each other again, and Mama hugged me a lot.
But she coughed a lot, too, and I knew we would not see
each other again. With all my mixed-up feelings about
her, it made me sad, and I sat down in the dirt outside that
tacky little shack and had a good cry. Then I said goodbye
to the shack and all that it stood for forever and walked on
to the Dinsmores'.

Life rolled along. I went to school, watched little Sara,
who grew more charming by the day, and read everything
I could. I went through the American transcendentalists,
the English essayists, all in great bunches, even though I
didn't understand much of what I read. Dr. Dinsmore took
to guiding my reading program, though always gently.

"If you're reading Thoreau, you ought to read some
Emerson next," he'd say, explaining the connection to me.

I followed his directions carefully.

Things between the Dinsmores didn't get any better. In fact, Mrs. Dinsmore seemed to get worse. A thin, somber woman, she grew daily more withdrawn and unhappy, not that she ever was unpleasant. She appeared to be grateful for my care of little Sara, and lots of days I did think how dull the child's life would have been if I had gone West, to say nothing of my own life. But still, I wondered how Sara could be so bright and happy in the midst of such an obviously unhappy household. I decided it was Dr. Dinsmore, for somehow he retained his cheerfulness much, if not all, of the time.

Now that my family had left, I was no longer quite the outcast with many of the schoolchildren my age, and I would take Sara on long walks through town. It was a relief to be able to walk without being teased and without having to run errands for someone or the other just to earn another nickel. I guess I vowed right then I would never be someone's servant, and it probably never occurred to me that was my status at the Dinsmores'.

Mary Jane Canary reminded me of it one day, though. "Look at the little nursemaid," she taunted from her front yard when I had made the mistake of walking by her house. She was all dressed in fine clothes, and though my wardrobe had improved some thanks to Dr. Dinsmore's insistence, I still felt the distinction.

Fixing my eyes straight ahead, I said, "Come on, Sara, ignore the nasty lady."

"How dare you call me nasty? You're the one who's nasty! Letting your mother go off and leave you to take charity from someone else. And who needs to say more reading my way through that library, and——"

"And you're beginning to learn about my medicines, and you're taking good care of Sara, who is very happy these days. So you've got a lot to be proud of. But it doesn't matter if Mary Jane knows that or not." Once again, he towered over me, even when I raised up from my knees, and I was aware of his strength and authority.

"It's not that . . ." I remember being thoroughly confused.

"Think about it a little, Mattie. I know it's unpleasant to have to listen to her, but at least you don't have to go with your mother while Mary Jane models dresses anymore." He got sort of a wry grin on his face. "And we all have unpleasant people to deal with. Come on, I need help measuring out some medicines . . . Sara, you can come, too."

Laughing a little now, he picked Sara up with one arm and draped the other around my shoulders.

Mrs. Dinsmore seemed to get worse every day. I couldn't understand why someone like her, who had so much, could be so sad and solemn when Mama, who had nothing but trouble, had managed to smile at least half the time and never, ever just sat and stared like Mrs. Dinsmore did.

I guess I had no conception of how bad she really was even though I saw Dr. Dinsmore daily grow more tired and worried-looking. He still had a smile for Sara and lots of encouragement for me, but I would catch him, sometimes, staring off into space as though lost in thought. And he was careful of Mrs. Dinsmore, as always, but he about your mother? Where's your father?"

Try as I might to be bigger than such taunts, like Dr. Dinsmore had told me, I had a hard time, and this day I ended up clutching Sara's hand too tightly and walking her home far too fast for her little short legs, while tears streamed down both our faces.

Mrs. Dinsmore saw us but never said a word, never offered to comfort either of us. She just turned and walked away. But Dr. Dinsmore found us in the hallway, both of us crying and me trying desperately to wipe away Sara's tears.

"Good heavens, what's the matter with both of you?"

"Nothing," I muttered. "I guess I got upset on our walk, and it scared Sara. I'm sorry. It won't happen again."

"Whatever could upset you that badly?"

My instinct was to bite my lip, lapse into stony but strong silence and tell him it was nothing. But something overcame that instinct. "Mary Jane Canary," I said.

"That spoiled child? What did she do?"

"She called me a nursemaid, and said I let my mother go off and was taking charity and all kinds of things." Tears crept down my cheeks again.

"Are they true?"

"What?" I stopped feeling sorry for myself long enough to think. I had let my mother go off, and I was taking care of Sara, which meant I wasn't really taking charity. "I guess, but Mary Jane doesn't understand."

"Why should she? What do you care if she does?"

"Well," I said defensively, "it's my pride . . ."

"Are you proud of yourself, of what you're doing?"

"Sure. I'm doing better in school than ever, and I'm

seemed to spend more time around her, as though he was worried and watching her. One night I guessed maybe he had been worried indeed.

I was wakened from a sound sleep by an awful screaming, a loud wailing that sent shivers through me and made me want nothing more than to burrow under the covers, pillow over my head, and hide until the noise stopped. After a minute I realized, of course, that I couldn't do that. I had to take care of Sara.

She was terrified and clung to me, sobbing, "It's my mama, it's my mama."

I wanted to say, "Nonsense, Sara, that's not your mother." But I knew it was indeed her, and I said nothing but "It will be all right. Your father will take care of her. Maybe she had a bad dream."

The screaming probably only lasted two or three minutes, though it seemed like hours, and then it stopped abruptly, as though someone had clamped a strong hand over her mouth. Someone had, I suppose.

Mrs. Dinsmore did not appear at breakfast the next morning, though the doctor did, looking much the same as usual. When Sara trotted off to play with her dolls, he pushed his chair from the table and talked softly to me.

"I don't know, Mattie, that I've done you any favor by bringing you here. Things appear to be worse than they were when you were with your mother."

"You mean Mrs. Dinsmore?" Filled with curiosity about the night before, I perched on the edge of my chair and forgot the rules against elbows on the table.

"What else? You're really too young to have to worry about this, but I guess you've worried about other things that were beyond your age." Taking a deep breath, he said, "Mrs. Dinsmore has a serious mental disorder from which I doubt she will ever recover. She is quiet now because I gave her a sedation last night."

I nodded sympathetically, but my stomach lurched. Was I going to have to leave after all? Was that what he was working up to?

"I thought, for several years, that she would improve," he went on, "and I did the things accepted by medical science to get her better, but nothing helped. She has, ah, a family predisposition to this type of illness."

Sara, I thought. Maybe she'll turn out that way, too. I looked at her, playing happily with her dolls, and couldn't believe it was possible. Dr. Dinsmore saw me and read my mind. Shaking his head, he said, "It's possible, but I hope not. Certainly, without your help, Sara would be growing up in the same dismal atmosphere that her mother did, and I think that contributed. But as long as she can see a brighter side of life, I think she'll be fine."

I had never felt that I was too good at seeing the bright side of life, but I guess I was better than that poor woman sleeping upstairs, and I vowed to be bright and cheerful from then on. It was, of course, a vow I couldn't keep, but I meant it at the time.

Meantime, I thought Dr. Dinsmore would never get to the point of what was going to happen in the immediate future. He sat calmly in that chair, looking intently at me while I fidgeted, my mind filled with questions. Was I to leave or stay? Would he commit Mrs. Dinsmore? I doubted that, knowing that mental institutions were hell-holes for the patients, who were often chained to their beds, fed the barest of diets and generally mistreated. I can't remember where I had learned that, but every schoolkid in those days had a grim picture of how awful a mental institution was. They still believed that the mentally ill were no better than animals, and they were treated accordingly.

Dr. Dinsmore did answer one of my unspoken questions. "She wasn't always this way. I want you to know that. Once she was young and pretty and always happy. I don't know what happened, really, to make her change gradually, but she surely wasn't this way when we married. And I guess that's the reason I can't institutionalize her. I will keep her at home as long as it's safe for Sara."

He never said anything about safety for him, and I wondered if she had threatened him when she was yelling and screaming.

"Mattie, the whole question is what you should do. Sara and I have no choice. You do. If you can accept and understand, I would like you to stay. Both for your sake and, selfishly, because you're the closest thing to adult companionship that I have. But if you don't feel you can live with this new problem—and you can guess what Mary Jane will say about this when it becomes public— I'll arrange for you to join your family."

Maybe it wasn't realistic, but I never doubted for one minute what my decision would be. "I want to stay," I said quickly. In retrospect, it was the best choice, but at the time, I made it for all the wrong reasons, among them a growing recognition of how important Dr. Dinsmore himself was in my life.

I guess I thought Mrs. Dinsmore would go on staring

out the window. This was not to be the case. Something had broken loose in the poor woman that night, and from then on, she no longer sat and stared. She paced and fidgeted and raved wildly and was never still a moment. Dr. Dinsmore took to locking her in her room, which he had taken special pains to make safe so she could not hurt herself or anyone else. But Sara and I still heard her each day as we sat at the dining table or read in the parlor. Sometimes she would sing softly, and other times she would moan long and low. It was eerie, and as long as the weather was good, Sara and I were outside as much as we could be.

If it weren't for Mrs. Dinsmore, life would have been pretty grand. School was going well, and I liked it. Even better, I liked learning about Dr. Dinsmore's medicines. Now that he had no one else to talk to except the housekeeper, Mrs. Evans, who wasn't very good company, he talked to me about his theories on medication, what he thought made the body healthy and why people got sick.

"That's the most puzzling thing, Mattie. Why did she"—he nodded his head upstairs—"suddenly change? What body chemistry in her changed to make her snap loose like that? Someday I suppose medicine will know, but it's a terrible puzzle now."

I didn't understand how body chemistry could have anything to do with Mrs. Dinsmore being, well, crazy, as I called her to myself, but I was willing to believe it was so if Dr. Dinsmore told me so. And I wanted so badly to be intelligent for him, to be worthy of the trust he placed in me by discussing these things with me.

"If it's chemistry, I would think you could do something

about it, give her some medicine."

"Maybe someday we can, Mattie, but we don't know enough about it now. Look how they treat most people in her condition. They lock them up like animals and claim it doesn't make any difference to them. But she's not an animal. She knows me, knows herself. I couldn't lock her up."

"Of course not. We can manage." I tried to sound confident.

"Mattie, Mattie, what would I do without you?" He put an arm around my shoulder and hugged me, and I glowed with a kind of comfort and security that had been denied me all my life. Dr. Dinsmore and I filled a real need for each other.

It wasn't that I replaced Mama with him, but rather, obviously, he became the father I never had. Instead of Mama, who was at once parent and child, I had a parent, someone I could respect and model myself after. And he had a semiadult, someone who would listen and never, no not ever, criticize. I was so wrapped up in my new life and what I saw as my new status and position in the world that I barely even missed Mama and Will Henry.

I did hear from them. They were settled comfortably in what they called a soddie. Strange to think I had no idea what a soddie was, me who lived a good portion of my life in one. It sounded dirty and nasty to me, and I didn't see how Mama would ever get better. Truth was, that was the one topic missing from that letter. There wasn't one word about Mama's health, and the omission made me nervous, as it well should have. But I brushed that worry from my mind and went on with my new life.

Mary Jane Canary continued to tease. "Living with a crazy lady, aren't you?" Word had gotten around town, of course, about Mrs. Dinsmore. I suppose it was because Mrs. Evans never talked to us, but outside the house, had a tongue that wouldn't stop. She was horrified by the noises Mrs. Dinsmore made and used to shake her head and cluck her tongue and mutter to herself, making almost as much racket as the poor woman herself. But somehow, Dr. Dinsmore had helped me with Mary Jane, and I no longer paid attention. Vaguely, I felt some kind of pity for her, but it was a feeling I would not recognize for years to come.

I guess we would have gone on like that a long time, although I had a growing feeling that we couldn't, that something had to be done about Mrs. Dinsmore. I think he felt it, too, because each day he seemed more worried. But as he confessed again and again, he had no idea what to do.

"I can't put her in one of those places, Mattie, I can't. But last night, she . . . when I took her a tray, she . . ." He sat at his desk, head sunk in his hands in despair.

She had, as I had feared, tried to harm him by attacking him with a knife, making only a small scratch but trying hard to do him real harm. I wanted to go up and slap her. How dare she injure him? Didn't she know he was special?

"Why did she do it?" I asked incredulously.

He shook his head sadly. "Who knows? I doubt she does. Maybe she wanted to leave her room. Maybe it was anger at me, maybe a combination of those things, but mostly, the act of a mind that's lost touch with reality and is probably frightened. Maybe the violence came from her own fright."

Dr. Dinsmore knew at that point that it would happen again, and that someday he would have to do something. If he were a wealthy man, I am sure he would have hired a keeper for her, but there was not enough money for that.

Mrs. Dinsmore solved it for us one day, or rather, one night. In spite of Dr. Dinsmore's care, she found a way to damage someone—herself. With a bedsheet tied out the window, she hung herself from the second story of the house. I was always thankful Sara and I were spared the sight. Someone saw her early in the morning and alerted Dr. Dinsmore, who ordered us to stay in our rooms. By the time we were released, the body had been taken away and the house was crowded with people, all offering sympathy and trying to satisfy their curiosity.

"Mattie, dear, you're so strong and such a help to the doctor in this terrible time" . . . "You've been through so much, Mattie. First your poor dear mother, and now this" . . . "How, I mean, does anybody know why . . . ?"

Finally I said to one curious lady, "Sorry, I think Sara needs me." I scooped the child up and ran from the room, nearly colliding with Dr. Dinsmore, who was talking with the minister.

"Terrible shame, just terrible. Don't suppose there's anything a man can do to prevent it in cases like this."

"Perhaps I should have put her into an institution, but I couldn't bring myself to do it, just couldn't. Maybe this is all for the best."

"Oh, never, man, never must you say that. It's a sin, what she has done, a terrible sin."

"She didn't know sin from right, Reverend. I think she only wanted to be free of her torment."

The funeral was held the next day, instead of the customary three days later, and there was no large funeral party. Only a handful of people gathered around the gravesite as the reverend implored God to forgive her for she knew not what she did.

I didn't think Mrs. Dinsmore's death would make as much difference in our lives as it did, except that we'd be spared that sense of a shadow looming over us and those awful noises she used to make. But I guess I was young and didn't realize about hidden tension. Things changed dramatically around the Dinsmore house, almost immediately, and for the better. Dr. Dinsmore, my rock and my protector, became almost a playmate for Sara and me. It was as though he took a day or two to reconcile himself to the inevitability of what had happened, then shook off the past and determined to build himself a new life.

"Come on, girls, what are you doing with your noses in books on a day like this?"

"Sara was studying her ABCs, and I'm trying to finish—"

"I don't care what you're trying to finish!" He said it with a laugh and grabbed *The Last of the Mohicans* right out of my hands. "We're going on a picnic."

"A picnic!" Sara squealed, running to Mrs. Evans to demand, "I want fried chicken for my picnic."

That grim lady, unlike her employer, had not reconciled herself to the death, and she said harshly, "You'll get sandwiches of yesterday's roast. I ain't got no time to fry chicken."

But even Mrs. Evans couldn't put a damper on our day, and soon we were loaded into the carriage, a picnic hamper of our own packing on the floor. Dr. Dinsmore drove way out into the country, or so it seemed, even though it probably was no more than two miles. We spread a blanket under a large oak tree.

He and Sara wandered, picking wildflowers, while I unpacked the lunch of cold roast, carrot sticks, homemade bread (Mrs. Evans could make wonderful bread even if she was the sourest lady in all of Missouri!) and a chocolate cake which I had made in an effort to become domestic as well as widely read. It was all delicious except the cake.

"A trifle dry, Mattie," Dr. Dinsmore said carefully. "You'll get better. Then again, maybe you won't. Maybe you weren't meant to bake and sweep and clean. You could learn medicine from me, you know."

I guess he planted the idea in my mind right then. Anyway, I didn't answer, just stared off at Sara, who was playing with something in the grass. But my thoughts were on the future, because suddenly I saw a way out of the trap set by my childhood and background.

"Sure," I answered finally, trying to be casual. "I can learn medicine." But I meant it seriously.

After we ate, we all lay on the ground and listened while he told stories of his boyhood in Philadelphia and how he had come to be a doctor and why he had come out to Missouri to practice instead of staying back there even though doctors weren't really well respected on the frontier. I was thrilled to my bones to hear of his early life.

Mrs. Dinsmore had died at the beginning of summer,

and for the three of us, it was a glorious summer, unkind as that sounds. Sometimes we went picnicking, sometimes Sara and I went on house calls with Dr. Dinsmore, and once we went fishing, though Sara was much better than I about getting a worm on the hook.

"Have to get over that squeamishness if you're going to work with me," he teased. "Got to develop a strong stomach."

I bit my lip and forced the wriggling, squiggly thing onto the hook, but I have never to this day liked fishing and don't really like to eat fish. I think it all comes from that memory.

When fall came, we settled more into a routine. Sara was six and off to school for the first year, and I was busy with high school. Unconsciously, I had somewhat taken over the running of the household, not that Mrs. Dinsmore had ever done much of it in recent years. But the doctor would ask me to check this or that with Mrs. Evans, and soon I found myself selecting what we would have for dinner for the coming week and reminding her that the rugs needed beating. To this day, I don't know how I knew how to keep house, for certainly, in our little shack, Mama had never beaten the rugs—there were only two. I think that housekeeping knowledge was another gift to me from Dr. Dinsmore, a gift given so subtly I was never aware of it.

We went on that way for three more years. Sara grew and flourished, an adorable and sweet child in whom I thought the sun rose and set. She filled the void left by Will Henry. When she was seven, she lost her first tooth, and I stitched her a small sampler about the tooth fairy, trying to remember all the fine stitches Mama had tried to teach me and doing a poor job of it. That was probably the last needlework I ever did in my whole life, except for emergency mending. My stitches were always clumsy and obvious, not fine and delicate like Mama's, and because I didn't sew well, it bored me. To this day, I'm a little suspicious of women who sew for the pleasure of it.

But back to Sara. When she was nine, she broke her wrist. I remember it distinctly. I was more frantic than any mother could have been, alternating between wringing my hands and scolding her for unladylike behavior. If she hadn't climbed that tree, she never would have fallen.

"Mattie, Mattie. It's unfortunate, but broken bones are often a part of growing up. And I'd rather she take risks and have fun than sit in a chair and never experience the world."

I looked doubtful. It was the first time that I was clearly aware that Dr. Dinsmore might not always be right, but I guess I didn't know that he was thinking of his wife and the risks she never took, the narrowness of a constricted life that finally led to madness and suicide.

Other incidents stand out more happily—Sara giggling with a little friend over a book they had sneaked from the library, Sara dressed for her first communion or riding the pony her father bought her for her eighth birthday. She had a wonderful childhood, and my teen years, which could have been awkward and miserable, turned wonderful because of her and her father. But inside, the whole time, I nursed a secret plan. I knew Sara would be grown one day, and I couldn't be her nursemaid forever, but I knew what came next for me.

The only question was, how?

The death of my mother was the only blow that came to me in those years, but it was a major one. Mr. Reeves wrote the kindest of letters, explaining that she had simply continued to lose strength, and nothing he could do had revived her. He was, I remember sensing, even more heartbroken than I, and I felt sorry for him. He promised to keep Will Henry with him and said I had a home, too, any time I wanted it. He expected they would move from Kansas to Nebraska soon because he had heard the farming was good there, and he felt the need to move on to a place with fewer memories.

I was a little angry that he would move and leave Mama buried alone in strange soil, but I knew enough to recognize that as an irrational thought and didn't mention it when I wrote back. Neither did I mention the awful sense of guilt that tore at me because I had let my mother go without me, a sense of guilt that perhaps I never did work out the rest of my life.

I thanked him for all his kindness and assured him that I was comfortably settled where I was and would remain in Princeton for years to come. I didn't bother to tell him about my secret plan for the future, mostly because as yet I had no idea how I would implement that plan. It was a fantasy that I clung to tightly.

Mama used to say to me that fate works in mysterious ways. That's truly how it was when Dr. Dinsmore announced one day that he was moving to Omaha, where he had accepted a position with the new medical school. With my usual selfishness, I could not see beyond my own nose and saw, not possibilities, but closed doors in his announcement. It had happened to me once before—the family I loved had left me behind—and now it was going to happen again. He was moving to Omaha, and I would be left in Princeton, where I now had neither family nor friends and certainly no way of making my dream come true.

"Mattie, aren't you glad? Why can't you say something?"

"I'm sure you'll be very happy there," I said stiffly, my back straight and my face tightly set.

"What do you mean, you're sure I'll be happy there? What about you?"

I stared, silent, and a look of awareness broke on his face, followed by a grin. "You're to go, too, you silly thing. Do you think Sara and I would leave you behind? I thought you'd be delighted. We'll be at a medical school, a chance for you to learn more about medicine." He paused, seeming lost in thought, though now I wonder if he wasn't after a dramatic effect. "You could, you know, go to medical school."

I almost sagged with relief. Here was the key to my plan. Yet experience had taught me caution.

"Women don't go to medical school," I said, testing him.

He had anticipated my arguments and had his answers ready. "They do back East. I admit, none has ever gone to the college in Omaha. But that doesn't mean you couldn't be the first."

"Me?" It was what I wanted, yet when it was presented to me, I wasn't sure I could do it.

"Yes, you. You could do it, Mattie. You're a good student, you've got a background in medicine, at least a little from me. And you are interested, aren't you?"

"Yes, I am," I admitted. "I really would like to be a doctor because, well, because there ought to have been some way that Mama didn't need to die." It wasn't a new thought on the spur of the moment, but something I had been thinking about. If I had been trained, had more knowledge, would Mama have lived? She wouldn't, but I didn't know it back then. And in the back of my mind still was the thought that I didn't tell him: Medicine was my way out of Princeton and poverty.

"Good. It's settled. I'll sponsor you."

In those days it didn't take much to get into medical school, not like today, and one of the surest paths was to get another doctor to sponsor you. There would, I thought, be no question of my admission to the next class, since I already had my high school training. With Dr. Dinsmore speaking for me, there would be no problems unless the school objected to women.

He must have read my mind. "It's time that school admitted women, started looking ahead. I'm going to change some things there, and you're going to help me do it, Mattie. It's perfect."

No, I didn't feel like a tool he was using. I knew Dr. Dinsmore really did want what was best for me, and that, to his mind, was for me to be that first woman doctor, no matter what problems I faced. Of course, we hadn't heard of Pygmalion at the time.

❧✳❧

OMAHA was school to me. The two run together in my

mind now, and I can remember little else. Oh, I remember we arrived by train from St. Louis, after an awful, long ride, and Dr. Dinsmore settled us in a two-story brick house, not as big as the one in Princeton but much more elegant, with walnut wainscoting in the downstairs rooms, little gas sconces that were decorated with brass, big, wide steps up to a grand front porch, and a window seat that Sara loved.

Actually, Dr. Dinsmore only bought the house. I did the work of getting us settled, because he began his duties at the medical school right away. We moved in the late spring, when both Sara and I were through with school for the year, and that gave me the summer to settle us in. I knew enough about housekeeping, even without Mrs. Evans, to unpack dishes and clothes and put them away. You do what you have to.

Omaha was a surprise to me, just because Princeton had been so small. It was a big city, even back then in 1885, with office buildings, an opera house, real asphalt paving on the streets and an electric light company. Sara and I walked to Capitol Hill, where the Territorial Capitol was until they moved it to Lincoln in 1867, and we wandered past the Douglas House and the City Hotel, wondering about people who stayed in hotels and supposing they were very glamorous. We didn't know that most of them were drummers, like Mr. Reeves had been, hawking their wares from one city to another in an existence that was anything but glamorous. We stayed away from the gambling houses, which were plentiful in those days, and from the huge, sprawling stockyards with their strong smells and bawling cattle. Sometimes we walked through residential sections, making up stories about the people we imagined lived in the houses. Omaha had its share of grand, big homes, and we made up equally grand, big tales about their owners.

I made Sara work that summer, and she rebelled some.

"Mattie, why do I have to sweep?" She pouted, leaning on the broom.

I stirred the simmering meat too strongly in my impatience with her. "You have to sweep because there's dirt on the floor, and I'm fixing dinner."

I didn't realize Dr. Dinsmore had been listening from the doorway until he came into the kitchen with a soft "Bravo, Mattie, you're finally being firm with her. Raising children doesn't always consist of making them love you, you know."

I thought that one over while he watched me cut up potatoes and turnips for the stew. I guessed he was right. I'd grown into a role with Sara that grew out of the days when I was responsible for keeping her amused and happy, and I still tended to think that was my responsibility.

"She needs more than fun," he finally said. "If she is to grow into a lady we can like to have around, I suspect she needs discipline and order in her life. I won't have time to give her all she needs."

"I think I know what you're saying," I said, pausing in my work to look at him, "and I'll try to see Sara gets what she needs." But inwardly I thought grimly that Sara was going to have to take more responsibility because I was going to have less time.

I finally did hire a housekeeper, at the direction of Dr. Dinsmore. Her name was Kate, and she was probably only a year or two older than me. Like me, she came from a poor family, only there were five other children in her home. She allowed as how she'd rather live in, and only visit home occasionally, so we agreed on that. But Kate was all business. She swept with a vengeance, cooked a fair meal—Lord knows, better than I did—and seldom played with Sara. Poor Sara. Maybe she, of everyone, got the worst of my decision to go to medical school.

Dr. Dinsmore was pleased with his duties at the college of medicine. He was to lecture in general medicine, which meant a chance for him to explore and develop his theories about medicines and health and the human body. He found some opposition to his ideas at the school, where traditional doctors, who had been teaching not much longer than he since the school was only three or four years old, objected to his stinginess with medicines. They tended to operate on the theory that if a little was good, a lot was better, and they would dose patients heavily with cathartics, diuretics or emetics, all strong potions for the human body.

Dr. Dinsmore would talk to me about it in the evenings, when I generally found time for my reading. Sometimes he raised his voice in anger.

"If God had meant the human body to become a receptacle for laudanum, he'd have made that drug less harmful and dangerous! Don't they understand when they lessen someone's pain a little, they're causing more grief by starting an addiction?"

Once or twice, he casually tossed medical books in my direction, and I was thrilled but baffled. *Gray's Anatomy* had fascinating drawings of the human body, and I studied them carefully, but a text on obstetrics was beyond me and awfully intimidating.

One night he talked to me about the attitudes he thought I might face at the medical school. "They've not had a woman before. You'll be the first, and they're not likely to be pleased."

"Will they accept me?" I looked up from my book to see that he was standing staring at me in what I had come to think of as his lecturing pose.

"Oh, I think so, with my standing for you. But they won't be happy about it. Some people don't think women should be doctors."

"Why not?"

"Well, they think it's unseemly. You should be more modest than to pry around people's anatomy, especially that of men."

"There's a reverse to that," I insisted. "Women should be glad to have a woman who's done that. I mean, they should prefer a woman doctor."

"Some might. But some will think every bit as badly of you as men do. And some men may refuse to let you care for them."

"I'll handle that when it happens," I said with a bravado I didn't really feel. "When should I apply?"

"Pretty soon, I suspect. The new term begins in about three weeks. Remember, Mattie, I'll help you any way I can, but you're pretty much going to have to fight your own battles . . . and they may indeed be battles . . . with faculty and students. Back East, you know, quite a few women are going into medicine, and they've even opened special women's medical schools. But this is Nebraska, a different world."

"I've survived prejudice before," I said stubbornly, thinking of the way everyone in Princeton gossiped about Mama and whispered and pointed at me when I went to the store. Maybe I had learned from those awful days.

I went to the medical school the next day to present myself and apply for admission. And I went with knee-shaking, heart-pounding terror, the kind that made me think, even as I mounted the stairs, that I'd have to turn and run. If Dr. Dinsmore hadn't been there, no telling what I'd have done.

The Omaha Medical College, some four years old, was housed in a dark, two-story frame building with a steep row of steps up the front to the door, a sign that said "Free Dispensary" and absolutely not a bush or blade of grass on the barren earth that surrounded the building. Dr. Dinsmore explained that the free dispensary was a way of providing patients to give students more practical experience, something missing from many medical schools.

He gave me a tour of the school from classroom and dispensary offices to the anatomy lab, where I remember avoiding a sheet-covered mound on a table, and then took me to the office to apply for admission.

It was nothing like today, with complicated requirements and the likelihood of being turned down. They pretty much accepted almost anyone who could write his name, and I was well qualified. But I was a woman.

"We haven't had a woman here before," the dean said. He was a dignified-looking man, tall with a white goatee and shining bald head. He wore the traditional white coat and sat behind an impressive big desk while he studied a letter from my schoolteacher in Princeton testifying to my ability to learn.

"What have you read?"

I was sure my voice would squeak and quake, but I managed to sound calm enough as I started to reel off the list of books I'd read, from Emerson and Thoreau to the European classics. He interrupted me abruptly.

"No, no. What have you read in medicine?"

Feeling foolish, I replied, "*Gray's Anatomy* and some texts in general medicine. I've helped Dr. Dinsmore some, and I've talked with him a great deal about his ideas on medicine."

"Yes. Well, you'll have to realize his ideas don't necessarily speak for the school."

"They're sound ideas," I protested, beginning to be fed up with his air of superiority.

"No doubt, no doubt. Well, do you think you can stand to be the only woman in a class of eighteen young men?"

"Yes, sir." I really didn't know what to expect. I'd read that Elizabeth Blackwell was greeted with spitballs and jeers when she entered school, but that had been forty years ago. Still, the students in a Nebraska school might still be every bit as crude and resentful. But I was determined to stay. If I didn't study medicine, what would I do with my life?

When Dr. Dinsmore came home that night, he was jubilant. "Well, Mattie, you did it!" He stood in the doorway, hands in his pockets and a broad smile on his face.

"Did I?" I tried to ask casually, as though I had not been waiting all afternoon for him to come home.

"Dean Lacross said you were a most determined young lady and that the faculty would, ah, attempt to let you enter the class."

"Attempt? What does that mean?"

"I don't think it means much except that you can start school," he laughed. "Don't get so upset by one little word."

"It has a feeling to it," I persisted stubbornly, "a feeling like they don't think I'll make it or I'll ruin the school or . . . I don't know, something awful will happen just because they're letting me enter medical school."

"They probably feel that way." He turned and left, leaving me with a strong urge to throw something at him. Instead, I wiped my hands on my apron and went after Sara, who was curled up with a reader.

"Sara Dinsmore, you get right in here and put out the plates and flatware."

"What has happened to you, Mattie?" she asked curiously as she put the book down and unwound her skinny legs from the chair.

Three weeks later, I started medical school. At least ten times while I was dressing that first morning, I thought, "I can't do it. I'll just go down and tell Dr. Dinsmore that I can't possibly do it. It's all a mistake." And then I'd brush my hair or buckle a shoe and think, "Nonsense. I have to do it."

At breakfast I was calm, hiding the storm that raged inside me, but I ate little, afraid the next bite would send me running from the table to be sick.

"Ready, Mattie?" To him this was just another day, and he showed no signs of understanding my dilemma.

"Yes," I said, picking up the sort of notebook we had decided would be appropriate for me and gathering my handbag.

We walked in silence at first, me still afflicted with that desire to bolt and run. Home, I thought, never seemed so comfortable.

"Nervous, Mattie?"

"Of course," I muttered.

"Good." That was all he said until we were almost in the door of the building. But at the foot of the steps, he stopped and looked at me. "You can do it, you know. I wouldn't have suggested, pushed or urged unless I was quite sure. You may have some unpleasant experiences, and God knows, medical school is never pleasant for anyone, but you'll survive, and you'll do it gracefully. If you're going to be the only woman, do it with a flair."

With that encouragement, I began two of the hardest years of my life. Medical school is noted today for being difficult, but it was another world back in those days. It hadn't been too many years, of course, since people simply apprenticed themselves to a physician if they wanted to become a doctor. Medical school was virtually unheard of, especially in frontier parts of the country like Nebraska had been not too many years before, and medicine wasn't the respected profession it is today. Too many doctors were unprofessional in their conduct and unsuccessful in their treatment of patients. By the time I went to school, the profession was just beginning to see organization of its education and some enforcement of standards that were restoring the respect doctors had enjoyed since ancient times. Would I, I wondered, add to that respect or bring disgrace?

"Nonsense, Mattie Armstrong," I scolded myself, very nearly talking aloud. "You are going to do this and do it well, because you don't want to go back to Princeton, Missouri, and you have got to do it to make people like Mama live." And that, sentimental as it sounds, was the thought that kept me going.

The entering students met in a lecture hall that morning, all nineteen of us seated at wooden student desks while a Dr. Henley, balding with glasses and a gray mustache and a pocket watch stretched across his thin middle, paraded back and forth, waiting to begin the class. The room was small, with fading paint and a brand-new blackboard. The school was fairly new, I remembered, but it had been established in a former boardinghouse.

I stole a look at the others in my class, all men, of course, and decided they didn't look threatening. They were mostly young, as young or more so than I, and they looked like freshly scrubbed schoolboys. There was one a slight bit older, with a mustache and a cynical look on his face. I was later to learn that his name was David Kimberly, and he was thirty and had been an undertaker in Iowa.

There was no commotion or fuss when I entered the room, though I saw one young man poke another and point in my direction, whispering in his friend's ear.

David Kimberly nodded at me, and one or two others stared outright. Dr. Henley had been warned, it seemed, for he addressed me directly.

"Good morning, Miss Armstrong."

I managed to return a weak "Good morning, sir." That, of course, brought further looks from my classmates, none of whom had been addressed personally.

Finally, Dr. Henley very obviously counted our heads and announced, "I see we are all gathered, so we will begin."

Dr. Henley was, it seemed, professor of surgery, which in those days meant any and all kinds of medicine. He was what you call a general practitioner today, and he was in effect to shepherd us through medical school, "loaning us out" to various other professors who taught anatomy and pharmacology and other scientific subjects.

"Gentlemen . . . and, uh, Miss Armstrong . . . welcome."

I blushed and hoped I was not to be so singled out for the next two years.

"You are about to begin the most important phase of your life. Look at those around you. Some will be strong enough for this rigorous training. Others will not."

Was it my imagination, or did everyone look at me?

"There will be no special favors, no leniencies granted to anyone. Each of you will be expected to perform flaw-lessly, for the responsibilities you are about to undertake are grave indeed. Fellow human beings will place their lives and well-being and that of their loved ones in your hands."

Dr. Henley droned on, and I decided he was a misplaced minister as he talked about awesome responsibilities and the like. If this, I thought, was medical school, it had been vastly overrated to me. We spent the entire day listening to Dr. Henley.

I went to Dr. Dinsmore's office when we were dismissed late that afternoon. He sat behind a rolltop desk, with books and papers cluttered on top of it and a great anatomical chart hanging on the wall. His head down in his hands, he was unaware of my coming into the small office, and I wondered if I had caught him in an unguarded moment. He had seemed, lately, to have recovered so well from the tragedies of his life and to have been so delighted with his new work. Yet I sensed a fatigue or even despair in that posture of defeat.

"Dr. Dinsmore?" I spoke softly.

He brightened immediately. "Mattie! How was the first day?"

"Fine," I lied, preferring to save the story for home, where no one might overhear my candid opinion of Dr. Henley.

"Good, good. I was just waiting for you, so let's get home and check on Sara."

On the walk home, about two and a half miles, I told him in detail about Dr. Henley, laughing at some of his statements and trying to be more serious about others.

"I take it you're amused by all this?"

Was there disapproval in his voice? "No, not amused. But I expected something different from medical school. I expected, well, maybe to be ushered to a cadaver right away or at least to memorize the bones in the body. Some awful assignment that it was impossible to complete. Instead, we got a daylong sermon."

"But an important one. On the ethics and responsibilities of medicine."

Chastened, I was quick to say, "Oh yes, of course. An important lecture."

Then he laughed. "Henley's all right. He's a bit of a bore, but he takes all that very seriously. And it is important. You've worked with me, and you know about responsibility and ethics. But what about some kid just off the farm? How do you know he doesn't take medicine as a lark, better than plowing all day? How do we know why he's here? He's the one who needs that daylong lecture. And you'll get your cadaver soon enough."

Indeed I did. Cadavers and impossible assignments and long hours of studying that left my eyes burning and my back aching. We were in school every day from eight in the morning until five at night, then we rushed home with an armload of books to sit up until nearly morning poring over the day's work and getting ready for the next. Many nights, Dr. Dinsmore would knock at my door and stick his head in to find me asleep over my books.

"Mattie." He'd shake me gently. "Get up and go to bed. You've done enough for one day."

"Can't. I still haven't memorized this muscle group and its relations."

"It will be there tomorrow."

Sometimes I'd take his advice and crawl, bone-weary, into bed, and other times I'd defiantly sit and begin again to read the material I'd just read three times before without understanding a word of it.

I remember still one student, Pete Rendon, who became

my friend, studying with me and often choosing to eat his lunch with me. We all carried sack lunches from home, for none of us could afford to eat at the boardinghouse near the school, and besides, we preferred to study while we ate. Pete was a farm boy with a high school education and, like me, a burning desire not to live as his folks did.

"What about helping other people?" I asked one day.

He stretched a bony leg down the steps on which we sat, ran his hand through his straight blond hair and thought a minute. "I'd like to be honest about that, because I've thought a lot about it. I guess you have to want to help people to be able to do the things medicine requires, but I'm not sure if that's the real reason I'm here. I mean, I don't know if it's burning dedication . . . or a chance to get off the farm."

"Don't let Dr. Dinsmore hear you," I warned. "He thinks you'd better be dedicated or else."

"Oh, I reckon I'm dedicated enough to satisfy him. At least, sure more than that Kimberly fellow."

David Kimberly had rapidly become the least popular student in our class, especially with me. He ingratiated himself with teachers, tried to buddy up to students who were smarter than he was and kept asking to walk me home.

"I walk with Dr. Dinsmore," I said frostily, because the man's too smooth ways infuriated me. At another time, smoothness would, to my misfortune, make a big impression on me, but I wasn't ready to meet men at that point, at least not as men.

"Ah, now, Mattie Armstrong, I know we can be friends, and you need a friend in this place." He leered at me, or so I thought, not being sure what a leer was but having heard the word.

"I have friends, thank you."

"We could study together, and I, ah, I could help you with your work." He leaned close to me, ever so barely taking my elbow with his hand, grinning all the while.

"Or do you mean I could help you?" I jerked my elbow away and marched defiantly in the other direction. One would have thought, or at least I would, that such rudeness would have been enough to discourage Kimberly, but it was not. I had to contend with him during the entire two years of school, because every once in a while he'd decide to offer to help me with my studies or walk me home. I think he wanted an invitation to the house so he could get closer to Dr. Dinsmore, but he never got one.

Christmas of the first year came and went, with only two days off in recognition of the holiday. There was no time off in the summer. By the end of our first year, we were well into our studies and were given the privilege of seeing patients, with a faculty member, of course, at the free dispensary. I was, without exception, assigned to female patients.

"But I might have to treat men someday," I protested in Dr. Dinsmore's office, pacing back and forth across the tiny room.

"Sit down, for heaven's sake, Mattie. You'll kick over my stacks of papers."

"I . . . well, I'm upset. But I don't know who to complain to."

"You probably have a point, but there's that old-fashioned notion still going around out there. Nice ladies would never treat men."

"A lot of men would have died in the Civil War if that was true," I shot back. "I'm not man-crazy or anything like that. I mean, if my reputation was questionable . . ."

He leaned back in his chair, stretching his arms over his head, and smiled at me. "No, your reputation is without a blemish, maybe too much so for your own sake . . ."

"What's that supposed to mean?" Looking back, I know this was a difficult moment for him.

"Do you intend to be a spinster doctor?"

"I . . . I hadn't thought about it. But no, I don't think so."

"Well, Mattie, you're nearly twenty now, and no young man has ever come courting, mostly because you don't encourage anyone."

"I . . . how do you encourage them?" I had never felt more awkward and inferior. I remembered Mama and how men always found her attractive, even when she was sick. I suspect my own sense of inferiority was planted by Mama, unconsciously, when she teased me about being plain and solemn.

"Oh, Mattie!" Dr. Dinsmore was laughing now. "We'll have to teach you how to bat your eyes. Never mind. I like having you to myself. Come on, let's go home."

"No," I said stubbornly. "I may not know how to encourage young men to court me, but I still want to know how to treat men who come to me as patients."

"I didn't distract you, did I? All right, I'll speak to Dr. Wolfe, who's in charge of the dispensary. Now can we go?"

But he left me with that strong feeling of inadequacy, one that later was to surface in my marriage to Em Jones.

I was well aware that I was not attractive, with big, dark eyes that usually had circles under them these days, those high cheekbones and lots of dark hair that I simply pulled back into a knot. Too, I was tall, nearly as tall as Dr. Dinsmore, and I never felt graceful. All those years of comparing myself to Mama had done nothing to improve the way I felt about myself. Years later, when young girls came to me for advice, I always tried to find some way of complimenting them, some way of letting them know they were attractive, because I knew how awful it can be to think of yourself as an ugly duckling.

Pete Rendon courted me in a way. He came for supper on Sunday several times, even went to church with us, and he did walk home with me when Dr. Dinsmore was busy or on the rare days I left earlier than he did. But I didn't take Pete seriously. He had country-bumpkin manners, slurping his food and talking with his mouth full. I once had to kick Sara because I could see she, who had been corrected so often herself, was about to warn him, "Don't talk with your mouth full!" The manners were indicative of a certain polish that Pete lacked and Dr. Dinsmore had taught me to appreciate. None of us were sorry when Pete stopped coming around the house. I saw him later with a pretty blond town girl.

In the fall of my second year, Pete was replaced as my study companion and friend by the second girl to enter the Omaha Medical College. Cora Strothers was from Omaha, twenty-three years old, and very bright. She was the first woman friend I'd ever had. In childhood I'd missed the girlfriend part of growing up, and Cora, because she was such a good friend, made me realize what I'd missed. We became inseparable, in and out of school, and I even thought of asking if she wanted to move in to Dr. Dinsmore's because it was so much closer to the school than her home. Besides, she came from a large family and a noisy house, and she often complained that studying at home was difficult for her.

"No, Mattie, I don't think that's a good idea." Dr. Dinsmore surprised me, because I thought he would be enthusiastic about my plan. "I don't think Cora Strothers has the quality you do."

"Quality?"

"I don't think she will be the physician you will. And frankly, I'm jealous. You spend all your time with her and have none left for me these days." He said it lightly, with a casual arm around my shoulders as we stood in the parlor, but some instinct, some feeling I wasn't used to, told me he meant it more than casually. I was uncomfortable.

Mr. Reeves and Will Henry came to Omaha that year. It was the first time I'd seen my brother in five long years, and I was like a little kid when I got the letter saying to expect them. They took the railroad from a place called Fort Sidney, some thirty miles from where they were living in a soddie.

"All these years, I've heard about soddies. Tell me exactly what a soddie is." I remembered they had lived in a soddie in Kansas before Mama died.

"Oh, Mattie, it's a house." Will Henry was thirteen that year, gangly and all legs and awkwardness. He would be tall, like me, you could tell from his huge hands and feet, but he hadn't gotten there yet. He had a thick patch of brown hair, pale like Mama's, but his eyes were like mine, large and dark. On him, they were attractive, I thought. Now he bubbled over with laughter at my ignorance. "You build it of chunks of sod from the prairie."

"A house made of dirt?" I was incredulous.

"Well, kind of, yeah, but it's warm inside, and the dirt doesn't bother you much. Pop put net over the ceiling to catch the worst of what falls down."

"It falls down! Will Henry, you must come to visit me often, because I swear to heaven I'll never set foot in a house made of dirt where the ceiling falls in." I stamped my foot jokingly to emphasize my horror.

He laughed all the harder. "Tell her about a dugout, Pop."

I had noticed before that he called Mr. Reeves "Pop" and that there was a strong affection between them. His Pop was the father neither of us ever had, and I was glad he had that relationship. It was the same as what I fancied I had with Dr. Dinsmore.

Mr. Reeves just sat back, grinning, and said, "You tell her, son. You lived in one long enough."

Will Henry chortled gleefully. "It's half a house and half a hole in the ground," he told me. "You dig out a place on the side of a rise in the ground, and you shore the edges up with lumber and put a sod roof over it. We lived in one for two years this time before Pop got our soddie built."

"Sounds awful," I shuddered. "Worse, Will Henry, than that little tiny house we grew up in."

He grew sad. "Mama would have loved it out here. She

never liked Missouri, and she was so much happier after we left there. I miss her."

"So do I," I lied. Strange, but I hadn't really missed Mama, because she was part of a life so different from what I was living now. But Will Henry would never have understood that.

When I asked about school, Will Henry twisted his cap in his hand, studied his toe, and mumbled something.

"He isn't much of a student," drawled Mr. Reeves, "but I keep after him. I know it was important to your ma. Will Henry, he's goin' back to school this fall." He said it with such assurance that the boy just nodded.

They stayed two days, shopping and treating themselves to a meal at the City Hotel. I was glad to see them but relieved when they left and I could get back to my studies.

"Now, Mattie, you come on out West and be a doctor, soon as you get out of school." Mr. Reeves put a huge arm around my shoulder and hugged me. "You got a home out there, you know."

"I know, and I appreciate it, but I'll probably stay right here in Omaha when I finish school." I hadn't thought about that, but I guess it was like staying with Dr. Dinsmore. I hadn't considered any other possibilities. "Besides, I told you, I don't want to live in a house where dirt falls from the ceiling all the time." I laughed as I said it, but silently I was remembering that I would never again live poor. Omaha, with its big houses, was the place for me.

We put them on the westbound train and watched until it pulled out of the station.

"Do you miss them, Mattie?" Dr. Dinsmore took my arm and guided me back to the street, where a carriage waited.

"No," I said honestly. "I love Will Henry—he was such a sweet little boy—and Mr. Reeves is an awfully nice man, good to Will Henry. But I don't feel related to them. I feel, well, different."

"You are. You live in a totally different world."

"I guess both Will Henry and I are fortunate," I said. "We both found fathers."

He looked like I'd hit him. "I hope there's a difference," he said grimly, and was silent the rest of the way home.

I told Cora about Will Henry and the soddie, and she laughed brightly. "Mattie, you better go East with me. I'm going to practice in a city and live in a comfortable house and drive fine horses."

"Dreams, Cora, just dreams."

"You wait and see," she challenged.

I found I liked taking care of patients. I liked talking to them, hearing about their lives, helping with their problems.

There was the young mother with the colicky baby, both of them exhausted from lack of sleep.

"You need to get your husband to take care of the baby some, so you can rest," I told her brashly.

"He can't do that. He works in the stockyards."

"Well," I leapt in, "when he's home at night."

"He's not home," she said, as though I were a dolt. "He's down to the tavern, drinking beer. Can't stand to hear the baby cry."

Indignation did me no good. I showed her how to hold the poor little thing over her knee and put some slight pressure on the stomach to ease the pain.

My supervisor, Dr. Wolfe, upbraided me severely. "You must not pry into your patients' personal lives. You are here to help them with their health, not to reform the world."

"But it's not right," I fumed. "Why should that man be allowed to run away from a crying baby and probably spend all their money at the tavern while this poor woman is stuck at home, dead tired?"

"Really, Miss Armstrong, if you wish to be a physician, you are going to have to learn to control that sense of, uh, self-righteousness. Try giving the baby a very mild dose of laudanum."

"I will not! Infants do not need to have their bodies disturbed with poisonous drugs."

"Miss Armstrong, I am instructing you on the proper care of a patient, not asking for your opinion."

I bit my tongue to keep from mentioning his righteous indignation, but of course I heard about the incident later. Dr. Wolfe wasted no time in complaining to Dr. Dinsmore.

"Mattie, you must have been a terror. He came into my office with coattails flying, literally fuming. I had to calm him down before I could get the straight of the story."

"You didn't get the straight of the story," I told him crossly, slamming shut the book I'd been trying to concentrate on. "You got his version. The man was insufferable."

"Maybe so, maybe so. I know he has that capacity. But, Mattie, he is the teacher, and you are the student."

"That doesn't matter if he's wrong. And you know he was. You wouldn't give anything like that to an infant."

I'd caught him, and he knew it. "No. Everyone has his own way of practicing medicine, and you're right, I prefer to avoid strong potions."

"What would you have done for the baby?"

"Advised frequent small feedings, I guess, and maybe rubbing its back. Did it suck its thumb?"

"Yes."

"Maybe that's the problem. Taking in too much air with that thumb. They might have to cover the hands or something."

"Poor little mite. It would probably cry all the harder then. And that poor woman, taking care of two children, one an infant and the other not quite two. But her husband sitting in a bar! Men are awful!"

"Give us a chance, Mattie. Not all of us are like that." He turned serious. "But you must try to be a little more respectful to the faculty, even if you disagree. And Dr. Wolfe has a point, you know. You'll just wear yourself out for nothing if you try to solve all the personal problems of your patients."

It was a lesson I never learned.

By the time I was nearing completion of my studies, I had earned a good reputation at the school. I knew it not only from the comments of my instructors, even that stick Dr. Wolfe, but from my own feeling about my work. I enjoyed medicine, more than I thought I would. I had probably gone to medical school for all the wrong reasons—because of Mama and Dr. Dinsmore and my need to escape Princeton, but not because it was what Mattie Armstrong wanted to do. But once I was there, I found it was the thing I wanted to do with my life. I was lucky. Most people who choose to do something on the basis of what other people need make themselves miserable.

Anyway, it appeared that I would stand at the head of my class. Now, mind you, it wasn't a very big class, only nineteen students, but I was the first woman, and I was proud of my accomplishment.

I shared the news first with Sara. "Oh, Sara, the most wonderful news. I made the top of the class. When we graduate, I'll be the first woman and the best student in the class."

She jumped up to hug me, and we whirled around again together. And that's where Dr. Dinsmore found us.

"Can I join this dance, too?" He laughed and put an arm around each of us.

Somehow, his presence canceled my dancing mood, and I stood still, though he didn't take away the arm he had laid casually about my waist.

"I was . . . celebrating," I said, but before I could go on, he interrupted me.

Eyes twinkling, he turned to me and said, "Dean Lacross gave me the news about your academic standing this afternoon. I am proud, of course, but I have to tell you, Mattie, that I knew all along you could do it."

"Thank you," I said. His praise, of course, meant much more to me than anything Dean Lacross could say, but right that moment I was feeling uncertain and I didn't know why. "I'm glad I made you proud. I . . . I'm rather pleased myself." Now, I'm not given to crying, and wasn't then, but I couldn't help a big tear that welled up in my eyes as I thought that I wished Mama could know. She'd have been proud, too, and much as Dr. Dinsmore had to do with my education, Mama had sewn some seeds, set some standards that had helped set the course of my life.

"Mattie, have you given serious thought to what you will do after you complete your studies?"

"Not really." That was a bald-faced lie, but sometimes the future is so hard to face, you just put it off. I'd thought a lot about it. Cora wanted me to wait until she finished her studies, another year, and then we would open an office together, specializing in the treatment of female complaints. It sounded like the most logical thing to do, but I wasn't sure what to do in that year until Cora finished. I couldn't envision myself setting up an office in Omaha alone, and I felt it was time I left Dr. Dinsmore's house. I was afraid to commit myself to any course of action.

"Well, Dean Lacross spoke to me about something else this afternoon," Dr. Dinsmore went on, apparently unaware of the tangle of thoughts in my brain. "Sara, dear, why don't you run help Kate and let me talk to Mattie."

Sara pouted at being sent from the room, but she went promptly.

"Dr. Lacross would like you to stay on at the college, working in the infirmary. You wouldn't, of course, be directly involved in teaching students until you've had a little more experience. But you would see patients and help with the overseeing of cases."

I was furious! "Dean Lacross told you that and didn't tell me this afternoon?"

"Now, Mattie, don't be so angry. Of course he did. You know Dr. Lacross' attitude about women. Even if you are a doctor, he probably doesn't think you have enough sense to decide your own future."

"Well, I do, you know, and I don't think I want to establish myself in an atmosphere dominated by someone like that." I turned abruptly and began to gather my things from the table, feeling all the while the flush rise in my face.

"You're prettier when you're angry, Mattie," he said softly, "but anger isn't going to get you anywhere. Common sense is. I think the offer is a good one. You could continue to live right here, and for the first time, you'd have an income. Try it for a year and see what happens."

"I'll see," I said stonily. That night I cried into my pillow for the first time in years, tears of frustration and confusion. Was I always going to be dependent on Dr. Dinsmore and always beaten by the prejudice I met around me? My pleasure in my profession seemed to sour.

The next morning I marched into Dean Lacross' office. "Sir, I understand you wish to make me an offer concerning next year."

"Ah, Mattie, yes. I see Dr. Dinsmore has talked to you." He still had the slightly stiff, patronizing air he'd demonstrated at my first interview nearly two years before, and I still resented it mightily.

"Yes, he did. But I must tell you, Dr. Lacross, that I'd prefer you discuss my future with me rather than with

Dr. Dinsmore."

"Oh, now, I didn't mean any harm. I know he advises you and is responsible for you."

"He isn't responsible for me," I said indignantly. "Dr. Dinsmore has been very good to me, and I rely on his advice. But I am responsible for myself, and I will make my own decisions."

Dr. Lacross looked at me a long time, and then he apologized. I was surprised by the apology and tried to be graceful in accepting it, but it threw the proverbial monkey wrench into my plans. I had come to refuse the offer, haughtily, of course, and after talking with Dr. Lacross, I was mollified enough to say that I would consider it.

Cora encouraged me to take it. "Who knows what will happen in a year, Mattie? I think you should do it. Then, if we still want to go into practice together, you can resign. Besides, my plans might change."

She meant, I suspected, that she might have other plans, both professional and personal. One of her classmates, Dwight Peterson, had been courting her rather strongly, and that probably was behind her change in plans. I accepted the job with the school.

One of the things I felt I had to do was to write Will Henry and Mr. Reeves about my decision. I knew they both kind of harbored a hope that I would settle in western Nebraska, and I hated to disappoint them. But I simply could not see myself leaving Omaha, especially for what sounded to me like a wild country.

Their answer, written jointly, came quite quickly, considering the state of mail service in those days. They were disappointed but wished me well, and wouldn't I come to Benteen to visit before I began my new duties at the college? I toyed with that idea but ultimately rejected it, urging them instead to try to come to my graduation.

Dr. Dinsmore had been partly responsible for my decision that I could not visit them. "Mattie, how would I get along without you?" he asked jokingly. There was an underlying seriousness in his tone that alarmed me.

"Someday, you know, it's going to be time for me to grow up and leave this house." I said it lightly, but I, too, was serious.

So was he. "I hope not."

We wore the traditional mortarboard and black graduation gowns, and all during the ceremony I felt like I had to pinch myself. Had Mattie Armstrong, that ugly girl from the wrong side of the tracks in Princeton, really come this far? I felt a sense of panic that I would never be able to retain all that I had learned, alternating with a wonderful sense of self-confidence that I had really done it, I had completed medical school. I was proud, of course, to be the first woman, but that didn't mean as much to me as leading the class.

After graduation, there was a reception at the school, with champagne—the first I'd ever tasted—and tiny cakes. Everyone milled around, offering congratulations and asking questions about the future.

"Oh, Mattie, I'm so excited!" Sara nearly jumped up and down in her joy. "I'm going to be a doctor, too, when I grow up. I know I can do it, just like you."

"Of course you can, Sara, if that's what you really want."

"I don't know that I could stand to have two women doctors in the house," Dr. Dinsmore laughed. "One may be more than I can handle." Again, his arm rested casually around my waist, a possessive gesture that was becoming more frequent and was, to me, unsettling.

Cora congratulated me and confided the news that she and Dwight Peterson planned to be married as soon as they finished their studies. She thought I'd done the right thing by staying at the school, because Dwight talked of the two of them going to Chicago to practice. Chicago! The very thought intimidated me, and I was glad I had stayed at the college, too. It seemed the right thing to do.

Dean Lacross congratulated me, too, sincerely, saying that in truth he had had his doubts about my ability, but he now had to admit that he was wrong, and he was, indeed, proud of my achievement. He was a sophisticated man, dignified, you'd say, and to have someone like that praise me, a country girl from Missouri, was heady indeed. I forgave him all his slights to my womanhood.

Will Henry and Mr. Reeves did not come to graduation. I barely had time to miss them.

Working at the clinic seemed little different than my final student days, so my life went on essentially unchanged. I felt pretty smug, I guess, sure that I was settled. I would be a doctor and live happily ever after in Omaha. Reminds me of the Greek saying that whom the Gods would destroy, they first make mad with power. I wasn't mad with power, just smug with success. And, of course, I wasn't destroyed. Just pointed in a new direction which turned out to be the best thing that ever could have happened to me. But if you'd told me those first days in the clinic that within a year I'd be living in a soddie in western Nebraska, the only doctor for miles and miles, I'd have either laughed or cringed in terror.

I became active in the newly organized Douglas County Medical Society, working with public education programs, going out to churches and the like to give talks on the importance of cleanliness, proper treatment for cholera and things like that. Public speaking terrified me at first, but I found that I was good at it. People responded. I think a lot of young mothers responded simply because I was a woman, sharing with them, rather than a man preaching at them. I was so successful at the public education program and so willing to go out and speak when other doctors thought they were too busy that I was soon elected president of the medical society.

"Now, Mattie, that's a real feather in your cap. To think they'd elect a woman president." Dr. Dinsmore beamed as we rode home in the carriage after the meeting.

"Bother!" I answered. "Being a woman had nothing to do with it. They just know I'm the only one who's willing to do the work and will take the time."

"The medical college, of course, will let you take as much time as you need. They want to be closely involved in the local society, you know."

"Closely involved? You mean they want to control it!"

"Ah, Mattie, you do have a gentle way with words. Yes, they want to control it so they can maintain the quality of medicine in this area. It's not such a bad goal, you know."

"Still sounds like tyranny to me."

Dr. Dinsmore threw up his hands in mock despair and

said loudly, "Look what I've created! Educate a woman and you get yourself all kinds of trouble!"

We laughed together, and it was the last unrestrained laugh I remember that we shared.

It took me months to realize it, but Dr. Dinsmore was the fly in my ointment. The man who'd rescued me from Princeton, the man whose every judgement I respected and whose every word I dwelt on, the man to whom I owed everything that I was now proud of—he'd changed. Or I'd changed. Or somewhere, something was different.

I'd noticed for some time that he put an arm around me differently than he did Sara, or that he seemed to stare intently at me when he talked to me, whereas when I was younger he would discuss medicine with me in a kind of abstracted way, so that I knew I was a handy listening post, not really the object of his talk. Nowadays I felt like he was always talking directly to me, and his talks became more philosophical, less scientific.

I still regarded him as the father I'd lost or never had, and for him to step out of that role, with the casual hugs and soul-baring conversations, made me uncomfortable with a guilt I couldn't pinpoint. He would discuss life, love, children, health as a reflection of mental happiness. One day he startled me by saying, "You know, Mattie, man was not meant to live alone. Nor woman either. It's not good for emotional health. I shall want to remarry soon. Have you thought about marriage?"

I was making notes for a presentation to the medical society, and his remark caused me to press so hard on my pencil that I broke it. "No," I hesitated. "I haven't given it much thought, because I just always assumed that it was something I would think about when I met the man I wanted to marry." Vaguely, I knew what he was hinting at, but the idea of a romantic relationship with him was so foreign, so impossible that I blocked out the thought.

"And you haven't met that man?"

I laughed nervously. "You know very well you and Sara would be the first ones to know about that. And you also know there haven't been any men around here courting me."

"That's true." He fingered his watch chain and gave me that intense look again. "But I didn't know if you'd met someone at the clinic or perhaps the church."

"Well, I haven't." I tried to say it with finality and turn back to my work, but he disconcerted me by crossing the room to stand above me.

"That's good," he said softly, looking down at me until I was compelled to look away in confusion.

Dr. Dinsmore began to ask me to be his hostess on various occasions and to accompany him to some social functions. I was a little anxious about this but viewed it, truthfully, as another step in his prolonged training of me. By sitting at his dinner table, I learned to watch after the guests' needs, to signal Kate when more water or wine was needed, to judge the moment to have the first course cleared away and the next served. Not that I've used any of those skills lately. People in sod huts tend to eat a lot more casually than those at the dinner parties we gave and attended. There was quite a round of social events in Omaha, and now that I was out of school and had more time, I was free to accompany Dr. Dinsmore.

I still addressed him as Dr. Dinsmore. Do you know a teacher for ten years and suddenly start calling him John? I couldn't do that, even though he brought the subject up.

"My dear, don't you think, especially when we are out in public together, that you could call me John? Dr. Dinsmore sounds so formal. It makes me think I'm escorting a schoolgirl around."

In my mind, he was still escorting a schoolgirl, and for me to call him Dr. Dinsmore was the most natural thing in the world. But after that, I called him nothing but merely waited until I had his eye if I wanted to speak to him. I'm not sure if he noticed my evasion or not.

Things went on like this for several months. Even Sara noticed the difference. "You and Papa go so many places without me these days," she complained. "Why are you always going out at night to dinner parties?"

"Shhh, Sara. It's important for your father's work at the medical school." I repeated the justification he had given me, word for word, because I wanted to believe it.

"Not your work?" The child was perceptive.

"My work isn't as important. Someday your father will be a well-known, even famous doctor and educator, and that's what's important."

"Are the parties fun?"

"Your father enjoys them a great deal."

"And you?"

I hesitated, wishing she weren't quite so smart and knowing that I had rarely if ever misled Sara by the tiniest of white lies. "I enjoy them, too, but because they're showing me a whole new world, a way of behaving and a set of manners that I know nothing about."

"And Papa already knew about these manners? What can be so different from the manners he drums into me all the time—don't eat with your elbows on the table, chew with your mouth closed, butter your bread on the plate and not in the air!"

I laughed at her recital, dismal as it was. "Those things are important, of course. You wouldn't go to a fancy dinner party and chew with your mouth open, would you? And yes, your father knew all those things from long ago when he lived in Philadelphia, not Princeton."

Dr. Dinsmore had grown up in the East in a wealthy family and had reached young manhood without fighting in the Great War because he had come West at that time to ride with a physician. He once explained to me that he abhorred war to the extent that he left his family, who, being loyal Northerners, disinherited him, although they gave him a kind of nest egg which enabled him to keep himself comfortable. He had simply ridden west until he found a place to stop, and that place had been a small town in Missouri where he spent three years studying under the local doctor. It was there, too, that he'd met and married Mrs. Dinsmore. And when he felt he'd learned all that doctor could teach him, he packed up his wife and the medical books he'd acquired and rode again until he found a town that needed a doctor. That was Princeton. But he hadn't always lived the unsophisticated small-town life, and once in Omaha, his city tastes and sophistication, which had always distinguished him in Princeton, made him part of a very fashionable crowd. I was a tagger-on.

Our relationship came to a head one night after one of those dinner parties, some eight months after I'd gone to work at the clinic. We arrived home late. Kate and Sara were both asleep, and the house was quiet and dark.

"Stay a moment, Mattie. Don't rush off to sleep."

"Oh, I'm really very tired," I yawned. Being so ladylike and watching my manners was always exhausting to me, and I really was tired.

"Come sit here on the sofa beside me. I want to talk to you."

So I sat, primly, with a distance of maybe a foot between us. Before I could say a word, Dr. Dinsmore was next to me, his arms around me, his lips brushing my cheek.

"Mattie, Mattie, you must know that I'm in love with you. I want to marry you." And he kissed me, a kiss that began gently, inquiringly, and then became demanding and firm, even as I tried desperately to pull away, my fists pushing against his chest, my heart beating wildly.

Finally, released, I fairly leapt across the room to stand and stare in shocked and frightened disbelief, outraged that he had stepped out of his role as father and tried to become a lover. If I had loved him in return, response would have been automatic, but I felt no awakening surge. Fleetingly, I thought that I wasn't feeling the things that I was supposed to when a man kissed me that way. But this wasn't any man. This was my beloved Dr. Dinsmore.

Before I could gather my senses, he crossed the room to grab me again, one hand fumbling at the buttons of my dress, the other holding me immobile. I fought an urge to scream only because I didn't want to alarm Sara.

"Mattie, don't fight me. It's meant to be. We belong together." His breath smelled of wine, heavy and unpleasant.

I don't know how I broke away from that iron grasp, but I remember finally stumbling and running from the room in tears, slamming the door to my bedroom and not caring by then if I wakened Sara and Kate. I threw myself on the bed and sobbed loudly, the kind of great sobs that come from confusion too strong to be borne. How could he have done that? The man who stood for everything right had done what I thought the most unpardonable thing he could. He had violated not only my physical body but my relationship to him, my respect for him. In one drunken moment, he had wiped out almost ten years and destroyed the foundation on which I had built my life.

Next morning I stayed in bed. When Sara knocked on the door to tell me breakfast was ready, I pled a headache.

"Can't I bring you something, Mattie? Perhaps some tea?"

"No," I said, my voice as feeble as I felt. "Just leave me alone." I burrowed under the covers, hoping she would not come into the room. My eyes were red and puffy, and my head throbbing from all my crying. Every time I thought of the previous evening and the dilemma I now faced, a slight wave of nausea crept over me.

I appeared at the dinner table, pale but, I hoped, composed, and tried to carry on as normally as possible. Dr. Dinsmore was quieter than usual, barely speaking during the meal, and Sara, well aware of the tension though baffled by its cause, tried to lighten the atmosphere by incessant prattling about her schoolwork, her friends, an upcoming party. Each time she addressed me, I smiled as brightly as I could and made some appropriate comment. But I had only to look beyond the dining room table to the mirror on the wall to see how pale my face was, how false my smile. Dr. Dinsmore avoided looking at me, for which I was grateful. A direct look from his haunted face would have sent me running from the table.

"If you're feeling well enough, I'd like to speak to you after dinner," he said as we rose to leave the table. Neither his face nor voice betrayed the emotion he must have been feeling.

"Certainly," I said formally. "Sara, will you excuse us?"

She nodded mutely, and Dr. Dinsmore, walking erectly as always, led the way to his study. I followed, obediently. Hadn't I always done what he had told me to? And yet, I fought with every step the urge to run and lock myself in my room. I knew he would make no more advances, but sorting out the previous night's scene promised to be even more uncomfortable than the scene itself. My heart pounded as before, and I felt a flush cover my face.

He closed the door firmly, while I stood awkwardly in the center of the room, waiting to see where he would go, what he would do.

He crossed the room slowly, as though walking were almost painful for him, and sat at the round oak table where Sara had done so much of her homework. Without looking at me, he said wearily, "You have no cause to worry. I won't repeat last night's bitter scene."

I knew then that he was angry with himself, desperately

angry, and not with me. For the first time, I felt a rush of pity, an urge to go to him and comfort him in the way I might have done before. But my own inner turmoil was too strong, and I simply stood there, shifting nervously from one foot to the other, my hands nearly tearing a handkerchief in half behind my back.

"You can sit down, you know."

Obediently, I sat on the edge of the sofa, looking, I'm sure, as if I were poised for flight. And in truth, I was. Every fiber of my being wanted to run from the room.

"You must know that I wish to apologize, Mattie." He spoke in a soft, controlled voice, but one more distant than he had often used of late in speaking to me. "I . . . There is no way to tell you how much I regret attacking you . . . There is, unfortunately, no other word for it. I will not, cannot change the emotions I expressed. I had thought, perhaps, you were aware of my feelings, and I had hoped you shared them. But that is no excuse. I realize you are inexperienced, and I apologize for trying to take advantage."

I sat silently during this long speech, still twisting my handkerchief and looking at the floor. I ached for him, for the humiliation he must be suffering, but still I could not bring myself to reassure him. It wasn't that I wanted him to suffer but more that I myself could not yet get the past evening out of my mind.

He waited a moment, as though hoping I would speak, and then went on. "I assure you it won't happen again. I had, as you well know, drunk too much wine last night, and I'm afraid that contributed to my loss of self-control. After this, I will see that neither the wine nor the loss of self-control will be repeated. I hope in time you can for-give me." He rose then, as though his having said what he needed to had solved the entire matter.

I wasn't sure whether he was coming toward me or leaving the room, but in one breath I blurted out, "I have decided to leave."

He stopped, surprised and indignant, and when he answered, there was anger in his voice. "That's entirely unnecessary. And foolish."

I saw then what I had blinded myself to in all the years of my devotion to him. He was a fair, honest and kind man, but he expected things to be done as he wished. He could not tolerate disagreement. Yet there I sat, having had the nerve to cross him in a major way, perhaps the most major way for both our lives.

"It may be foolish, but it's very necessary." I tried to speak calmly. "I have spent the day thinking about it, and it's the only answer for me."

"You really mean that, don't you?" His anger paled as he saw that I was sincere.

"Yes," I said firmly, and watched as he bowed his head and muttered, "What have I done?"

I couldn't tell him. I didn't know how to explain how much I admired and respected him, how he'd become the father I never had and how I couldn't, wouldn't change my relationship to him. That tangled web of thoughts was beyond explanation. And the force of his apology made me reluctant to express my anger and indignation. He had hurt himself enough. There was no need for me to hurt him further.

"I'm going to join Will Henry and Mr. Reeves. I'll write

them in the morning."

"You'll leave Omaha and the college?"

Looking directly at him this time, I said, "Yes. I feel I have to."

"Now, wait a minute!" Now his voice thundered, indignant anger returning. "I will not believe that one incident will chase you away from a life you've been building. I won't bear that responsibility."

"No. It's not your fault. It's my decision. It's what will make me comfortable. I want to build a life out there."

"In a sod hut? You're the one who couldn't bear the thought of living in a house where dirt fell from the roof!" He was sarcastic now, as though he would make me see the utter folly of my decision.

"You remember," I smiled. "Yes, but I imagine I'll learn to live in a sod hut and a lot more. I think I'm going to like it."

He was quiet again, the bravado of the last minute changed to sadness, and I was almost alarmed by these sudden changes in his mood. "Mattie, Sara will miss you. I will miss you. I meant it last night. I love you."

"You know, I love you, too. But in a different way than you mean, and we would make each other forever uncomfortable, even at the medical school. Besides"—I hesitated, feeling bold to add what I wanted to say next—"I don't think you love me as much as you think. You're lonely, and it's time for you to remarry. I suspect that you'll be remarried within a year." As I spoke, I felt composed and in control of the situation. My decision, forced on me, was one I should have made alone much sooner.

He looked anguished when I predicted his remarriage,

as though I'd accused him of infidelity. "Never. I love you, Mattie Armstrong."

No use to tell him that he loved what he thought he had created, but that I couldn't be Pygmalion for him. The story wouldn't end that way.

"I'll tell Sara that I've been thinking this over for some time, and that I feel it's time for me to join my family."

"You won't tell her that her father attacked you?" He said it bitterly.

"Please don't," I said. "I'd like to forget that last night ever happened. I want to go on feeling that you're the person I most respect and admire, and I hope you'll go on feeling proud of me. Maybe you'll be proud of what I do in Benteen." I rose and left the room, leaving him standing there.

Sara and I had a tearful talk. I thought I was composed and brave and would not break down, but when I looked at her and saw those huge tears welling up in her brown eyes, I broke down and cried, too. Hugging each other, we cried and talked through the tears.

"Mattie, you never said you missed them. I thought we were your family."

"You are, dear, you are. But it's time for me to get to know them. You're growing up nicely, and you're well settled here. You'll do fine without me."

"No, I won't. I'll come to Benteen."

"Of course you will, someday. I want you to. I'll miss you very much."

"When are you going?"

"Oh, I imagine it will take a month for me to make

preparations, and I have to give notice at the college."

Sara cheered a little at that. When you're thirteen, a month seems forever, and you don't have to face things until they are right upon you, until the day they happen.

I wrote to Will Henry and Mr. Reeves, telling them of my decision, asking them to arrange living quarters for me (with an ironic comment that I retracted all my horror about soddies) and asking what I should need to purchase to set myself up in housekeeping. At twenty-three, I owned none of the necessities, because I'd always lived with Dr. Dinsmore. Fortunately, because of his generosity, I had been able to save much of my salary at the medical school during the last months, and he had agreed to loan me the balance that I needed to establish myself. My plan was to purchase household furnishings in Omaha and have them shipped west, a plan that Dr. Dinsmore agreed was the only sensible thing to do. In spite of the tension between us, I still relied on his advice.

I spent the next weeks gathering the things I would need. I had my medical supplies—bag, books, some anatomical wall charts for my office to use in demonstration to patients. I was woefully unaware that I would have no office for nearly four years, and an anatomical wall chart would do me precious little good when I had to ride horseback five miles and more, usually more, to see my patients. But I forged ahead, blissful in my ignorance. I gathered a supply of the usual medicine—cathartics and emetics, diuretics and so on, though I intended to use them sparingly.

But it was household goods that caused me more grief.

I had been supervising the Dinsmore household long enough now to feel fairly comfortable about pots and pans, linens and bedclothes, but the idea of starting from scratch was appalling. So, I thought, was the money I spent, though today it wouldn't buy one towel. I decided to equip my house sparingly. After all, people did have supplies sent in to small towns like Benteen, and it would be better to arrive with too little than too much.

Mr. Reeves and Will Henry had written as soon as they received my letter. Rather, Will Henry wrote, and Mr. Reeves asked him to add some words of welcome from him, too. I don't think Mr. Reeves wrote much, if at all, but that wasn't uncommon in that day. The only thing I ever knew him to write was the letter telling me of my mother's death, and I guess he felt he had to do that himself, no matter how hard it was for him.

Will Henry was delighted that I was coming, his letter so full of plans that he never thought to ask why I had changed my mind so abruptly. I was grateful.

He assured me they would have a soddie for me, and said they had already picked out a claim. It was on the river, like theirs, only mine had the only three trees in the whole valley. Horsemen from miles around used it as a landmark, because there was quicksand on either side, but at my trees the crossing was safe. They would, said Will Henry, have a soddie built within a week or two, and when would I arrive?

It was February when I made my decision, and by mid-March, I was ready to set the date. I would take the Union Pacific to Fort Sidney on April 15. I wrote to Will Henry that I would expect him to meet me, with a large wagon, unless I heard otherwise. As the days went by, and I heard nothing from him to cause me to cancel my plans, April 15 became a red-letter day in my mind.

It would be sensible to say that I left Omaha with mixed emotions, but that wasn't true. Once I had decided to live in the western part of the state, it seemed that there had never been another choice for me. I left Omaha without a doubt, sure that I was sailing into a bright new future.

Sara, of course, did not see it as a good decision, and the closer the actual day came, the droopier she got. I tried to cheer her with tales of sod huts, tales that I made up of whole cloth, I confess, but she remained unconvinced that life would be worth anything after I left. Leaving her was a wrench for me, and though I tried hard to sympathize with her point of view, I sometimes wanted to scream at her, "Don't you realize this is hard on me, too? Can't you make it easier on me?" I even occasionally had the wicked thought of telling her to ask her father why I was leaving, but I would never have done that.

Dr. Dinsmore was reserved, but he made it clear that he wished I would change my mind, and he frequently sided with Sara in a kind of litany of pleading that suggested I stay. He would pretend it was a joke, that he was simply teasing Sara when he said, "I don't know why she insists on leaving. Have you been cruel to her, Sara? Of course she should stay here. Things would be much better if she did, but Mattie has to do what she wants, regardless if she breaks our hearts." I knew there was nothing funny about what he said, in spite of his droll look and his mock posture of defeat.

Finally the day came. Dr. Dinsmore hired a dray to take my luggage to the station. The furniture had been shipped earlier, but still, it seemed I had an inordinate quantity of goods to take with me. Even Sara teased me about it.

"Goodness, Mattie, are you moving into a castle? There'll be no room for you once you put all this stuff into your soddie. Is that the right word?"

"Yes, dear, that's the right word. And you may well be right. My supplies may crowd me out of house and home." I laughed, too loudly, I'm sure, and turned to her father, wanting to reach out and touch him and yet equally afraid he would touch me.

"I don't know . . ." I began tremulously, starting to extend my hand for a rather formal handshake.

He grasped it in both of his hands. "Mattie, you don't have to say anything. You've been a godsend to both Sara and me, and whatever we've been able to do for you is merely a trifle in terms of repayment. I . . . I wish things had turned out differently." He stared intently at me, the look I had learned to dread, but now, once again, there was concern, a flash of my old Dr. Dinsmore, in his eyes.

I didn't want to say I wished things had turned out differently, too, because at that point, I didn't. I was pleased that his behavior, which he now regretted so much, had given me the impetus to do something that I should probably have done long before. I could only say thank you.

Sara threw herself into my arms, sobbing loudly—she was, remember, thirteen, a most dramatic age—and I tried to comfort her, but I was teary again myself. They had both been my family for so long that it was awful for me to part with them, no matter how much I looked forward to my new life. My excitement about the future was balanced, too, with a fear that occasionally crept up behind me to proclaim that I was an utter fool, throwing my future away on a whim and leading myself into a grim and bitter life.

As the train pulled out of the station, I waved while I could see them and then settled back in the plush seat of the coach section, where Dr. Dinsmore had insisted that I ride. From then on, the wheels sang two songs to me. The first, encouraging, was, "You're going to a new life, a new life, a new and good life." But it was countered by, "You've been silly, Mattie, silly Mattie, silly, silly, silly." I slept a little, stared out the window a lot on that trip.

I don't know what I expected of Fort Sidney, but it wasn't much of a town. All I really was aware of as Will Henry and Mr. Reeves encompassed me in bear hugs was a wooden railroad station with one dusty street stretching out behind it. I later came to know, of course, that there were stores—a general merchandise store, a saloon, a bank of sorts, and the lawyer's and doctor's offices, a dressmaker's shop and all the signs of struggling civilization. But that first day I was too confused and uncertain to register much of any thought except, "Is this what I left Omaha for?"

I turned from the disappointing town to look at Will Henry and our stepfather. Mr. Reeves hadn't changed at all. Oh, maybe a touch of gray tinged that curly dark brown hair, but he was still big and kind and gentle, and I still thought he could do anything in the world.

Will Henry, though, he was sixteen by then, and in the

three years since I'd seen him, he'd changed from a gangly and awkward kid to a young adult. I stared appraisingly, sensing that one day soon he would also be able to do anything he put his mind to.

"Sight for sore eyes, isn't she, Will Henry?"

Will Henry swiped at a stray bit of that thick brown hair that had fallen onto his forehead and said, almost shyly, "She looks like Mattie to me."

I suppose I did look the same, my hair pulled back in a bun that emphasized my large eyes and high cheekbones. What I didn't know then was that my skin would never again, after exposure to the prairie sun and wind, be as soft again. It would become leathery, like Mr. Reeves'. Even Will Henry's face looked tough and tanned to me.

Of course, Fort Sidney wasn't my destination. Benteen, miles away across the prairie, was where I was headed. Will Henry and Mr. Reeves—he insisted right off that I call him Jim, and it made it easier for both of us, although he tried to call me Dr. Mattie, and I had to put a stop to that on the grounds that it wasn't fair—anyway, they were most efficient about loading my worldly goods, which had been unceremoniously dumped on the station plat-form. Boxes of books and dishes and medical supplies, clothes and linen, and all that I owned were loaded, and we were on our way before the reality of the situation could register. You know how you can be kind of caught up in the moment and later think how unconscious you were through a string of events.

I came to consciousness, however, during the ride to Benteen. It took one whole long day, what with the horses pulling a heavily loaded wagon. I became aware of the endless prairie, rising and dipping and extending as far as the eye could see with not a tree to break the sight. I hadn't learned the prairie then, didn't know about the bluestem and gamma grass and the rye, didn't realize there would be creekbeds with wild grapevines and plums and berry thickets. I didn't know about the jackrabbits, prairie dogs and gophers that add life to the land, the quail that flutter out of the grass or the wild ducks and geese. I couldn't see the lushness and life of the prairie for all the space in front of me. It frightened me some, and I have always since understood the frontier women who went stark raving mad out in the midst of the prairie.

In mid-April the weather was crisp and clear, cool enough that I was bundled up and glad to be protected from the wind that bent the grasses and carried a spring chill. Still, I could feel the intensity of the sun beating straight down on me, and I wondered what summer would bring.

"See over there, Mattie? That's a dugout."

"Dugout? Let me see, you said that was a hole in the ground with a wall built in front of it, right?"

Jim laughed. "Well, sort of."

I peered into the distance, barely able to distinguish the timbers that marked that particular rise in the ground from countless others in the endless roll and swell of the land.

My first soddie was more recognizable, though, and from a distance, I simply thought it was a house, not a very grand one, but someone's home. As we drew closer, I saw that it was made of dry dirt, just as they had told me, and spring wildflowers and grass grew from the roof. But it had windows of isinglass and a door. A woman stood in the doorway, seeming to stare at us, and both Will Henry and Jim waved heartily.

"Do you know these people?"

"Out here, Mattie, everyone is your neighbor. Sure, we know those folks, even though they live miles from us. Name's Nelson. Came out here from eastern Iowa. Mrs. Nelson, she ain't too happy. Misses her kin and all, but Lars, he's planning on making it big. And he'll do all right. Like as not, you'll get to know them once they hear there's a doctor in the area."

I stared at that woman, and a memory of her sadness imprinted itself on my soul. She was probably the first link in a chain that bound me to prairie women. In that instant, she gave me my first glimpse of their hardships and disappointments and their occasional joys. It's a trite saying now, been said so often, but it's true that the West was great for men and dogs but hell on women and horses.

We passed more soddies and an occasional dugout, but if I was expecting a community, I was sadly disappointed. The houses were all far apart and looked lonely. About the time Jim told me we were nearing the end of the ride, we began to drive along next to a river. I remember being amazed that it was so wide, and Will Henry told me that old, now familiar saying about the Platte River being a mile wide and an inch deep. We rode across it at a point where there were three trees—the only trees in sight—and Jim pulled up in front of a soddie that was ringed by a picket fence, newly painted.

"Well, Doc, here you are at home."

"Home?" I echoed with disbelief. There was not another

house in sight, nothing except the river beyond the soddie and the three trees I had been written about. This was my tree claim!

"But where's Benteen?"

"Further on, about five miles."

I don't suppose I fooled them, even though I tried to be bright. "Well, it looks wonderful. I want to go inside."

"Aw, Mattie." Will Henry was plainly a little uneasy. "It ain't wonderful, and it'll take some fixin', like window curtains and all. But it's the most solid soddie I seen in these parts. You'll be warm and comfortable here; Jim and me made sure of that."

For a moment I felt like an ungrateful wretch. They had broken their backs to get things fixed for me and to build me the nicest house they could, and there I stood, thinking with longing about my comfortable bedroom in Omaha, the well-furnished kitchen I had supervised, the proud dinner table at which I'd sat. All that was a thing of the past, but sometimes it's hard to be as adjustable as you'd like.

"I appreciate it, Will Henry, and you know I do. I'm sure I'll be comfortable. It's . . . it's just going to take a little time for me to adjust. Come, show me the inside."

We entered a dark room, medium-sized, with a great open gabled ceiling, at least ten feet at its peak. The rafters were exposed, and cheesecloth had been tacked to their underside to keep falling dirt out of the soup and stew, as Will Henry explained to me. The floor and walls were covered with rough boards, and cheesecloth had been tacked over the walls. I could, they said, choose whatever wallpaper I wanted, and they would put it up.

Many families lived in one-room soddies in those days, but those two men had built me a second room, a sort of lean-to affair with a much lower roof, to serve as a bedroom.

They had worked hard in the month since I had told them I was moving and had even dug a well about twenty-five yards from the house. Will Henry told me later how they did it by putting a two-by-four post in each of the four corners. As they dug the dirt out, the corner posts slowly traveled down. Then side boards were set between them. When it got too deep to shovel, the dirt was loaded into a carrying bucket and hauled out by a windlass.

Will Henry and Jim had even stocked my pantry with coffee, salt, flour and canned goods. There was enough for me to make a meal for us, though it was much different from the kitchen in Omaha. Still, while they unloaded the wagon, I fixed supper. I pointed out the dish barrel first and got out enough utensils for three people. Then I opened some cans and was just getting ready to crack the eggs they had brought as a housewarming gift when I realized I had nothing to cook on. A Franklin cast-iron stove, they told me, was being shipped. They hadn't wanted me to buy it in Omaha because they were afraid I wouldn't know anything about buying cookstoves and would not buy one that could use the coal of the prairie, cow chips, corncobs and hay. Of course, they were right, but it would be several days before I could cook. We had a cold supper of canned tomatoes, coffee, crackers and that staple of the frontier, sardines. Never did like those fishy things.

By dark, they had me settled in. I never felt so welcomed in my life . . . And as they rode away, promising to be back first thing in the morning, I never felt so alone. All night, I lay in bed and listened to the wind blow across the prairie and wondered whatever I had done.

"Wake up, wake up!"

"Come on, Mattie. Is the coffee ready?"

"I can't make coffee without a stove," I called from the bedroom, where I had been brushing my hair. "I didn't expect you so early."

"It's not early," Will Henry protested. "Must be near eight o'clock."

"I don't have a clock," I reminded him.

"Put it on your shopping list. We're taking you to town this morning to the general store so you can meet folks and get whatever you need."

"I don't even know what I need. How can I?" I smoothed my gabardine skirt, tucked in the crumpled white shirt and appeared in the doorway.

"Mattie, you sure do look professional. Everybody's going to know you're the best doctor around. Course, you're also the only doctor around."

"Thanks, Jim," I said, laughing a little at his partial compliment. "I wonder when I'll have my first patient."

"Word will travel; just you wait. You'll be called on before you know it. Come on now, we got to get to town before you do have a patient."

Town was a cluster of four houses, three of them sod and one frame, a general store which carried everything from groceries to overalls and fabric, and a one-room school-house.

"How many children are in the school?" I asked, incredulous that there could be enough children to fill the classroom.

"Seems like they have about ten this spring," said Jim. "Two families live here in Benteen so the children can go to school. Means the fathers commute to their claims. Then the rest of them kids, they ride in whenever they can. Weather's not bad, they aren't needed to work, then they can come to school."

I thought about Sara and the regularity with which she attended her large school.

Jim had pulled the wagon up in front of the general store, a wooden structure with a large front display window broken into several small panes, all dirty and dusty. Peering through them, I could make out only a hodgepodge of things—canned goods, a sad iron, some dishes and several pairs of work boots.

Inside, the store smelled of coffee and spices, dried fruit, old tobacco, vinegar, cheese, pickles and ham, all blended together in a rare mixture that existed only in old general stores out in the midst of nowhere. No city store ever smelled like that, and I miss the aroma still.

"Whittaker, I want you to meet my stepdaughter, Dr. Mattie Armstrong." Jim threw one of his huge hands around my shoulder and beamed with pride. I offered my hand to the middle-aged man who stood behind the counter, an apron over a large midsection on which his hands rested. He was bald, with a fringe of hair around his head and a round, cheerful face. Right now, though, he had a puzzled look on his face, which clearly indicated he hadn't expected me.

"Dr. . . . uh, how do you do? We . . . we were expecting you, well, sort of, that is . . . Jim, you didn't tell me the doctor was a woman!" His eyes shot up nearly to the top of his head, and he turned accusingly toward Jim.

Jim grinned and ducked his head. "I told you it was my wife's oldest child, didn't I?"

"Jim!" I was indignant and a little bit embarrassed. "Have you brought me out here on false pretenses?"

"Now, Mattie, calm down. It don't make no difference. I just didn't want to get folks all stirred up before you arrived."

"Jim," Whittaker broke in, "don't get upset. It doesn't matter. You just should'a told me. I mean, I wasn't . . . well, hell, I wasn't expecting a woman."

"I assure you, Mr. Whittaker, I am a competent physician. I graduated at the top of my class at the medical school in Omaha a year ago, and I—"

"Land's sake, what's all the ruckus about?" Sally Whittaker, a pleasant lady with graying brown hair and an expanded middle to match her husband's, bustled into the room. "Why are you all yelling at each other? Oh, hello." When she noticed me, she turned directly and introduced herself. "I'm Sally Whittaker . . . And you must be . . ."

"Mattie Armstrong. Jim's stepdaughter, and your new doctor, I hope."

"How wonderful! A woman doctor! Oh, Ralph, what a surprise. I declare, this is the nicest thing that's happened in a month of Sundays." Her face brightened with a grin, and she came to put an arm around my waist with a squeeze. "Welcome to Benteen, my dear. We're really glad you're here."

After that, it was all confusion and smiles as I gathered up the items on my list—chintz for curtains, the only flowered wallpaper they had, matches, a clock and a list of small things that I had either forgotten or not known I needed until Will Henry and Jim made their suggestions. After all my careful planning, I had, for instance, forgotten needle and thread.

Another woman came into the store while we were there and was introduced as the wife from one of the two families who lived in town. She was cordial and glad I had moved to the area, and as we left, laden down with packages, I had an optimistic feeling.

"Now, you let us know if we can help," Sally Whittaker called. "Don't you let Jim and Will Henry scare you any about life out here. You're going to love it."

"I'm sure I will," I called back, adding my thanks.

"They liked you," Jim said on the way back to the soddie.

"Good. I liked them."

"Not everybody's going to, you know." He stared straight ahead, hands on the reins, eyes on the horses.

"Aw, come on, Jim, everybody'll like Mattie," Will Henry protested as though he were trying to protect my feelings.

But I knew what Will Henry didn't. "Because I'm a woman?"

"Yep."

"Jim, I know that doctors aren't that popular . . . or maybe respected is the word I want . . . and the idea of a woman doctor is still fairly new in these parts. But the only thing I can do is show them that I'm capable. It will all depend on whether or not I can take care of people when they need me." This was a problem I'd given a lot of thought to, and I saw no easy answer, nothing except patience, doing the very best I could and waiting for people to accept me. Since I never was a patient person, the waiting part might be hard, I knew.

"Well, I hope you get your chance to prove it," he said, still without expression.

"Why did you encourage me to come out here if you don't think I'll have patients?" I was indignant again, but my indignation only drew a smile from him.

"Because Will Henry and I can look after you. Couldn't keep my promise to your ma if you were in Omaha and we were clear out here."

"I don't need looking after," I said primly. "I can take care of myself."

But he just smiled at me and looked sideways, and I wondered if he suspected more about Dr. Dinsmore than I had told him. Jim Reeves wasn't a stupid man by any means, and he would have guessed that there was some reason behind my move other than the sudden and total change of mind I had lamely offered as my reason for joining them.

My chance to prove myself as a doctor did not come with any sudden dramatic event, though sometimes I thought an epidemic or major accident would be a blessing in disguise, allowing me to perform some outstanding, miraculous act of healing that would forever endear me to my neighbors. Of course, I knew better than even to wish tragedy on someone else just so I could show off how smart I was, but the thought did flit through my mind once or twice. Later, when I did have a dramatic case or two, I regretted even the thought.

But in the first months I was on the prairie, I treated a fairly steady stream of minor ailments, using mostly the contents of my medicine chest that I had brought from Omaha—calomel as a cathartic, a solution of tartar to induce vomiting in a child supposed to have eaten poisonous berries, lemon and honey for a spring cough that wouldn't go away. Remembering Dr. Dinsmore's advice on medicines, I always used them sparingly, sometimes diluting them with water to minimize their impact on the human system.

"Why's this medicine so watery?" asked one old man who had come to me for a catarrh.

"Because I put water in it. It's too strong as it is," I replied.

"Water!" he snorted. "Never heard of making medicine weaker. Always thought it should be stronger, the stronger the better. Suppose you used that river water out there."

"No," I laughed. "I used fresh water from my well."

But that was how my "river water" cures got known, and folks talked about them for years afterward. I still hear someone mention them now and again.

Summer came, and with it the endless burning sun, the heat that seems to blanket the prairie and suffocate you. Omaha had hot summers, of course, being a river town, but it had hills and water and trees, and that, I found, made all the difference. There's no way now to make a summer in a soddie real to someone who hasn't lived through it. Oh, the soddie, with its thick walls, did stay some cooler, but I think if we'd had today's garden hoses and could have wet it down periodically, it would have been all that much cooler. Of course, we didn't have that kind of water, and I never tried it. At night, the prairie breezes would be cool and lovely, and you'd never think it could be so awful hot during the day. But the next day, there it was again.

I treated some heat exhaustion those days, and snakebite, and lost only one patient, a woman who had simply lived out her life span. She wasn't old, maybe fifty, but she was worn out with work and hard living, and she just lay down in her bed and died. The family understood and accepted.

"Folks like you," Jim said one evening as he sat at my kitchen table.

"I knew they would," proclaimed my young champion, Will Henry.

"I like them. I've not met anybody who was reluctant to be treated by a woman doctor. Well, not too reluctant, anyway." I grinned as I thought of the old man who had christened my river water cures.

"Learning your way around, aren't you?"

"Day before yesterday I must have gone three miles southeast of here across the prairie. I thought I'd get lost, but I did as you told me, kept track of the landmarks. It's amazing to me that there are so many things to go by out there on the prairie, because when you first look, it's all the same."

"You're learning, though, Mattie. No two inches of that prairie is the same. I'm almost ready to turn you loose on it."

Jim had carved himself out a big job in teaching me to go alone on the prairie. First he had to teach me to ride a horse.

"Never knew a girl that couldn't ride," he exploded when he found out I'd never been near a horse, except to pat other people's horses on the nose when they were tied up at a hitching post.

"Jim, there was no horse around when we were kids. You know that."

"Will Henry knew how to ride. Not very well, but he knew."

I glanced at my brother and found him looking determinedly the other way. I knew but wouldn't tell that he had probably never been on a horse until the first time Jim Reeves put him on one, but he'd lied and pretended he knew how to ride. Out of sheer determination, he'd managed his bluff. And now he rode better than he walked.

"You're gonna have to learn to ride astride. None of this sidesaddle stuff. You was to get in a hurry to get somewhere, you'd slide right out of that sidesaddle. Here, I brought you a pair of pants to practice in. Go on, put them on. They're clean."

"I know they're clean," I laughed. "But how will I make them stay up?"

"Use pins or something. Come on, Mattie, we don't want to spend all day on your first riding lesson."

Pretty soon I found myself mounted on the oldest and calmest of Jim's horses, a mare that he loudly proclaimed wasn't much good for anything but kids and timid lady doctors. I knew a touch of Will Henry's determination, though, and before long I was riding, having listened carefully to every bit of advice Jim gave me. Soon I graduated from Belle, who really did plod along, to Brownie, a frisky but well-broken gelding.

I rode with Jim almost daily, and as we rode, he taught me how to "read" the prairie, so that I wouldn't get lost.

"See that buffalo wallow? Remember that's on your left as you go out, so you want to come back to the right of it, and you want to begin to angle back north just after you pass it. Course you can kind of tell if you keep track of the time and the position of the sun," he said wryly.

"Thanks," I said with equal dryness. "I can pretty well figure that out."

"Well, that's good. Least you won't be like the feller I heard about who thought he was headed north and ended up in Texas."

"I'm glad you think I'm a little better than that, Jim."

"Some," he said, and I took it as a compliment.

I did get called to various soddies to treat patients before Jim judged I was safe to send out alone, and he either went with me or sent Will Henry. It meant that one or the other of them was at my soddie most of the time, and I enjoyed the company.

"Let's go to the baseball game," Jim said one night when they had both come for supper. I'd fixed one of my less imaginative meals—red beans and beef—but they seemed to relish it, and I'd given only a fleeting thought to a delicately sautéed piece of chicken, cooked in wine, the way Dr. Dinsmore liked it. Sometimes I truly did miss Omaha so much it was hard to bear.

"A baseball game? Out here? You're teasing me again,

Jim Reeves."

"No he's not, Mattie. They really do play baseball. In fact, I'm going to play on the team this summer." Will Henry never understood the teasing between Jim and me, and he always rushed to the defense of one or the other of us.

"Will Henry, you play? That's wonderful. Of course I want to go."

We hitched up the wagon and horses. Jim made me do most of the hitching as part of my continuing learning process, but he admitted I was getting pretty good. Will Henry glowered a little, from jealousy I think.

"Okay, Mattie, take us to town." Jim leaned back in the bed of the wagon, pretending to take a nap. "Don't know if I can sleep or not. You won't take us to Texas, will you?"

"Careful, or I'll take you back to Missouri!" I warned.

"No, not that." He pretended alarm, and before I could stop myself, I turned solemn for a moment.

"You're right, not that. Anyplace but Princeton, Missouri."

Jim knew when to lighten the moment, change the subject, move on to the future. "Go on," he said. "You gonna let those horses sit there all night and make Will Henry miss his game?"

I got them to Benteen fine, in plenty of time for the game. Will Henry got to bat once and struck out, but it was his first attempt, and we praised him highly. I was surprised at the number of people the game attracted. Oh, there weren't quite two full teams, though the rivals from a town not too far up the river had eight on their team, while Benteen had only seven. Each man seemed to have brought his family, so there was quite a crowd, and I found myself the center of some attention.

"You're the new doctor, aren't you? Pleased to meet you." A strong hand was thrust at me, and I looked into a bearded face, wrinkled with exposure but not really old. The man stood with his hand on the head of a bright, tow-headed boy about eight who smiled at me, exposing great gaps in his teeth.

"Dr. Armstrong, remember me? I'm Billy, the kid that carried your stuff out of the store last week."

"Sure, Billy, I remember. And I'm glad to meet your family."

Billy's mother spoke up then. "We're glad you're here, but of course, we hope we don't have to see you." She smiled nervously at her own joke. She was pale and looked to be old beyond her years, with dull brown hair hanging limply behind her ears and a tired look in her gray eyes which failed to come alive even as she tried to joke. With a nervous gesture, she pushed her hair back. Billy looked healthy enough, but I suspected his mother would be my patient at one time or another.

Then there was Rastus Wolf, the old man who had teased me about river water cures, and Sally and Ralph Whittaker, young Mary Eberhardt, whose child I'd cared for during a siege of the croup soon after I arrived, and an endless list. I found that I knew the people, they knew me, and I felt a strong sense of community.

Omaha was far from my thoughts in moments like that, but there were other times, especially when I was alone in my soddie with a long day stretched before me, that the thought of Omaha and the Dinsmores brought pain. Dr.

Dinsmore had written only twice, both letters correct and distant, commenting on a case that I'd told him about and expressing concern about my possible rides alone on the prairie. They both missed me, he wrote, but said no more about my returning.

Sara wrote more frequently, lamenting her lonely life, how bored she was, how strict Kate was, how unhappy her father was, how awful life in general was. I took none of it seriously except the portions about her father's unhappiness, and then I felt guilt. He had been good to me, given me the chances my own mother could never arrange, and if it weren't for him, I'd still be stuck in a shack in Missouri or maybe farming out here with Jim and Will Henry, like the many worn-down prairie women I cared for. Maybe my debt of gratitude was to be what he wanted me to, and yet I couldn't make the switch in roles. I couldn't go from being his pupil to being his lover.

Then another voice would come out of my head, asking, *Have you given up your only chance at romance? Are you destined to live alone the rest of your life?* That thought scared me enough to consider the possibility of returning to Omaha.

Yet a stubborn streak in me would not consider the possibility of Omaha. It was as though I felt I had to show my independence by carving out a life of my own in Benteen. And so, I stayed and made myself a home, found myself a community and, eventually, found myself a family.

⸺✳︎⸺

FOLKS wondered why I married Emory Jones. I knew it at the time, because they told me so. Some of them tried to discourage me, gently, of course, because I was grown and independent, but they tried nonetheless. My own brother, Will Henry, told me he wondered if I was doing the right thing but that he'd stand behind me, no matter what I decided.

And I decided to marry him. Married him in 1895 and it lasted until 1910, fifteen long years. It seemed like forever at the time, but now when I think back on it, fifteen years is such a small chunk of my life. Still, it was an important chunk.

I married Jones because he was the first man who really wanted me, who made me feel like a woman. Oh, Dr. Dinsmore thought he wanted me, but he really needed me, and there's a big difference between the two. Emory Jones would have gotten along just fine without me, but he wanted me with him. He made me feel desirable and attractive and all those things that I thought I was not. For a girl who is plain, sensible and responsible, love, or infatuation, can be pretty heady stuff.

Em was wild and crazy, too, a nice balance, so I thought, for my practicality. Not that he was wild and crazy in destructive ways or that he thought about being an outlaw or any of those things, though there was a strong streak of dishonesty in him, which I tried to overlook for years.

But I am getting ahead of my story. I met Emory Jones in 1892, two years after I had come out to the plains. He had come to work in the mercantile store for the Whittakers, and the first time I ever laid eyes on him was when I went in to purchase some dry goods. A patient was going to cut me a blouse and skirt as payment for my services, and I was to pick some plain serge and a good cotton for the blouse.

Ralph Whittaker greeted me cordially, then called to the back: "Come take care of Dr. Armstrong."

And Em appeared through the curtained door that led to the small quarters behind the store. He was tall—taller than I, at least, and that was something—and darkly handsome, with hair that he tried to plaster down but which always escaped into curls. His smile was just a bit crooked, but it was his eyes that told you when he was laughing. They were dark brown and fairly danced when he was amused.

Those eyes danced when he first took a look at me and then repeated, with disbelief, "*Dr.* Armstrong?"

I was never poised and sophisticated around men, and now, strangely, I felt a fluttering uncertainty, an almost physical sensation deep within. Blushing, I replied, too formally in a tightly controlled voice, "Yes, I'm Dr. Armstrong."

"Em Jones," he said, still grinning as he put out his hand to shake. "Pleased to meet you. Don't know that I've rightly seen a woman doctor out here before. It's a real pleasure to know you."

If I was disconcerted, he appeared completely at ease and sure of himself. Remembering his job, he became businesslike and helpful. Eventually he did talk me out of the sensible dark gray serge, coercing me instead into choosing a pinstripe, which, he said, had more "life" and suited my personality better. I left the store feeling dizzy, sure that his laughing eyes were following me.

After that, I saw Em from time to time when I went into

the store or once or twice at local parties when the neighbors all got together for a dance in the schoolhouse. And each time I saw him, I felt that strange flutter. I will say, though, that old saying, "Out of sight, out of mind," applied. There were long stretches when I never saw nor thought about Em Jones.

But then Em got the cholera, a bad case, and I was called to treat him. For two days he had a fever so high that he really didn't know where he was or who was taking care of him. I wrung sheets out in milk to wrap him and try to get that fever down. Yes, milk! The things we did in those days without knowing better! Now I know the milk may well have carried bacteria and been sort of a double jeopardy to my patients, but at the time I thought it held the coolness better.

Em lived in the small room behind the Whittakers' store, a tiny, dark space without much fresh air, and I thought it an unhealthy spot for him to recuperate. Even after his fever broke, he was weak and needed much care for almost two weeks. So I had some men wrap him up good and put him in a wagon to bring him out to my place, where he could rest in my bedroom, which when needed was put to use as an infirmary, causing me to sleep on a pallet in the main room of the soddie.

Of course, he protested. "I can't be so much trouble to you," he said while they were carrying him out to the wagon. "I'll be just fine in my room if you'll look in on me occasionally, and Mrs. Whittaker will bring me food. She does from time to time, anyway."

"You'll tire yourself talking," I told him, and got on my horse before he could say any more.

Fortunately, it was spring and the weather was warm, so he didn't suffer any from exposure. Even the five-mile trip from Whittaker's out to my claim was tiring for him, though, and he slept most of the first day he was in my soddie. I'd go around to feel of his forehead and listen to his chest, but he barely waked at all, and I let him sleep.

But as the days went by and he began to feel better, Em and I started to talk, trading stories of our childhoods, our hopes for the future, the reasons we were out on the prairie and everything about ourselves. My practice was slow and I spent a lot of time sitting in the rocking chair in the infirmary, keeping him company, even though there was much I could be doing outside.

I did manage to keep the horses fed, and one day I plowed up my small vegetable garden, using Tony, my gelding chosen by Jim as a safe and stable horse, and a borrowed plow. My growing herd, six head of cattle, was turned out, and with the weather nice, the cattle rarely came up from the buffalo wallow.

I learned a lot about Em in those long days. He grew up in St. Louis. "My father's a newspaperman," he said. "Owns the biggest paper in the city. Quite successful. And Mother, she's a leader in St. Louis society. Knows all the right people, gives fashionable parties. They live in a big house with servants and everything."

"Why ever are you out here, then, instead of back there enjoying the life of luxury?" I rocked gently and stared, genuinely puzzled. My early life made it nearly impossible for me to believe that anyone would walk away from a life like the one Em described. I forgot, I guess, that I had done almost the same thing, though not quite so drastically, in leaving Omaha.

"Luxury isn't everything, Mattie." We had reached a first-name basis by then. "They had expectations for me that I just couldn't meet. Matter of fact, they wanted me to be a lawyer. Then, of course, I'd have gone to work for the newspaper as their legal counsel, married a very rich and very proper and probably very boring girl from St. Louis society, raised a passel of spoiled kids and grown old and tired before my time. No, it wasn't the life for me. I simply told them I had to be free to do what I felt was right, and then I came West.

"I've worked several jobs. I can ride, I can do a cowman's job, string fence, you name it. I've learned the way of life out here by doing it. I spent one harvest threshing, and another time I worked on a little newspaper in Kansas. Thought my father would have appreciated that, me sneaking into journalism through the back door, but when I wrote and told him, he apparently wasn't amused. He never answered the letter."

Em stared lazily into space from time to time as we talked, as though remembering was painful. His hands lay out of the bedclothes, and occasionally he clutched them nervously. I remember now wondering why his hands were so delicate if he'd done all that, but I dismissed the thought.

I told him we were like the prince and the pauper with our very different backgrounds, and I found myself telling him all about Mama and my miserable years in Princeton and how I had all these fantasies about who my father was, but I really didn't know. He was the first person I'd poured all that out to since years ago when I'd hinted at it to Dr. Dinsmore. To my surprise, Em was neither shocked nor overly sympathetic.

"Must have been rough," he said matter-of-factly. "Of course, when everyone kowtows to your folks like they do mine, it's hard for me to imagine being teased about my mother's bad reputation. But I think I can see some of what you felt. You're strong to have done all that you've done."

"No," I said, self-conscious again and feeling a blush rise, "just determined to get out of Princeton."

He laughed then. "And is a soddie in western Nebraska any better than Princeton, Missouri?"

"Yes it is," I said fiercely. "It's the beginning of a better way of life for me and a chance to practice medicine, which is all I want to do."

"All? Oh, Mattie, surely you want more from life than medicine." His eyes were laughing, and I knew he was teasing me.

The question made me both nervous and happy, and I excused myself to go and fix some supper. As I left the room, I could feel him laughing behind my back, and I knew his eyes would still be dancing.

As Em got his strength back, he began to get out of bed some each day and, slowly, to do some chores for me. There were always things I needed a man to do around the house, and I used to lie in wait for poor Will Henry to come through. I'd have a list as long as my arm of things that needed repairing, from the sod roof to a window frame that wasn't right to mending some bit of my harness. Em began to do some of those things, though I refused to let him do too much in any one day, and I would hound him to get back to bed and rest.

But he did mend my bridle, and one day I caught him brushing both horses, which I thought was too hard for him. Then, just before he had recovered enough to move back to his own dingy little room, he dug me a bigger vegetable garden so I could plant a little more corn, beans, turnips and pumpkin.

"Not, Dr. Armstrong, that you're much of a cook," he teased, leaning on the shovel. "If I have any complaint about my care while in your, ahem, hospital, it's the quality of the food."

I tried to bluff as though it didn't matter and take it in good grace, for he had no idea that I used to pride myself on the meals I prepared and supervised. It was just that out there, it was all different, and I had somehow lost the impetus to cook. "I'll do all right with beans and turnips. Can't do wrong just boiling them." I tried to laugh lightly.

"You'll probably boil them too long," he said.

Em left my soddie, less because he was cured than because he got a roommate in the infirmary, a farm woman named Mrs. Goyne who had a brand-new baby I'd delivered some days earlier but who was suffering from fever and couldn't nurse the baby. I couldn't keep running eight or nine miles out to see both her and the baby, so I had them brought into the infirmary, where I could bottle-feed the baby frequently and watch the mother's infection closely. Em left the day they arrived, and though he was lighthearted about it, I could tell he was a little put out.

"You're sure you're all right?" My concern was more

personal than professional. After the work he'd done around my place, I knew he was in good shape and probably should have gone back to work earlier. But personally, I was reluctant to pronounce him hale and hearty. I would miss him, and I knew it.

"I'll be fine, just a little weak. I will miss the company and, of course, the larger, brighter quarters." Then, with a mock bow, he added, "It's been a delightful stay, Dr. Armstrong."

Trying to match his bantering mood, I answered, "The pleasure was all mine, sir."

But as he climbed onto Tony, the horse he was to borrow for the ride home, Em gave me one of his long looks and said, "You know, I think I'll have to marry you."

Then he was gone, before I could answer, and I was left standing there bewildered and excited. My thoughts were jumbled, but from that moment, I believed him. He would marry me.

Em began to court me, and since I'd never been courted before, it was a wonderful time of my life. We'd go on picnics, far out on the prairie, spreading a blanket, eating cold roast and talking about the meaning of life. It reminded me a little of the picnics with Dr. Dinsmore and Sara, but better. Other times we'd go if neighbors got together, which they occasionally did at kind of a potluck supper where everybody brought something and had a chance to visit with other people and break what was an isolated life for many families. Some of those women went months and months without ever seeing anyone but their own family, so that they were even grateful when someone got sick, because it meant I'd come to visit.

When the Literary and Debating Society met in the schoolhouse, Em always rode out from town to get me. And if there was a dance, we were there. Em was a wonderful dancer, light and sure on his feet, and when I was with him, I became almost a dancer myself, me who had always been awkward and unsure the few times I'd danced in Omaha. Poor Dr. Dinsmore, he never could teach me the steps. But with Em, I seemed to fairly fly across the floor. Sometimes, early in our courtship, I was still too shy or self-conscious to try some of the faster dances, those that I thought were kind of attention-getting, so Em would dance with someone else.

I remember one night, at a dance in the schoolhouse, when they played a polka, and he danced with a neighbor girl, younger than me and prettier by far. I ached with jealousy as I watched them whirl across the floor, both laughing heartily. But the minute the dance was over, Em was back at my side.

"Don't come near me," he warned. "I'm all sweaty and hot." And then he swept me into his arms as the fiddler played a waltz, and I felt like the belle of the ball.

Sometimes Em drove me on my calls, in the new spring-buggy that Ed Landman down to the stable had fixed for me. It had extra-strong springs to give a smoother ride and could be all closed up with isinglass in the winter so I didn't have to freeze to death. It worked fine and was a big improvement over those lonely horseback rides across the prairie, except when the snow was so bad the buggy couldn't get through. Then I'd have to leave it, tying one horse to the buggy and riding the other.

By the time winter came that year, Em and I were a pretty constant couple. He seemed proud that I was the only doctor for sixty miles and never questioned when a patient came before my pleasure or before him.

Once I was gone three days delivering a baby. Em was at my soddie, which he was a lot of the time, when a skinny young boy, maybe about twelve, rode up, frantically calling, "Doctor, Doctor!"

"Whoa, son," I said, coming out the door. "Calm down, now. I'm the doctor. What's the matter?"

"It's Ma. She sent me for you. Says her time's come. Please hurry. She . . . she looked awful scared when I left."

It was a procedure I was used to, and by now Em was, too. "Hitch up the buggy for me, would you, please, Em. Son, what's your name?"

"Ralph, ma'am, Ralph Grubbs." He was a solemn child, pale with big brown eyes that stared at me uncertainly, as though not sure of my response. His clothes fitted him poorly, the pants too short, the jacket too big, and his shoes were obviously worn and old, perhaps too small.

"All right, Ralph. While Mr. Jones hitches up the horses, you tie yours to the back of that buggy. That way you can ride with me."

We were on our way in minutes. I had gathered my bag, put on my long cowhide coat and an extra scarf against the cold and found a blanket to wrap Ralph in since the poor child looked half-frozen and poorly dressed for a winter afternoon. We took off across the prairie, in the direction Ralph pointed. Em had decided to stay behind this time, since I had company, but promised to wait for me and to check the chickens and my cattle, now up in a hay barn for the winter.

"Is your father with your mother, Ralph?"

"No, ma'am. He's . . . well, he's gone. He is a lot. I ain't seen him for several days now." The child avoided looking at me as he spoke. Somehow, as he mentioned his father, I could easily imagine fear in his eyes.

"Is your mother alone?"

"Oh, no, ma'am. I got three sisters and a brother. I'm the oldest."

"That's quite a family," I said, and he missed my ironic tone completely.

"Yes, ma'am, Ma calls us her pride and joy." Then he bit his lip. "Pa, he says we're trouble and nuisance."

I already didn't like Pa too well. When I got to the Grubbses' soddie, I liked Pa a whole lot less. The place was a mess, and a tired, frightened woman lay in the bed. I shooed all the children out of the room, drawing the curtain to give what privacy I could. If the weather had been at all decent, I'd have sent them outside, but the wind was beginning to howl, and I knew a good Nebraska blizzard was brewing.

Mrs. Grubbs wasn't a frail woman, just tired out like so many on the frontier. She'd used all her strength hoeing and plowing and cooking and giving birth, and she had precious little reserve left to help this new baby into the world.

"I'm scared, Doctor. I . . . It's never been like this before."

"You're doing fine," I soothed her, not wanting her to know that I, too, thought the labor was going too slowly. There wasn't much I could do at that point beyond cleaning her up, smoothing and changing the bed and generally making her comfortable. After I brought her a cup of tea, I turned my attention to the rest of the soddie, telling her to call out if she needed me.

I began with the children, each of whom needed a bath and clean clothes, a good scrubbing of the face and a hairbrush. It seemed to take forever, with cries of "That's not my dress. It belongs to Elizabeth."

"No, it doesn't. That's mine."

"I want Ma to dress me."

"I'm hungry. What's for supper?"

Finally I had them all sorted out. Ralph was the oldest and the one I could always identify. Next was Rachel, a smug and proper young lady with perfectly braided hair, then Elizabeth and Kate, at eight and seven only a year apart and scarcely distinguishable, even to their strawberry-blond and perfectly tangled hair. Littlest of the lot was Henry, an amazingly plump five-year-old who doted on his oldest sister and followed her everywhere.

I tried to be gentle but ended up being quite firm and even swatting lightly at a couple of bottoms with a hairbrush, but finally I had all five of them clean and neat.

"Now, sit and read a book. Ralph, do you read?"

He looked at his toe. "No, ma'am. Not too well. Never is time for me to go to school, 'cause I got to help Pa and do the chores when he's away."

Pa again, I thought.

The oldest girl, Rachel, piped up. "I can read real good.

Ma taught me, and sometimes I even read to her."

"Fine, Rachel. You read to all the others, quietly now, over there in the corner."

Then I started on the house. Of course, every few minutes I had to go to Mrs. Grubbs, who called every time a contraction set in.

"You're doing better now," I said. "I think this baby is about ready to come in the next hour or so." That meant I had to turn my attention to the birth and forget that messy house for a while. The birth actually went much more smoothly than I expected, and soon we had a healthy, nice-sized baby boy. When I got the mother straightened up, the baby cleaned and in her arms, I called the other children in quietly to see their new brother. As always, the mother looked like a different woman than the one who had just screamed and struggled her way through labor. Now she beamed in proud happiness, staring down at the little thing.

"Isn't he beautiful, children? We'll call him William."

"That makes three of each," announced eight-year-old Elizabeth.

"Yes," sighed the mother. "Three boys and three girls. I think that's enough for this family, don't you?"

"No," said Elizabeth. "We need another girl now, so there'll be more girls than boys."

"Pa's going to be mad," said Henry, the littlest of them.

"Oh no, Henry," his mother answered. "He will be very proud."

"He says we're trouble." Henry confirmed his own opinion. "He's going to be mad there's another one."

I couldn't keep out of the conversation any longer. "I'm

sure he knew, Henry. It's unfortunate he had to be away just at this time."

Mrs. Grubbs looked away and didn't say anything. I wasn't sure if she thought it was unfortunate or if, perhaps, she was relieved he wasn't around.

I told the children their mother needed sleep and put them to work helping me to straighten. Each child had to pick up his own things, and the older girls were to help me set the table for supper. Outside, I could hear the wind howling, and I was hesitant to send Ralph to check the animals, but it had to be done.

"Don't worry, Dr. Armstrong. I'm used to it. We ain't got but a few cows, and they're in the barn right close. I'll hold on to the rope."

I went to the door with him and recognized the blizzard I had thought was coming. Fine, hard snow, blowing almost straight across the prairie, was already piling up at the side of the house. By morning, we'd be snowbound.

"Be sure to check the horses," I called, my voice whirling in the wind.

Ralph turned and said something over his shoulder, but I couldn't hear it.

With my cooking skills and the lack of supplies I found in the soddie, dinner for the children wasn't much that night, just oatmeal, bread and honey. Mrs. Grubbs had done her best to prepare ahead, and there were several loaves of bread, some canned preserves and dry staples, but I hadn't thought to ask Ralph to saw some meat off the carcass I presumed hung in a shed somewhere, and I wasn't sure he knew how to do it anyway. But somehow I got them all fed and off to bed, checked on mother and baby, who were doing fine, and fell into the one big chair in the house to sleep myself.

I woke stiff and sore in the morning and found that we were indeed snowed in, tight as the proverbial drum, and the snow was still blowing. I settled down to straightening up the cabin, keeping the children occupied and not fussing at one another, and trying to care for Mrs. Grubbs and little William, who, fortunately, needed me far less than the others. Briefly, I remember wondering if Em had gotten back to town before the blizzard and then fantasizing, as I worked, about marriage to Em, with our own children. As Elizabeth shouted at her sister and Henry screamed for attention, I decided there wouldn't be six of them, not ever!

I was at the Grubbses' soddie for three days, and by the time I left, Mrs. Grubbs was up and about and back to her routine. She apologized for the shape her house had been in, and I could see she really was a good housekeeper when she was in control of things. But I felt sorry for her. No one mentioned Pa much, and of course he never showed up, couldn't have gotten through the storm if he'd wanted to.

Mrs. Grubbs was grateful for all the work I'd done in her house, and she was profuse with her thanks. But one thing I did scared her, I could tell. In straightening and cleaning, I'd found six bottles of whisky. Now, mind you, I never was as militant as Carrie Nation, and Em had given me an occasional glass of homemade wine, which I enjoyed. But I knew whisky was expensive, and there wasn't any money to spare around this household. Besides, I figured Pa, whatever he was like, probably drank too much, neglected his family and ran off to drink more. So I poured all that whisky on the ground, choosing a spot where the wind had swept the snow clean. I heard later that nobody could get anything to grow on that spot for years.

When I got home, there was a note from Em. "Had to get back to town before the storm. Hope you got home all right." He was enough of a prairie dweller, I guess, not to worry about me, and I appreciated that. But I was a little sorry he wasn't there to greet me.

Sometimes it was days, even a week or more, between times when I saw Em, and he would greet me with "Miss me?"

"Of course," I'd reply, and the truth was that I did.

"Good," he'd smile. "I'll stay away more often, so you'll realize how important I am to you."

He was important, though I was hesitant to let it show too much. But I couldn't imagine life without Em or what it had been like before I met him. Yet sometimes I couldn't imagine life forever with him either. There were nagging doubts that bothered me, like his stories about the various places he'd worked. If he worked that many places, he must have started when he was six! And his parents. Why didn't Em ever hear from them or talk about them? That early conversation about his newspaper-owner father and socialite mother was all I ever heard about the Jones family of St. Louis. And why, I wondered, was a man with so much ability and so much future clerking in someone else's mercantile store? At the very least, he should have his own store or be buying a farm or whatever. Em's future was always right around the corner, if he got the right break, met the right people. He never talked about earning his own future. I closed my mind to my doubts.

Will Henry was more open about his doubts whenever he came to call. "Em Jones still hanging around you a lot?" he asked bluntly one day as he sat at my kitchen table.

"I believe, young man, the word is courting, and yes, he is. I feel rather special about him." I stood with my hands on my hips, ready for an argument.

"Well, Sis, I got my doubts that he's the man for you." He said it straightforward, though I could tell the conversation was difficult for him.

"Well," I replied, uppitylike, "fortunately, you don't have to make the choice. I do."

"Now, come on, I worry about you. You know that."

"Will Henry, I'm seven years older than you, and the worrying goes the other way."

"You may be seven years older, but you ain't seven years smarter about some things."

"Aren't," I corrected automatically.

"Ain't, aren't. Okay, you're smarter about grammar." He laughed as he said it. Will Henry had grown into a fine young man, nearly twenty years old now and strapping big and strong from all the work he and Jim Reeves did. He never had liked school much, and neither Jim nor I could persuade him to stay beyond about his fourteenth or fifteenth year, so grammar didn't matter much to him. But Will Henry would be all right, I knew, with his own place someday and a good, solid future. Add to that his good looks, and I thought it was about time he worried about his own romance rather than mine. What didn't occur to me that day, or what I ignored, was the difference in what I sensed about Will Henry's future and that of Em Jones.

Will Henry knew, though. "What I'm trying to tell you is, just think real carefully before you do anything. I . . . well, I hear things from time to time, you know. And I like Em, don't get me wrong. He's fun, but . . . well, is fun what you want for the rest of your life?"

"Will Henry Armstrong, you've been listening to gossip. You know how I feel about trying to sew a button on your neighbors' lips. You can't do it, but that doesn't mean you have to listen to what they say. Now, go on, get out of here. I've got things to do."

When you're twenty-six and unmarried, you don't want to listen to the gossip about the man in your life, and I was afraid Will Henry would elaborate on the things he'd heard. I didn't want to know. Just because I was a doctor, a woman in that masculine profession, didn't mean, like most folks thought, that I had given up all ladylike things. I wanted a husband and family and home, and I saw in Em Jones my chance to have them. So I loved him, without questioning, and sadly, without listening to myself or others.

Jim Reeves never mentioned Em to me. I later decided he figured I was old enough to make my own mistakes, and he'd stand by me no matter what I did. And neither Sally Whittaker nor her husband at the general store where Em worked talked to me at all about our courtship. But Lucy Gelson mentioned it in no uncertain terms. Lucy was the only close friend I'd made, and I was delighted with our friendship.

Lucy lived in a soddie about an hour's buggy ride out on the prairie, with her husband, Jed, a hardworking, no-nonsense man, and their three sons. She worked from dawn to dark every day milking cows, picking up eggs, collecting what cow chips she and the boys could find, all the chores that went with living that kind of life. She cooked over a wood stove and was lucky to have that, scrubbed clothes in a copper kettle, attacked the dirt in her soddie with ferocity and yet remained cheerful.

After I got to know her, I asked once why she liked that life.

"I don't know that I do, Mattie," she said slowly, raising a work-hardened, strong hand to tuck in a wisp of pale hair that had escaped from the knot in the back of her head. She sighed and frowned, her hazel eyes strong with concern, and her face, with its sun and wind lines, temporarily lacking its usual smile. "But I won't shrug my shoulders and tell you I'm here because Jed brought me. There's got to be more to it than that. I love Jed, and I adore the boys, so that explains in part why I like the life. But there's still me, and I have to explain that. I think I do it because there's a sense of adventure, doing something new like we never did back in Illinois. And there's a sense of future. Jed and I won't live like this always. We'll have a grand house and a big, prosperous farm for the boys to run, and we'll sit on the porch with our feet up and sip whisky . . ."

"Shhh," I laughed. "The preacher will get you."

"Shaw, I don't even like whisky. It's just that's the men's idea of the lazy life. But it'll be good someday; I know it will. So I stay and do what's given me for all

129

those reasons." She smiled, the kind of truly happy smile that was rare in frontier women, and went on with her mending. Jed and the boys had gone to town and dropped her off for a visit. But even as we sat that afternoon and talked, her hands were busy while mine were, I thought, conspicuously empty.

Probably Lucy had no choice about staying on the prairie. Women alone rarely left the frontier to return to their families, but many chose other ways to relieve themselves of the strain of frontier life. Some became nagging, whining, complaining and unpleasant witches, others were soon chronically ill and often died young, a few simply lost their reason trying to cope with it all. Lucy chose none of those alternatives.

I got to know her, after a couple of brief meetings in Whittaker's store, because she brought her youngest son to me with a case of the croup, and we spent a long night together in my soddie boiling water and helping the youngster breathe. He would sleep fitfully at times, and during those moments we talked. And it was then I confessed to her my hopes and dreams about Em Jones. It was strange, of course, to become so familiar so quickly, but I think it was a combination of the need to talk to someone, particularly another woman, and Lucy's warm, outgoing personality. Unfortunately, I didn't really listen to both sides of the conversation but only heard myself talking.

"Mattie, the best of marriages are bad maybe half the time. There's no way you can be happy through all the little troubles that life brings you, let alone the big ones, but what you have to hope is that you've chosen someone who will work through all those long, difficult spots."

"Em and I have no difficult spots," I told her naively, and she smiled gently at me.

"Of course you don't. Neither did Jed and I back in Illinois when we each lived with our parents and only had the moments of courting. Life together is a different thing, Mattie. Are you sure Em is the kind of man you want to see first thing every morning the rest of your life, no matter if you feel rotten or he does or the crop hasn't come in or you've been up all night with a patient or who knows what?"

"Of course I'm sure."

She looked long and hard at me without saying a thing. Then, finally, after I had fidgeted uncomfortably, she said, "Just be sure you're not getting married to be married. You have to be sure Em is . . . well, there's a saying out here that if a man is true and trusted, he'll do to ride the prairie with. Are you sure Em will do to live a life with?"

Fortunately, the baby awoke, crying, and saved me from having to answer.

All thoughts of Lucy and Will Henry fled when Em said to me, as he did one day, "All right, when are you going to marry me?"

"Sometime, I suppose." I was evasive because much as I loved being courted by this handsome and laughing man, and though I knew the marriage was going to take place, I wasn't quite ready. I don't know what held me back unless it was some inner warning that I should have heeded.

"You have to be sure about this," I told him. "How

many men do you know whose wives may have to get up in the middle of the night, ride twenty miles and be gone for two days?"

"Not many, not many, but I don't know any other women like you. It's the other fellows' losses, not mine."

"Em, be serious. You know my work could become a problem between us . . . or between me and any man."

"Aha, is there another man?"

"Em!"

"All right, I'll be serious for a minute. I'm very proud of what you do, and I know you need to do it. You wouldn't be Mattie Armstrong if you weren't doctoring, so what's the problem? It may be inconvenient, but it's the best choice. I don't believe I could stand a woman who stayed home all day every day baking and cleaning. I'd get fat as a hog, for one thing." He was sitting in my rocker and got to laughing so hard at the idea, sticking his stomach out to demonstrate, that he nearly went over backward.

"Serves you right," I said without sympathy.

We went on that way for almost two years, maybe even a little longer. Em driving me on my calls, Em tending my vegetable garden and the few flowers that I'd planted by my soddie, Em doing all the repairs that I needed and, in short, acting like the man of the house, except that I made him ride back to town each night. Things weren't the same then as they are now, and I've often wondered since if I would still make him take on that long ride morning and night. I think I would. Of course, he still worked at Whittaker's store, which meant that he worked six days a week, so it was mostly Sundays that we spent together, if I didn't get called out. Sometimes, though, Em would come out during the week, protesting that a whole week was too long to wait to see me, and often I'd stop in the store several times during the week.

Em was the polite gentleman for a long time in our relationship, progressing slowly to kind of brotherly kisses when he left me, affectionate little pecks that I, in my innocence—and it was an appalling ignorance!—accepted as appropriate and normal. But one night he came up behind me as I worked, muttering, on some mending that I could not avoid.

"Must be why I love you, Mattie. You're so domestic! Such fine stitches!" His tone was sarcastic, but laughingly so.

"You know how I feel about mending," I fumed. "I'm intimidated by Mama and her fine work." I stood up, throwing the shirt down in disgust, and turned, only to find Em right in front of me. He held out his arms and simply enfolded me in them, kissing my forehead gently and murmuring that it was all right.

I stood trembling, expecting something to happen, and when Em's mouth found mine forcefully, a new world exploded for me. As a doctor, I had of course studied all those things—the birds and bees, if you will—but there's nothing like experience, and Em wakened feelings in me I had never dreamed could exist.

After that evening, Em was a gentle and patient teacher, though it must have been difficult for him. I learned to explore and to let him explore with those wonderful strong hands, but there was a harsh Puritan streak in me which held to the sanctity of the marriage bed. I would not compromise what I considered my honor, and still being naive, I had no idea how unfair I was being to Em. But he never pushed me. I guess, however, our physical relationship, in its halfway state, was one of the things that made me decide to marry him.

Strange that after all these years, I can't bring him to life in my mind. When I write about him, I feel that he is vague, shapeless, lacking all the dash and charm that captivated me. Maybe it's because all that dash and charm were part of an act, or maybe it's because so much unhappiness came between those years of courtship and my memories that I can't erase it. My memory is fully of happy days—I know they were happy for him and for me —and of silly fun, our last chance to be young again. But Em Jones no longer comes alive in my mind, not the man I knew at first. It embarrasses me to think about that past.

I did ask Em once why his parents never wrote.

"They prefer not to write too often. Black sheep, you know." He said it lightly, and I thought at the time he must be hiding a great sadness.

"Don't you ever visit them?" I wanted to reach out and comfort him, yet I was puzzled by this distance between parent and child. I had been unable to do anything about my separation from Mama, but it seemed to me Em and his parents could be doing things differently. As I have said, I was naive in more ways than one.

"I haven't visited them in four years. It didn't work out too well the last time I was there. They don't seem to understand me or what I want to do with my life."

Now there's a statement that should make any girl wary. This world is so full of misunderstood men! But I simply asked, in all seriousness, "What do you want to do with your life, Em?"

"Why, marry you, of course!" He said it with a laugh, and came around the table to confirm it with a kiss. But he saw that I still was troubled.

"Why are you so concerned about my parents? You should know that relationships between parents and children aren't always the way they're pictured in *Harper's Weekly*. How old were you when you parted company with your mother?"

"That's different. It was a case of necessity."

"So's mine. It's necessary for me to be away from them to survive as an individual. I'll tell you what, though; after we're married, I'll take you in grand style to visit the family in St. Louis."

"Really? I think I'd like that. Have you any brothers or sisters?"

"One of each. Both younger. You'll meet them."

"Would any of them come here for the wedding?"

"Nope. I won't invite them. But does that mean you've set the date?"

"No, not yet." I smoothed my skirt nervously and got up to walk away.

When we finally did marry, it was under unusual circumstances. It all began one day late in September. I was in the soddie, working on my account books and records, and Em was doing I don't know what, inspecting my cattle or planning the next year's garden or whatever.

Matt Quimby, the hired hand from Old Man Gressler's farm, came riding hell-bent into the yard, yelling my name as loud as he could.

"Calm down, Matt. What's the matter?"

"It's Mr. Gressler. He's been shot!"

"Shot?" I turned automatically to get my bag, and Em went for the horses.

"No buggy," I called after him. "We'll ride. It's faster."

We left Matt behind as we fairly flew out of the yard, for his horse was tired from the trip over. But before we left, he had time to shout, somewhere in the confusion, "Alvin Jones shot him."

Em and I rode too hard for conversation, but we both knew that Alvin was another hand on the Gressler place, not a bad sort of fellow but not a dedicated worker either. I couldn't imagine why any bad feeling between the men should come to shooting.

When we whirled into the Gressler place, Em took the horses without a word, and I ran into the house. Mrs. Gressler, a long, lean woman who had worked years on the plains, stood on the stoop, almost in a trance. She was dry-eyed and seemed to look right at me, but she never said a word. I murmured something soothing and brushed by her.

Luke Gressler sat slumped over his desk, account books before him, a neat hole in his temple. I didn't know much about firearms, but I knew Alvin had been close when he shot him, and I knew that Luke Gressler was dead. I checked the pulse to make sure, but the man had died instantly. I would have been too late if I'd been in the next room.

Mrs. Gressler knew. When I said, "He's dead," she just nodded, still staring into space.

"Where's Alvin?"

"Gone." It was her first word.

"Did he just shoot him and run away?"

"Yes."

Conversation with Mrs. Gressler wasn't going to tell me much, but I doubted I could leave her alone. Em had been standing in the yard, still holding the lathered horses.

"Em, go back to town and bring Alice Short, will you? I don't think Mrs. Gressler should be alone."

Em nodded and left, riding more slowly this time, and I turned to the work at hand. After urging Mrs. Gressler inside, I settled her in the bedroom, where she couldn't see her husband's body, and began to brew a pot of strong tea. Then I settled to the task of caring for Gressler's body. Without professional undertakers, it was often my chore to prepare the body for burial, a chore that I despised but did nonetheless. Gressler would be buried in the clothes in which he was killed, and Matt Quimby would seek the help of neighbors to build the coffin and dig the grave.

I looked at the account book Gressler had open in front of him, but it told me nothing except that he was figuring pay for his hands, Matt and Alvin. But it gave me a strange feeling to think that one minute he had been sitting here working on his daily business, and the next he was dead. I've seen very few murders in my life . . . only two others that I can recall . . . and I feel fortunate. Gressler's wasn't messy, neat and clean, in fact, better than if he died from peritonitis or gangrene or some of the other horrible things that happened on the prairie, but the idea that it was the work of another man chilled me. Still does to this day.

By the time Matt Quimby rode in, I was sitting in the bedroom, tea in hand, trying to comfort Mrs. Gressler. She still wasn't talking, and I knew it would be some time before she came out of her shock.

Matt tiptoed into the house and then coughed loudly. I went out to talk to him.

"You didn't save him, did you?"

"There was no way I could. I suspect he died instantly. What happened?"

"All I know is I was outside by the barn, mending some harness, when I heard their voices raised real loud, then a shot, and Alvin comes flying out the door, grabs a horse out of the barn and takes off. Never said a word to me."

It seemed hours before Em came back, and it probably was, but he brought Alice, a widow woman who lived in the tiniest house in town and who spent most of her time caring for those who needed her. In return, most folks saw to it that she had plenty of food on her table and was generally taken care of. Alice had often been a help to me with patients who needed care and couldn't or wouldn't be taken to my infirmary.

Em also brought news. Alvin Jones had gone almost straight to the sheriff and told him what he'd done. His version of the story was that Gressler had fired him for no reason and refused him wages due. It was the culmination of bad feelings between them that had been brewing for some time, and Alvin's temper got the better of his judgment. He was not a bad man, however, and was immediately sorry for what he'd done.

"Nobody'll ever hear Gressler's story about why he fired him and whether or not he held back wages," Em said. "I suppose maybe his wife can tell some of it, but . . . wouldn't you know, it would be somebody named Jones that did the shooting. Now everyone will think I'm related to a murderer!"

He said it with a laugh, knowing no one would connect him with Alvin, and I thought how like Em it was to turn even such a somber occasion into a joke.

Alvin was transferred to the jail at Fort Sidney to wait for the judge to come through and try his case. It turned out to be spring before it came to trial. Judges, like the rest of us, didn't get around the countryside much in a Nebraska winter.

So it was April when I was notified that I must be in Fort Sidney to testify. Em and I decided to make a wedding journey of it, and once I had committed myself, I shut off the doubts and hesitations and went blindly ahead.

"Why in Fort Sidney?" Em asked. "Why not here, among our friends?"

"I just want to do it this way. We'll take Will Henry and Jim with us, and Lucy Gelson if she can come, and the judge can marry us after my testimony."

Em thought it was crazy, but he wouldn't cross me, and that's exactly what we did. We made a party of our trip to the trial, all going in one wagon and having a wonderful time even on the long ride across the prairie. It seemed a shame, in a way, to make a party out of so serious an occasion as a man's trial for his life, but that's another thought

I banished from my mind.

Em and I were married on April 22, 1895, in the court-room at Fort Sidney. Spectators and the accused had been cleared out, and only Will Henry and Lucy stood up with us. The judge pronounced us man and wife, and Em kissed me, and it was done, far more smoothly and easily than I suspected.

"Why, Em," I said, teasingly, "if I'd known it would be this easy, I wouldn't have waited so long."

"I tried to tell you," he said, feigning resignation.

We settled down into domesticity fairly rapidly and hap-pily. Em kept his job at Whittaker's, but only for a while, because he either had a long ride twice a day or he had to stay in town in the same old room he'd had when he was a bachelor.

"Besides, you've got fifteen cows and four spring calves this year," he pointed out, "and you need someone to pay attention to this place and drive you on your calls."

It was wonderful to have him drive me, mostly for his company but also so I didn't have to drive myself, so I agreed to his plan. We covered the western end of Nebraska in those years, or so it seemed. People since have told me strange stories that I hardly even remember, like the time a farmer about fifteen miles north went out in the morning and found our buggy between his barn and house. Em and I were inside asleep. Seems the horse had been there before, when I treated the family, and it just turned in and stopped. Others have told of seeing me grope my way out of the buggy, fighting to consciousness after a deep sleep on the ride, and I know I did that often.

People who got sick, and particularly babies, never cared about my sleep, and I as like went at night as during the day.

Em didn't like having patients in the infirmary. "It's our home, and I like my privacy," he complained. So I tried to keep that to a minimum, although at least once I reminded him that if I hadn't had the infirmary, he and I would never have become acquainted.

"I know, I know. I just don't want anyone else becoming acquainted."

"Mattie, come see how your corn is growing," he called one day as he came into the soddie.

"Isn't it our corn?" I asked, raising my head from the medical journal I was reading.

"Well, sure, but I still sometimes feel like I'm living in your house. We'll have to think about moving; time we got out of a soddie anyway. Then I'd feel like it was our house."

"Em, I never knew you felt that way."

"Neither did I till we started to talk about it. Come on, let's look at the corn."

It was early summer by then, and the corn was well along, almost knee-high, as it should have been. We didn't grow much, only enough for us to have some and to feed the cattle.

"Em, could we ever make a paying proposition of this claim?"

"Sure we could, Mattie. We could raise sorghum, wheat, potatoes, lots of things. But we got to have grazing land for the cattle, and this claim just isn't big enough to do all those things."

"Wait a minute," I laughed. "We need a bigger and better house, more land. Where is the money for all this coming from?"

He grinned at me. "Didn't you know? I married a woman with a good income, a doctor."

I didn't even hear the warning bell that went off in my head.

We stayed in the soddie two years after our marriage, with Em talking all the time about moving to town. "Mattie, Mattie, don't you see? Benteen's where everything's going to be. It will be important to your practice to be in the midst of things. You can take care of people better."

Em knew how to convince me, because I truly did want to take care of people, and it was indeed hard to do when I had to ride all over the countryside. The thought of having a central base of operations and not having to travel so much was tempting beyond belief.

But I loved the land around my claim. I remember walking out alone that day, after we talked, and standing and letting the prairie wind blow over me, the fresh grass smell coming up. The wild prairie roses were blooming, and down by the buffalo wallow, the plum thickets looked like there would be plenty of plums for canning. I'd have to take a bushel in to Alice Short, who always put up preserves from my wild grapes and plums. I never tried to fiddle with it myself.

But move to town? Give up the soddie now that it was home, with four-o'clocks blooming outside the door and bright chintz curtains in the windows? Give up the freedom and the privacy, such as it was with people coming for help at any and all hours of the day? Why, I wondered, was Em always convincing me to do something that I was reluctant to do? It had taken him three years to convince me to marry him, not that he hadn't been right about that. Marriage to Em was so wonderful that I used to wake in the night and put out a hand to touch him and make sure he was still there, that I wasn't dreaming. So much, I thought, for Will Henry and Lucy Gelson and their prognostications of doom.

But that old warning bell was telling me to consider carefully before I agreed to the move. Was it because I didn't want to leave the prairie, or was it something else?

Em finally wore me down.

"Will we sell the claim?"

"Of course not. I have to have work to do, too, you know, with you busy with patients all the time and never having much time for me." He paused just a moment to let that sink in. "The claim, the cattle and your vegetables will be my business. I'm thinking seriously of putting in a potato crop, and maybe sorghum, too. They're both selling well. Course, I'll have to hire a hand, and we'll watch for more land close by."

"But, Em, the reason you quit Whittaker's was so you wouldn't have to ride back and forth. Now you'll have to make the same ride, just going the other direction."

Those dark eyes that could dance with laughter now looked thunderclouds at me, and Em paced around the room, silently, picking up a small vase and fingering it, then staring at the picture of my mother as though he'd never seen any of those things before. Sitting in the big chair by the stove, I waited nervously for him to speak. I was, to be truthful, afraid of Em, never knowing when a casual word or phrase would anger him. And now, I wondered if I'd done it again.

When he did speak, it was slowly, as though he'd thought out each word and phrase carefully. "Mattie, why are you questioning my judgement about this move? I am the head of the household, you know, and I thought you truly had faith in my decisions. I didn't mean to marry a woman who would wear the pants in the family."

It was a low blow, and he knew it. I bit my lip and said nothing, because I could feel that I was about to cry. I was darned if I wanted to do that just then.

We built a fairly large house in town, and for some months Em was busy supervising construction of it. I was back to going on calls alone, and I hated it. Riding alone, I convinced myself that Em was indeed right; moving to town was going to be the best thing.

We planned the house together, sort of. "Where do you want your office, Mattie?"

"Office? Can't I just see people in the parlor?"

"No, I want you to have a separate room for seeing them; keep our living quarters entirely apart from your work."

"This surely is getting to be a big house."

He grinned, busily working over the drawing in his hands. "We need a big house. We'll have to have a nursery, too."

Both Em and I agreed we wanted children, and I thought after two years of marriage, it was time for them to come along. Maybe after I was settled from the move and not subject to quite so busy a life, I thought, though I already suspected my life would not be any less busy, just different.

The house was frame, one story but large and roomy, with an office in front and a room next to that that could be my infirmary. The back of the house, our living quarters, consisted of a parlor, kitchen and two bedrooms, one of which Em designated as the nursery. We moved some of the furniture from the soddie—the sofa and occasional table I had shipped from Omaha, seven long years ago, and the bedroom furniture, kitchen pots and pans and the like. But Em "surprised" me with a new parlor set, a lovely sofa and chair with ornate mahogany trim around the cut-velvet upholstery, and a mahogany table with a marble top and pineapple design in the base. Then there was a big rolltop desk for my office—"You really want me to look like a doctor, don't you?" I teased—and a new bedroom set with a poster bed boasting pineapple designs on each of its posts and a burled pattern in the headboard, chest of drawers, nightstand and a chair to match, all again of dark, heavy mahogany.

"Em, it's wonderful furniture. But can we afford it? I mean, where's the money coming from? First the house, then all this furniture."

He was beaming with pride in his surprise, but when I mentioned money, he turned cross. "Don't worry about that, Mattie. Couldn't you just for once like something without finding fault or worrying about the price?"

But worry I did. For a short while, I wondered if he had borrowed the money from his wealthy family or maybe they had given a belated wedding gift. We never had heard from them since the wedding, though Em assured me he had written, giving them all the details. He said that since they never even responded, our planned trip to St. Louis was canceled. I learned to keep his family a secret question in my mind.

I found out, of course, that Em had not received any bounty either from heaven or St. Louis. He had borrowed six thousand dollars, an appalling sum, I thought, from the bank.

"Em, how could you do that without asking me?"

His eyes flashed again. "Asking you?" He made his voice incredulous. "Why should I ask my wife if I can borrow money from the bank?"

I said the unforgivable, in anger. "Because it's my money, and I'm the one with income to pay it back."

"So that's it. It's your money. What happened to 'our'? I thought we were in this together. Well, you can just take your money and keep it . . . and this house, too!" He slammed the door hard on his way out, so hard the etched-glass pane, ordered from Omaha, rattled, and I feared it would break.

An awful blank feeling filled the pit of my stomach, not like fear but more as though everything in my world had just turned blank and the future had been wiped out. Surely he couldn't leave me with the house. After all, he was the one who wanted it, not me, and he wouldn't dare walk away, leaving me with a big house and a huge debt. Would he? And where would he go, what would he do?

Another part of me still rebelled. I had been poor once, and Em knew that. He knew my absolute terror at the

thought of being anywhere near poor again. I'd consented, only reluctantly, to using my money in the bank—
our money, if you will, but money that I'd saved before
we were married—to build the new house, because Em
had assured me it wouldn't take any time to replace it
once I was established in an office in town and he made a
paying proposition out of the claim. But to borrow beyond
that?

I waited until long into the night, but Em didn't come
home, and I finally went to sleep. Sometime in the early
morning, while it was still dark, he climbed into bed
beside me, smelling of whisky. We made up, passionately,
and I've always been sure that was when Nora was conceived. In anger.

Once I knew I was pregnant, I didn't tell anyone, not even
Em, for a while. It seemed like a grand secret to keep to
myself, though I suppose that was silly. Em and I never
mentioned that awful night again, and I had tried to come
to grips with the idea of being in debt. Em seemed to be
working hard, spending all his time at the claim and
reporting gleefully that we had eight cows that should
calve soon, the fields were plowed and so on. I was busier
than I thought I'd be, with between five and ten patients a
day and still having to make some calls in the country, so
I rarely got out to the claim to inspect his work. Sometimes, though, he hitched up the buggy and took me out
there for an afternoon drive, and I saw that he had accomplished a lot. He'd built a real barn instead of the annual
one blown from a threshing machine, and he'd fenced the
pasture away from the fields he had planted. The cows

looked sleek and healthy, and it seemed as if the claim indeed might prosper, not that anyone ever made that much from a small farm like this one.

So life was going smoothly, and I decided that the unfortunate evening was just an accident, one that wouldn't be repeated. Land's sakes, how we can fool ourselves when we want to!

Lucy Gelson brought up the subject of the baby one day when she'd ridden into town with Jed when he came for supplies. It was her first trip to see our new home and office, and I was glad for a chance to visit with her and, I guess, to show her that my marriage was fine.

"Mattie," she said, holding her cup of tea and laughing at me, "aren't you going to tell me about the baby?"

"Lucy Gelson, how did you know?" I guess in my exalted position as a doctor, I thought no one else knew much about the body at all, but I should have known better. Lucy had helped neighbors in childbirth many times as well as giving birth to those three boys of hers. She knew a thickening waist when she saw one.

"Have you told Em?"

"No, but he'll be delighted. I guess if you noticed, I better tell him soon before he asks why I'm getting so fat."

"Will you stop practicing?"

"Of course not, Lucy. Did you stop doing chores on the farm?"

She grinned and said simply, "I'm very happy for you. I hope everything goes just as you want it to. Boy or girl?"

"I suppose Em will want a boy, but I really don't care."

I knew Em would want the baby. He had always wanted

children and talked about it, and he was almost jealous of the Gelsons for their three boys.

"I wish we had three like that," he said one day after a visit to their farm, where the boys had taken him on a tour to show off all their treasures, such as an old surveyor's stake they'd uncovered in the high grass, or a muzzle-loading gun, without a stock, that Jed had unearthed for them to play Indians. "Won't be long," Em told me, "before those boys will be a big help to Jed on this place. He's a lucky man."

Having children was not something I had ever thought about doing, but then I guess I had never thought about being married either. Some girls seem to prepare for motherhood all their lives, but not me. I wanted children simply because I wanted to make Em happy, and it was what he wanted. Of course, raising Nora turned out to be important to me. Afterward, I couldn't imagine life without her and that experience, but that wasn't the way I felt back in the days before her birth. Children were something I accepted as inevitable without either positive or negative feelings.

Em was delighted, as I predicted. He whooped and hollered around the kitchen, sweeping me off my feet into some sort of wild dance.

"Em, you'll make me dizzy!"

"Oh, I'm sorry. Here, Mattie, sit right down here."

"No, no, I'm all right. I just don't want to whirl about the kitchen so." The wooden spoon in my hand was dripping onto the floor, and the oilcloth on the table had been pulled sideways by his burst of energy. I straightened it, listening to him ramble.

"Now, if it's a boy . . . and I kind of suspect it will be—"

"You do? Why?" I was amused, watching him and seeing his eyes dance with that special happiness.

"Well, boys just come first, or at least they should. Anyway, I think we'll name him, uh, David. Good solid name."

"What about Emory?"

"No, no juniors around this house. David. Don't you like that?"

"I don't know. I have to think about it a while. We won't need a name for several months, you know."

"It doesn't hurt to be prepared. I mean, hadn't you better start sewing for the baby?"

"Sewing? No self-respecting baby would wear anything I sewed. Lucy has some hand-me-downs, and I'll ask Mrs. Short to make some gowns. I did hear about a quilting coming up, and I thought I'd see if the ladies would make me a quilt." It wasn't exactly taking unfair advantage to ask that. I had doctored all those ladies' families, sometimes without pay and sometimes for a few eggs or an oilcan full of wild berries or some other trifle. They would be glad to do something that I really needed.

"You really aren't going to sew something yourself, just, well, I don't know, so the baby will know you cared?"

I laughed and hurt his feelings. "Em, the baby will have to know some other way. I can't sew well, and you know it. I gave it up after I tried years ago to sew something for Sara Dinsmore. I don't have the patience for it."

"Well, I thought you would want something to do while you wait for the baby."

"Something to do! I have more than enough to do right now, thank you, what with seeing patients and keeping up with this house and my records and studying some when I get a chance." I knew we were in trouble as I said it.

"You're not going to keep up your practice now." It was meant to sound like a question, but I knew Em didn't mean it that way. He wanted it to be an order, and he somehow got caught between the two inflections in tone.

"Yes I am." My own tone was defiant. I loved Em, and I wanted to do almost anything to make him happy, but I guess even then, as pliable as I was with him, I couldn't do something that went against my whole being. I couldn't quit practicing medicine. And if I did, who would mend the broken arm when Lucy's middle boy fell off the range cow he tried to ride, or who would deliver Amy Snellson's baby or tend to this one or that when they got cholera? Of course I would keep on practicing.

"I don't think it's right. You should put the baby's welfare first," he said righteously.

"Oh, for land's sake, Em. Prairie women do chores right up until the day of the birth. They work harder, physically, than I ever thought about doing. It's good for them. What's bad is sitting on a soft cushion all day doing nothing. I'll try to cut down on house calls when the time is closer," I promised.

"Well, shall we take you to Omaha to Dr. Dinsmore? I mean, who will deliver the baby? You can't do it yourself." He was getting excited again, his disapproval forgotten momentarily.

"I think Lucy can help me. She's delivered many babies before, and between us we can do it. I don't want to go to

Omaha and have to stay forever waiting, then wait until the baby and I are strong enough to come back. Em, it'll all work out. Just don't worry."

He looked at me fiercely. "I don't think you realize, Mattie, how much I want the baby. I don't want you to do anything to keep me from having it."

I felt like a brood mare.

We settled into the waiting phase of my pregnancy. I grew gradually thicker about the middle but was still able to wear my traditional plain skirts and blouses, and with an apron, most people couldn't tell I was expecting. I kept it from my patients and went on with my daily routine.

Sara answered the letter I'd sent to Omaha with the news and proclaimed herself delighted to be an aunt-to-be. Now eighteen, she was a young lady and had finished her schooling in Omaha.

"Father is relieved, I think, that I show no interest in medicine," she wrote. "Perhaps seeing you go through school was enough for him. I do have to decide on what to do, as no attractive young men have come along, and Father will not tolerate my sitting around waiting to get married. Would you like a nursemaid for the baby when it comes? I believe I could be quite good at it."

She went on to say that her father was busy at the medical school and seemed to be enjoying his work, but she felt he was still lonely. Occasionally he had a fellow physician in for a brandy and conversation, but he had had no regular female companionship since I'd left.

"Sometimes," she continued, "he talks about you and mentions how much we both miss you. We both hope you are very happy."

Dr. Dinsmore had never recently written to me, though I took that as hurt pride rather than anger, because I thought he truly cared about me. Perhaps his silence was more embarrassment than anything else. But I wondered what he would say about my life now. Oh, I knew he'd be proud of my medical practice, because I did a good job, just as he'd taught me, and my patients fared well. But Em? How would the two of them react to each other?

As for Sara, I began to mull over the idea in my mind. I would want someone to care for the baby and give it all the constant attention that I wouldn't be able to. Why not Sara? Probably it was time for her to get out of her father's house, and since I had raised her when she was little and needed love, it would be only fitting if she raised my child. I decided to mention it to Em. The baby would probably come in late April, and perhaps Sara would come out for the summer to see how it went.

"Where would we put her?" Em asked. "We only have two bedrooms."

"She can sleep with the baby," I replied.

"I don't know. I don't like the thought of someone else taking care of our baby. You should do it."

"Em, let's not go into that again. I have a medical practice. Do you want to give up your ranching and farming and take care of the baby?"

"It's not man's work," he said petulantly. "You know I can't do that."

"Well, neither can I."

"I'm not sure I want someone in the house all the time, someone who's not family."

"She's family to me. Believe me, Em, it will work out. And besides, it's kind of what you do for people. She needs a change right now, and her family took me in when it was very important to me. In a way, I'm repaying not just what they did for me, but the world in general. Do unto others . . ."

In the end, Em gave in but he wasn't happy about it, and I had no idea he was storing all those small unhappinesses, like a squirrel storing nuts against the winter. For him, winter would be many years away, yet it would come with a sudden eruption that left me devastated.

In some ways, doctoring was easier in winter than in summer. We were less likely to have a lot of cholera, maybe because people were closed into their houses and saw each other less, maybe because Nebraska's hard freezes quieted the bacteria that caused the disease. But there was still pneumonia and croup for babies and childbirth and frostbite. Today, if people get frostbite, we accuse them of carelessness. But back then, frostbite was sort of an occupational hazard. Someone had to go outside to check the animals, see that the horses and cattle had plenty of hay and straw, and hogs had a lot of straw bedding to wallow around in and plenty of swill. And even during a blizzard, cows give milk and hens lay eggs. Someone also had to gather cow chips for the fire and to dig away the blown snow from the doorway of the house. You couldn't decide to come inside just because you were cold. And so there was a lot of frostbite, or chilblains as we called it then.

The oldest Gelson boy, Jake, got a case of it on his feet

that year. Lucy packed him up in the wagon and drove him seven miles across the snow-covered prairie to bring him to me. It was like heading your horses off across a trackless white ocean, but like the rest of us, Lucy knew precisely where she was going, snow or not, and she knew she wanted me to see that boy.

Jake was twelve and not very talkative, the way boys often are. "Shoveling snow," he muttered when I asked him how he got his feet so cold.

"Those new boots didn't wear at all this year," Lucy said. "Got holes in them already, and winter isn't half-over. I've a mind to speak to Mr. Whittaker about it."

"Why were you shoveling snow?" I asked. "We haven't had a good blow in days."

He looked down. "No, but Ma decided I should shovel it out where it, well, collected over the cellar. She wanted some preserves."

"It's all my fault. Wanted a little something special, and now look what I've done." Lucy looked as guilty as she must have felt.

"His feet are going to be fine, Lucy. Just sore for some days. Keep them good and warm, and either get him some new boots or line those old ones better with cardboard." In truth, Jake Gelson probably never got full circulation back in those toes the rest of his life, but he was fortunate enough to avoid gangrene.

Amy Snellson's first baby was born that winter, almost in the midst of a blizzard, and Em was angry that I had to go. Fortunately, the Snellsons lived in town, so I didn't run the risk of getting lost on the prairie. In some of our blizzards, you could get lost between the house and the barn—people really froze to death that close to home, because the snow disoriented them—but this snow wasn't that hard, and by peering carefully through the isinglass in my buggy, I found my way to the Snellsons'.

"The baby's early," Amy said in a tiny voice. She was a frail thing herself, very blond and thin and young. She and William Snellson had been sweethearts for several years, and it was kind of a town celebration when they married. William was now clerking at Whittaker's, doing just what Em had done, and declared he wouldn't go back to the farm, because he didn't want Amy to work that hard. Fortunately, he didn't declare this out loud to many people but me, so he didn't offend all those good folk who did live on the prairie and did indeed work hard. That included his folks, and hers, too, for both families lived in the area, though Amy's were nearly twenty miles from Benteen.

This particular evening in early December, William hunched over the table in their parlor while I was with Amy. The minute I came out, he was on top of me.

"Well, Dr. Armstrong? Well?"

"I don't know, William. The baby's early from what Amy tells me, awful early, and we'll just have to wait and see."

Amy Snellson was in labor almost twenty-four hours. I sat by her bed almost the whole time, except for a couple of brief spells when William stayed with her and I could catch a nap. But William was too scared himself to be of any comfort to the poor girl, and I mostly had to shoo him out of the room.

"Don't let him come in here anymore," Amy said in her

weak voice. "He, well, I know he means well, but he makes me nervous. He looks so scared."

"It'll be all right, Amy. Don't worry. Just try to relax and push down when I tell you." I tried to sound soothing, but I was worried. The longer the labor went on, the less chance the baby had.

The baby was born in the wee hours of the morning, almost a full day after I'd arrived. She was a delicate little girl, beautifully formed but too tiny. She gave only one weak cry in spite of my best efforts. I wrapped her in a cloth and put her close to Amy, but she died within two hours.

Amy and William were inconsolable, and I didn't try to tell them that God knew best or anything, like many doctors did, because I couldn't believe it myself. I left them to their tears and went about the business of fixing up the baby, choosing the prettiest of the little dainty things Amy had sewn and wrapping the tiny thing in a blanket before I put it in the wooden cradle. Then I straightened up the house and gave Amy something to make her sleep. By then, William was able to talk to me, though he choked up every two minutes. I wasn't exactly dry-eyed myself.

"Thank you, Dr. Armstrong. I know you tried, and, well, I . . ."

"You'll see about a coffin?"

"Yes, ma'am. I can do that. Will you say a few words if we can bury her?"

The "if" meant if the ground was soft enough to dig a grave.

"Of course," I said, "but the reverend—"

"He'll understand."

This was not the only time I'd been called on to say a few words at a gravesite. That had happened to me before, out in the country where there was no one else, and I always dreaded it. What William meant as a compliment settled on me as a burden, like the final straw. I went home with the heaviest of hearts that early morning. Fortunately, Em was asleep and didn't stir as I crawled into bed. I dreaded telling him about a baby that didn't live.

Nora was born in the middle of a stormy night. It was probably the only predictable thing she ever did, but like most first babies, she came at the most inconvenient time, and she was late. Em had been nervous for three weeks, hovering over me, asking if I was sure I had counted the weeks right, didn't I think it was time to worry, maybe I should contact Dr. Dinsmore. I had a hard time to keep from losing my temper with him, but I knew he was excited and scared and anxious. And truthfully, underneath all that pose of "Don't worry, I'm a doctor, I know best," I was scared, too. Not, like some women are, of childbirth, but that something beyond my control would go wrong, that the perfect baby that I wanted to bring into the world wouldn't be healthy . . . or worse, like Amy and William's baby, wouldn't live.

I was good enough, though, at appearing calm and collected, covering the nervousness. It's always been one of my strengths, the ability to hide my fears and uncertainties from other people. So I tried to calm Em.

"Em, the baby's only a week late. You started expecting it too soon."

"Well"—he paced nervously around the kitchen,

picking up a cup here, a paper there, fiddling with an old piece of string—"you never can tell. Sometimes they come early. You should know that."

"Of course I do, Em. But first babies often come late, and this one just isn't ready to come into the world yet. They're healthier, you know, if they don't come early."

"But don't they, well, I mean, sometimes if they're too late, doesn't that mean . . ."

"Only in unusual cases, Em, unusual cases." I tried again to pay attention to the recipe that I was diligently trying to follow. All the women around could make corn-bread with a pinch of this or that and a handful of meal and so on. I had to ask Sally Whittaker to write down directions, and still, the first time I baked it, I got nothing but crumbs. But I was trying again, flour and cornmeal all over, and me as ungainly and big as a bear, when Em came and grabbed me.

"It's just that I'm scared, Mattie. Scared for you and scared for me, because I want our baby so badly." He looked like he might cry, though he was the kind of man who never did that, and I remember feeling, well, touched. To think that a man loved me that much, that he was that scared about something happening to me, and that he wanted our baby that badly.

"Em, it will be all right. Believe me, it will."

And like a little child, he looked solemnly at me and said, "If you say so, Mattie. I'll try to relax."

Nora kept him in suspense for another two weeks, though, and it was a strained time. Em refused to leave my side for more than five minutes, and he dictatorially announced that I would go on no house calls. I agreed, because I wouldn't have gone anyway, no matter what he said, but I let him think I was bowing to his wishes. Every once in a while, I guess I must have learned a lesson from Mama. Letting Em think things were his own idea was one of those lessons.

We had a late spring snow that year, one of those storms that blow off the prairie quicker than you can think. I saw the dark gray-blue of the sky off in the distance and knew, instantly, that it was too late to send for Lucy Gelson and that tonight I would need her. Somehow you know those things with an irrevocable certainty. Luckily, Em didn't have the same premonition I did.

"Sure is blowing up a storm," he said, coming into the kitchen and warming his hands by the stove. "Glad I got back from the claim in time. This is the kind of spring storm a man's a fool to be caught in."

"If he can avoid it," I said. "They come up so fast, sometimes you can't help yourself."

"Well, I'm glad we're all safe and warm here. Wonder if we should have asked Lucy Gelson to come in before this. I mean, if the baby comes tonight, who will help you?"

"Hush, Em. The baby won't come in a storm like this. And if it did, you'd help me. Who else?"

He turned green and grabbed a chair to steady himself. "Me? Not me! Oh no, Mattie. I couldn't."

I was sitting, resting, which was mostly what I did those last days before Nora's birth, and I stared long and hard at him and saw that he was right. He would be no help, might probably be a hindrance, getting nervous and not following my directions.

"We'll call Sally Whittaker. She could make it that far if she had to."

"Sally Whittaker has never had any children of her own!" He was indignant.

"Neither," I said, "have you. But she's a woman. I'm going to lie down."

Em heated some soup for our supper, took it out of the cold-keeper room, and I ate, but not very heartily. I still didn't tell him that tonight was the night, and we both went to bed early, ostensibly for the kind of sound sleep that is possible only when you're snug and warm inside and listening to a storm boil around you outside.

It was still early in the night, maybe before midnight, when I awakened Em.

"Em, Em! Wake up! I need for you to go get Sally Whittaker."

"Huh?" He was always foggy when he woke up, a sound and heavy sleeper who seemed to escape from the world when he dreamt. "Mattie? Why the hell are you shaking me? Oh, the baby? Is it the baby?" As consciousness came to him, he recovered all his nervousness and grabbed me hard as if to assure himself I was still there.

"Everything's fine, Em, but I think it's about time to get serious about having this baby. And I'd like Sally, I really would."

"I'll go right away," he said. And he did. He was dressed and out the door quicker than I'd ever seen him move.

While I waited, I lay back on the bed and worked hard at relaxing. One thing I'd noticed about childbirth was that the more tense the mother was, the harder the delivery was on her. Course, now that's almost a commonplace, but nobody had said much about relaxation in those days. Yet I lay back and willed my body not to be tense, took some deep breaths and tried not to fight back every time a contraction came. Nora, always feisty, was a hellion coming into this world, but she was quick.

Sally barely had time to get into the house, all breathless and full of "Oh, me!" and "My goodness, what shall I do, Mattie?" I gave her a few simple directions, such as to bring me water to drink, and showed her where the clean cloths were and how to rig up a blanket around the bedposts for me to pull on. Em, of course, had disappeared to sit, I later learned, whisky bottle in hand, at the kitchen table. Sally calmed down quickly and proved helpful and a comfort, and before we knew it, Nora Kathleen Jones made her appearance, caterwauling as though she'd tell the world instantly what she thought of it.

"Mattie?" Em heard her cry and stood outside the door, whispering, as though a loud voice would break some precious moment.

"Wait just a minute, Em." Pride made me want to be clean and covered before he came in, so I held the baby while Sally straightened and cleaned. Within minutes, the baby and I were ready for Em.

"I'll just wait in the other room," Sally said, sliding out the door.

Em said the obvious. "She's beautiful, Mattie, absolutely beautiful." But she was. She had dark, curly hair, lots of it for a newborn, and her face was neither wrinkled nor red, but rather, soft and feminine. Her crying had stopped, and she stared at the world with dark and suspicious eyes.

"She is lovely, isn't she?" I asked. Oh, I was the proud mother, full of dreams and hopes and longing for this fairy child I had brought into the world. Nothing, I vowed, would be too good for her. Never would she know the uncertainty, the pain of childhood that I had.

"Do you want to hold her?"

"Is it all right?" He looked scared, and I smiled a little, tired as I was.

"Of course it is. She's your daughter. Here, be sure to hold her head." I put my hands under her to give her to him, and he sat on the edge of the bed, cradling Nora and smiling foolishly at her.

Then he looked at me. "Thank you, Mattie. She's wonderful. And you are, too."

Never, I thought, had there been a family as complete and perfect as we made, and never had there been a man who loved a woman as much as Em loved me. I loved him because he had brought it all together, like a circle that had come full round. Em gave me back the baby, kissed me gently and went off to take Sally home. Nora and I were asleep before he closed the bedroom door.

The next day Em was beside himself with pure joy and bursting to share it with the world. Of course, once he'd taken Sally back home, every family in Benteen knew of Nora's arrival, so Em couldn't exactly surprise them with his news. And you know how it is with good news and sometimes bad; lots of times a person wants to be the first one to tell folks. I could see that was how Em felt, and I understood. As a new father, all he could do was stand and boast, while I was taking care of the baby and recovering my strength, fully occupied and not feeling like I wanted to share my happiness with anyone but Em and Nora. But I understood.

"Em, why don't you ride out and tell Will Henry and Jim?" I asked, as though it were of burning importance to me that they find out instantly about the baby. Actually, they had been checking on me every two or three days, and it was about time for them to wander along of their own accord. But it would make them feel important to be sent for, and it would occupy Em.

"Gee, Mattie, I'd like to . . . but, well, I don't think I should leave you and Nora."

"We'll be fine, Em. I . . . well, that's really thoughtful of you, and I appreciate it. But we'll be just fine. I think we'll both sleep most of the time you're gone."

Em left, and we slept. In a few hours he came stomping into the house. I could tell by listening that he was shaking snow on the kitchen floor, but I kept my peace. Then I heard voices behind him.

"Where is she?" boomed Jim, heading straight for the bedroom.

"Wait!" Em said, desperately trying to control the situation that should, by rights, be his moment of glory. "Let me see if it's all right for you to go on in."

"Pshaw! I ain't gonna hurt nothing. Just want a peek at my new grandchild." And in Jim came, grinning from ear to ear.

"Here she is, Jim, Nora Kathleen Jones, for your approval." I smiled and held the baby out to him, but he backed away.

"Now, Mattie, I just want to admire. I don't want to get

into holding her."

"Jim, you've got to hold your grandchild." It was unspoken between all of us that Jim, though no blood relative, was to be Nora's grandfather, the only grandparent she'd ever know, it seemed.

"Well, maybe I'll hold her a day or two from now, when she's had time to get used to things, but for right now, she sure does look comfortable right where she is. Don't you think, Will Henry?"

"Yeah" was the noncommittal answer. Will Henry stood in the doorway looking shy and uncertain.

"Come see her closer, Uncle Will Henry," I urged.

He tiptoed over. "She sure is tiny, Mattie."

"Tiny but healthy," I said.

"Came into this world yelling like a calf that lost its mother," Em said, proudly stepping to the head of the bed. "Mattie practically delivered her herself; did a good job, too."

They all looked at me in awe, and I was most conscious of being in a feminine position and state, surrounded by three amazed men. It was a nice feeling.

Jim cooked dinner that night, cutting a hunk of meat off the side in our storeroom and raiding my cupboard to find the makings of a stew more delicious than any I ever made. I ate ravenously, while all three of them stared at me.

"Hungry, Mattie?" Jim laughed.

"Well," I said indignantly, "I haven't eaten all day, and I've got to keep my strength up to feed Nora now, you know."

"That's right. She does," Em said solemnly.

Jim just laughed. "Have another helping, little mother."

Later in the evening I caught Will Henry kneeling by Nora when he thought no one was watching, extending a tentative finger toward her tiny curled fist, a big smile on his face. She'll be blessed with a loving family, I thought, and no child can ask for more.

The next few days people drifted by with gifts for Nora— a handmade blanket knit by a woman I'd once ridden out to see, a tiny sweater of wool that apparently once had been used for something else, then unraveled, washed and reknit. From Sally Whittaker there was a corncob doll dressed in scraps of old material with dried corn silk, saved from last year, for hair, and a ludicrous boa of chicken feathers. In later months, Nora would chew on the doll and rub the feathers against her face.

There's nothing like the feeling of being close that a first baby can bring to a couple. With Nora, we were a welded unit, strong against the world, or so I thought. She was a good baby, rarely fussy, though she didn't gurgle and bubble happily like lots of the babies I've brought into this world. Nora seemed to lie there and take it all in.

"She's seeing if she likes the world," Em would laugh. "Not going to rush into anything until she's sure."

Sometimes he would wake with me when I fed her in the middle of the night, and Em would spin glorious tales about the future, specifically about Nora's future. "I'll get her a horse pretty soon. Gentle, of course, but she's got to grow up riding, not like you having to learn when you're full grown, and not like me, never feeling sure of myself."

"Em, are you going to make her a cowboy?" I was

joking, but in a way I meant it. I envisioned a dainty little girl, dressed in ribbons, kind of a Mary Jane Canary that I had never been, and I didn't want Em turning her into a ruffian.

"No, not a cowboy, Mattie. Just a strong all-around person, who can do whatever she wants. Who knows? Maybe she'll be like her mother and be an independent woman with a career."

I was always on the alert for comments like that, but Em said it proudly this time and leaned over to kiss me hard.

"Careful! You'll smash Nora before she can get to that horse."

He pulled away again and stared at the baby, who was busily nursing at my breast and making no sound except that sucking noise.

"She is beautiful, isn't she, Mattie? Is she the prettiest baby you've ever seen?"

"I haven't seen that many, you know," I laughed. He sounded as though I'd delivered hundreds of babies, like some old country doctor who'd been around for years, and like I have by this time in my life. But my laughter turned silent, because I thought of one of the few babies I had delivered, the stillborn girl of Amy and William Snellson. I hugged Nora tighter, feeling how blessed we were, until she protested with a slight sound of disgust.

William and Amy came to visit when Nora was but two weeks old, bringing her a beautifully smocked little gown.

"I . . . I made it for our baby," Amy said hesitantly, "and I want you should have it."

"Oh, Amy, I'll treasure it. It's the most important gift Nora's had, and I can't thank you enough. It means . . .

well, you know." I truly was at a loss for words because of the enormity between my good fortune and their bare lives. But Amy confided in me later that she thought she was pregnant again, and I prayed for a safe and normal delivery. Realistically, I also told her to visit me soon and explained a little about the importance of taking care of herself during pregnancy.

With his usual extravagance, Em ordered a huge stuffed animal from Kansas City for Nora. He set it in the middle of our bed, then put Nora down beside it to see how she liked it. She stared long and hard without a sound. Then, apparently having accepted it, she stuck one hand out and shoved as hard as her little fist would go. We thought it was wonderfully funny, but I wonder now if it didn't say something about Nora. Em encouraged her by putting the bear back for her to knock it down again and roaring with laughter at her efforts. She fixed him with a long gaze that seemed to say, "Okay? You like that, do you?" And then she hit the bear again with that tiny but remarkably strong fist.

I made my first house call three weeks after Nora was born, riding out in the buggy, with Nora tucked safely into a basket on the floor. We went to see the Gelsons, partly because I'd heard Lucy was poorly, though nothing urgent, and partly because I was housebound and anxious to be out.

The late spring snow of the night Nora was born was long gone, and the prairie was turning green. It seemed to be blossoming with beginning new life, and I had a lot of dramatic thoughts about spring and new beginnings and

Nora. Even the air smelled fresh and new, and I marveled at how wonderful my life was. Omaha seemed far away, and Princeton, thankfully, much farther.

Nora took to the ride without complaint, just as she did everything, and I quieted Em's fears by telling him that contrary to what everyone thought, fresh air was wonderful for babies. He finally let me go, though with so much advice that I could hardly bear it.

"Yes, Em, I'll keep her bundled."

"No, Em, I won't let the boys hold her." I might fudge on that one, I thought.

Lucy was poorly, just as Jed had said on his last visit to town. "She, well, she just seems tired all the time," he'd worried aloud. "Can't get her strength up to do nothing."

I'll bet she is tired, I thought grimly, and Jed's idea of nothing would probably flatten two stronger women, but I said nothing to him at the time. Jed was an old-fashioned, noncomplaining type who accepted life as it came to him, and he expected the same stoicism of others. Even his appearance indicated his calm steadiness, for he was bigger than most men, with a solid, square face and a generally impassive look in his deep blue eyes. I had seen Jed smile only once or twice, but then, I had never seen him frown.

Lucy oohed and aahed over the baby, as I knew she would, and Nora fixed her with one of her solemn stares, which made Lucy laugh. "Land's sake, isn't she a solemn one, Mattie? Can't you ever tell her any jokes?" She reached a finger toward Nora's tiny fist.

"You know Em," I replied. "He jokes with her all the time, and she just stares at him like she's sizing him up."

Thirteen-year-old Jake paid little attention to us, kind of adopting that boyish attitude of "Bah, babies!" but the two younger boys danced and clamored around.

"Can't I hold her?"

"Her hands are so tiny. Can I touch one?"

"Let me see, Jim! You're in the way!"

Lucy's smile faded, as though she didn't want to have to deal with even this good-natured bickering. "Boys, hush, please. For my sake."

They hushed instantly, staring a moment at their mother, then standing downcast. We were still outside the soddie, and I asked Jake to look after my horses while we went inside.

"I hate to go into that dark, stuffy house these days," Lucy said. "Spring is so wonderful outdoors."

"True, Lucy, but I need to set Nora down and let the boys have a good look at her."

Inside, I guessed why Lucy didn't want to go into the house. Her usually spotless house was not quite up to her standards—not dirty, but things hadn't been picked up, and there were cobwebs, an inevitable problem in soddies, in places where Lucy would normally have gotten rid of them.

"I don't know." She gestured helplessly. "I just didn't seem to be able to keep up this winter."

"Boys," I said, "you keep an eye on Nora. No, Luther, don't pick her up, just watch her. Your mother and I are going to talk."

I pulled the curtain to the bedroom area to give us what privacy I could and then said, "All right, Lucy, how long have you been feeling this way?"

"Most since Christmas," she muttered. "I don't think it's anything. I just . . . Oh, Mattie, I'm so tired!"

"Let's have a look." And I gave her what examination I could, listening to her heart, feeling her back, looking closely at her eyes. She sat, apprehensive and quiet.

"I think you're right, Lucy. It's nothing, nothing but you're tired—worn out—and you need to get out of this cabin."

We talked a great deal, Lucy explaining that she couldn't work less, there were things that had to get done no matter how she felt, and my countering that the boys could help with most of her chores. I prescribed an hour's ride on the prairie, alone, every day that it was pleasant.

"You mean just ride out there all by myself?"

"Right."

"Jed would think I'd gone crazy."

"No. I'll tell him." Nobody thought much about time for yourself in those days, yet I knew that Lucy needed a little time to be Lucy and not a mother or a wife or a chore girl on a hardscrabble farm. I did talk to Jed, and I could see he thought it was crazy, but he liked me and generally accepted what I said, so he agreed.

The boys, meanwhile, had sat as requested, staring at Nora, who returned their looks with equal solemnity and occasionally waved a hand in their direction.

"She doesn't talk," Luther complained.

"Of course not, dummy," his brother crowed. "You didn't either when you were a baby."

"I didn't?"

Nora and I took the midday meal with the Gelsons and then headed back across the prairie. I drove the horses slowly, enjoying the ride and, truthfully, the solitude. I guess I knew the reception that was waiting for us.

"You've been gone four hours." Em was angrier than I had seen him but one or two times.

"It usually takes me almost that long to go out there."

"This isn't usually. You had Nora with you!" He looked about to burst, and I wondered if he'd thought about how he looked to anyone who might pass by. But as always, a part of me was afraid of Em, and I tried to mollify him.

"She's fine, Em, really she is. Enjoyed the ride, I think." I hated the pleading tone that crept into my voice.

Nora even smiled a little, as though to reassure her father, but he was enjoying his anger and the power it gave him.

"Well, I didn't like it," he raved. "I was damn scared that the horses had run away or stepped in a hole . . ." He waved a fist in the air furiously.

"Lucy needed me, Em. That's why I went, or at least partly why I went. Now, can we go inside and stop standing out here arguing in front of God and everybody."

He grabbed the harness to lead the horses to the barn but flung over his shoulder, "I don't care who hears that you're an inconsiderate and careless mother!"

Dinner was silent that night. It was the first blemish in our happiness since Nora was born, and I was both dismayed and puzzled. I didn't think I'd done anything wrong. In fact, I don't think I'd have done anything different, couldn't have. So it was unfair that Em was treating me like I was the one at fault when truly he was at fault with his temper. But the most unfair part of it was that I couldn't defend myself, couldn't lash back as he lashed out at me and tell him the things I thought about his being overprotective, unjustly angry and, to be blunt, childish in his anger. I bottled all that up inside me and walked tiptoe around him all evening. He played some with Nora, then stormed out of the house without a word and had not come home when I put Nora down and went to sleep myself.

Nora had been sleeping through the night lately, even at that young age, but this night she wakened, and I nursed her. Em was asleep in a big chair in the living room, and I left him there.

The next morning, he was loving and apologetic. "I just lost my mind," he said. "It won't happen again. I love you so much . . . well, there's no explanation. But I apologize." He drew me tightly to him, and I held on, wanting to believe that it would all be all right.

But I knew, even then, that a pattern was developing. Em would flare in anger over something that amounted to nothing, make a big and ugly scene out of it, then, when he calmed down, he'd be contrite and promise it would never happen again. But it always did.

I heard from the Dinsmores when Nora was a little over a month old. Dr. Dinsmore wrote a formal and stiff congratulatory note and sent a money order for Nora. Sara, by contrast, wrote an effusive letter asking all the details about the baby and hoping that Nora's arrival had made her an aunt. She had, she said, secured permission from her father to spend the summer with us, but no longer, and would expect to arrive in early June. She would, she promised, be a big help in taking care of Nora while I worked, and also in the kitchen because, she boasted, she had become quite a cook in the years since I'd left Omaha.

"I don't want an outsider in the house," Em said flatly.

"She's not an outsider. She's family to me." I said it calmly, certain as always that in the long run I would get my way, because my way was right. That was an irritating habit of mine, I'm sure, that tendency to think I always knew the right way something should be done.

"You know what I mean!" he fumed, but I simply walked away. Sara had her train ticket, and though Em would be angry, I knew he would do nothing.

As it turned out, Em decided to turn on the charm for Sara. From the moment she stepped off the train, a dazzling beauty at twenty, Em was chivalry and courtesy come to life.

"So this is Sara! Mattie, you told me to expect a young girl. How could you have misled me so?"

Sara blushed and I laughed. "She was a young girl when I last saw her, Em. Welcome to the prairie, Sara. You do look lovely."

"Oh, Mattie, it's so good to see you!" Forgetting all her twenty-year-old poise, she threw her arms around me, and though I was generally not a very demonstrative person, I was delighted. "I've missed you something fierce," she whispered.

"I've missed you, too," I told her, and it was the truth. Of all the people who were dear to me—Em, Nora, Will Henry and Jim—Sara had a special place on the list. "We'll have a good long talk later," I told her, "but first come, let's get you to Benteen and have you meet Nora."

Nora was duly rescued from Sally Whittaker, in whose care I had left her while we made the trip to Fort Sidney to meet Sara's train. Sara had been awed and surprised by the prairie, gasping at how far she could see, wondering how people ever lived in its bare open spaces, and Em was avuncular—that was then and is now the only word I could think of for his attitude. He was the indulgent, slightly patronizing uncle-figure, and each time she said, "No, really?" he preened a little and said, with all the wisdom of a born frontiersman, "God's honest truth, Sara." I was amused to see Em so beguiled by this charming slip of a girl. Jealousy never occurred to me.

"Mattie, I wish you still lived in a soddie. I wanted to see one."

"Our soddie is still there, empty right now. But Em can drive you out one day to see it. Sometimes I miss that house, Sara." It was true. Our new house was fine and grand, much easier to keep clean and much more convenient, but the soddie had been the start of a new life for me, and it held special significance. I had privately vowed that it would remain standing forever, even if Em had to plow around it, but I wasn't so sure I could convince him to go along with my private vow.

"Sure thing, Sara. I'll take you out to the claim. But wait till you see the house in town I've built for Mattie. It's really something special."

"I'm sure it is, Em. Mattie described it to me, and I can hardly wait to see it and meet Nora." She looked admiringly at him, with those big blue eyes, and Em sat a little taller.

I blessed her for tact, because our house in Benteen was small potatoes compared to her home in Omaha, and Benteen would, I knew, be a revelation to her.

"There it is," Em said, pointing a finger in the distance. "The town of Benteen, Nebraska."

Sara squinched her eyes and shielded them with a hand in order to stare at the buildings that rose from the prairie. "Is that all of it? I mean, I thought it was larger."

"No, dear," I told her. "That's Benteen. Just a few families, a store and a schoolhouse and church. Actually, four new families have moved to town within the last year. We're almost a boomtown."

Sara looked puzzled, but Em picked up the thread of my talk. "Going to be a big place someday. I mean, look at this river location and all. Can't hardly beat it for perfect places on the prairie."

"I'm sure," Sara said weakly, and I wondered what she would write to her father about Benteen, or Em, or me for that matter. I looked at my hands, rough from riding the prairie, and knew that my face was equally rough. Dr. Dinsmore would no longer consider me the perfect hostess for his smart dinner parties. A flicker of sadness took me from the joy of that day, and for a brief moment I longed for the past, for Omaha and my beloved Dr. Dinsmore.

Nora seemed to take to Sara, smiling at her occasionally and being most cooperative when she tried to feed her a little gruel. Sara, for her part, adored Nora, sang to her, carried her everywhere, rocked her to sleep and seldom left her for a minute.

"Sara," I protested, "I'll have the most spoiled child in

all of western Nebraska."

"Oh, Mattie, love can't hurt babies. It must be good for them."

Neither Sara nor I had benefited from that uncompromising, undemanding love as infants, and I guessed she was right. We had both missed love, though Sara had a doting father. And me? I had found it where I could, and I had grave doubts now about the wisdom of my choice. It would be good for Nora to have all the love she could. I've changed a lot of my ideas on child-rearing over the years, due to experiences good and bad, but I have never changed that one. The little ones need lots of love, and the big ones do, too.

Em continued to prance and preen for Sara, and I thought it was so much better than having him angry that I was pleased and paid them no mind. Sara did take much of the responsibility of Nora off my shoulders, and I was busy with my practice. Besides, I never was one to look for problems that didn't come up and hit me square in the face. So I went blissfully and blindly on.

I had a steady stream of patients that summer—cholera and diphtheria only occasionally, minor aches and complaints all too often. Much as I could, I encouraged people to come to see me in town, but I still rode the prairie whenever I was needed. That was the summer of one of my most dramatic cases, one that I'm still proud of today.

I was in the kitchen, doing dishes while Em played with Nora, when a young man I'd never seen rode into the yard, his horse lathered from a long, hard ride. He was calling frantically as he reined to a stop.

"Doc! Doc! Hurry! Quick!"

I'd learned to react quickly to these rare but terrifying riders, their haste backed by emergency. Still drying my hands on the dish towel, I tried to calm him down. "Now, tell me exactly what's the matter."

"It's Weatherby; he done knocked a hole in his skull."

"A hole in his skull?" I repeated somewhat stupidly.

"Yes, ma'am. Bucket handle hit him in the head. He's alive, least was when I left there, and we need you bad."

Em had come out the door and sized up the situation right away. "I'll hitch the horses," he volunteered.

"No, I'll ride, Em. Get my small bag, please."

Within minutes, this strange young man and I were off across the prairie at a good clip, riding the horses hard as long as we dared, then slowing them briefly for a rest. During those rest periods, he told me what little of the story remained untold. A group of men had been digging a well, and Weatherby had been turning the windlass, hauling up yet another heavy load of dirt, when somehow—no one knew yet how it had happened—his hand slipped off the handle, and the windlass turned wildly and hit him in the head, sort of above and forward from his ear, according to my escort, who turned out to be named Scovill. He and Weatherby were neighbors of the man who owned the well.

We reached the soddie where Weatherby was in good time for a long prairie ride, and I rushed inside. By this time, Weatherby's young wife had been brought, and she stood silently weeping in one corner, while one or two women tried to comfort her. The men in the party stood around looking miserable, and one motioned toward the bed with his head.

Weatherby was young and big and strong, and if anybody ever had a chance for recovery, he did. His head had been loosely bandaged, to stop the bleeding, I supposed, and if you could overlook that rag, with its one bloody spot, you might have thought he was sleeping peacefully. Even his color, far as I could tell in that dark soddie, didn't look too bad, and his breathing seemed regular and fine.

I was very careful, believe me, when I peeled that rag bandage away, and I was glad all those folks in the room didn't know how hard my own heart was beating. The wound I saw amazed and scared me—that windlass handle had just knocked a piece of his skull clean out. With a damp rag, one of the clean ones I kept in my bag, I wiped away the clotted blood and could see pale gray brain tissue gently pulsing beneath the gaping hole. Well, it wasn't all that big, no bigger than a half-dollar, but it seemed quite a gaping hole at the time. I knew right away that the problem was to cover the hole and protect the brain from injury and infection. It was remarkable, I guess now, that the brain hadn't been injured in the original accident, but there was never any sign of swelling or anything. Just that hole in his head.

I talked gently with the people in the cabin, explaining that I thought he'd be fine if I could find something to cover the hole with. They suggested almost everything in the soddie, and I rejected each suggestion just as quickly. Leather and wood were too full of loose material and would cause infection. It had to be metal. No, bits from a bridle could never be smooth and thin enough. I don't call it luck or anything that made me remember I had a silver dollar in my purse. Em had given it to me some time ago, and I'd hung on to it, carrying it with me as a good-luck piece rather than salting it away in my private hoard as would have been my custom.

One of the men pounded that metal as flat and thin as possible, and we used an auger to pound holes in it. Then I had the ladies boil it hard to sterilize it; then, of course, I had to wait for it to cool. All of this seemed to take forever, and I could feel the people getting more and more tense, the young wife still weeping, the men muttering.

"If we don't do this, he doesn't have a chance. Oh, he might wake up, but infection would set in sooner than I don't know what. And I want you to realize it still may. I can't guarantee this at all. They don't attempt things like this except in the big medical centers back East, but I see no choice. We certainly can't transport him anywhere, let alone to a big medical center." I think I was pleading with them to have faith, to will him to recover, and they seemed to understand.

"We're with you, Doc. You do the very best you can."

And so, I cleaned out that wound and sewed a silver dollar over the hole in young Weatherby's head, my hand miraculously steady in spite of the raw state of my nerves. I tried to give the wife the piece of bone to keep, but she was squeamish and didn't want it.

It was touch and go for some time, and we worried a lot, but Weatherby recovered fully. Fact is, I heard tell not too many years ago that he had ridden in a rodeo parade at the age of seventy-five. Still had that piece of metal in his head.

I was exhausted when I got home, but I wanted to tell Em the story. I poured out all the details of what I considered a remarkable experience, and all he said was "Really? You should have seen Nora while you were gone. Sara and I took her for a ride today, and she loved it. Mattie, are you listening to me?"

My disappointment in him was strengthened by sheer anger, and for a moment I even wanted to lash out at Sara, but I said nothing. Next day, Sara hung on every detail of my story and kept exclaiming, "Papa will be so proud, Mattie! You must write him immediately."

I suggested she write the letter, but I was warmed by her reaction.

That was also the summer Mary Jane Canary entered my life again, though at first I didn't realize who she was. Late one night, three cowboys pounded on the door, demanding in loud voices that I come immediately. I threw on a robe and went to the door, Em's protests echoing in my ears.

"Doctor! We need a doctor, now!"

"Quiet!" I told them. "I'm the doctor, and all that yelling isn't doing one whit of good. It's only disturbing my family. Who's the patient?" From the doorway where I stood I got a strong whiff of stale whisky, and I suspected none of them were sober.

Even as I spoke, there was a loud screaming in a deep but definitely female voice from the wagon that had been hitched to our gate.

"Out there," motioned one of the cowboys. "Don't know what's wrong with her."

"Can you bring her in here?"

"If we have to, reckon we can," said another.

When they approached the woman, her screaming became more frantic, calling all the while for Bill. I showed them into the office, praying that Em wouldn't come charging in to demand what the hell the ruckus was all about. They had to hold the woman before I could even get near her, for every time they loosened their hold, she began to flail her arms wildly and once tried deliberately to kick me hard. Later, that kick would ring a familiar bell in my mind.

I surveyed the group for a minute and was truly appalled. Sure, we had cowboys come through Benteen now and again, even though the days of the cattle drives were over. And most cowboys did look pretty seedy, but these were the worst I'd seen in a long while. Their boots were scuffed beyond repair, their jeans worn and thin, their shirts crumpled enough to have been worn a month without changing.

But the woman they so stubbornly held on to was the worst of the bunch. Her hair hung in dingy brown strings around her face, probably uncombed for days. Her face itself was as dirty as her clothes, and her eyes were wild, as though she saw something horrifying directly in front of her. All she could see, far as I could figure, was me. I hadn't treated any cases of drunkenness—I guess you'd call it the delirium tremens these days—but I thought I recognized one.

The men who held her kept trying to calm her, saying, "Easy now, Calamity. It's okay. Bill's not here, can't come to you. Calamity, calm down."

One finally lost his patience and yelled, "For God's sake, Calamity, shut up!" But she just yelled the louder.

I deliberated a moment, then took charge of the situation with the only cure I knew, a purgative to try to empty some of the alcohol from her stomach, followed by quantities of strong black coffee and lots of walking up and down the road in front of the house, held always by at least one of the cowboys, who, for some strange reason, seemed devoted to her and determined to see her through this siege.

We kept that poor woman walking for hours, until the rest of us were exhausted, and Em had, predictably, come to demand to know what was going on.

"You woke both Nora and Sara," he accused, "and scared them half to death. I tried to comfort them." Then he looked at Calamity, in her filth and wildness, and muttered, "Damn drunken scum. Has no right to take up your time."

"Hush, Em," I whispered. "Don't cause more trouble." But I was too late. One of the cowboys, who to this day remain nameless to me, heard him.

"What'd you say, mister? You insult my friend?"

Em considered the situation for a moment, a haughty look on his face, and then, fortunately, seemed to decide that he didn't want to tangle with all three of them. "No offense," he muttered. "I'll just go calm the girls. Try to keep it down, please."

"You try to keep it down," the cowboy said menacingly, but I took his arm and led him back to his charge, who was, finally, beginning to show signs of calming down.

Eventually Calamity quieted enough that we could put her in the bed in my office, and I even could make some attempt at cleaning her up. The cowboys held her hand until, at last, she fell into a deep sleep.

"She'll feel awful when she wakes, and I think I should watch her for a while," I told them.

"Yes, ma'am. She's never been this bad before. You do whatever you think necessary." And he peeled a number of bills off a wad and handed them to me. I never thought to ask where such poor-looking cowboys got so much money, and to this day, I don't want to know.

My patient slept soundly for over twelve hours, and when she awoke, she was weak as a kitten but her eyes still flashed. I moved around her, trying not to disturb or upset her. All the time, though, I could feel those eyes on me.

Finally she spoke. "Who are you?"

"The doctor," I said calmly. "You were, well, pretty ill last night."

"Drunk, you mean!" she snorted.

"Have it your own way," I said, not willing to sympathize with anyone who would drink that much.

"What's your name?" She was staring at me intently again.

"Jones. Mattie Jones."

"You married?"

I almost told her smartly that it was none of her business. My business was to get her better and out of there, and she should be quiet and let me do my work. But I answered, "Yes."

"What was your name before you married?"

"Why?" That, I thought, was pushing the limits of courtesy and everything else.

"Think I know you."

I looked at her strangely but could think of no one who would have known me as Mattie Armstrong. Still, I told her my maiden name.

She grinned wickedly, nodding her head, and mumbled, "Canary. Mary Jane Canary."

I nearly dropped the washbasin I had just picked up. A stream of images went through my mind . . . Mary Jane taunting me as I ran errands, Mary Jane trying on clothes like a princess and trying to kick me, Mary Jane reducing Sara and me to tears. Frozen, I stared at her.

"That's right. You heard me," she said brusquely. "Mary Jane Canary from Princeton, Missouri. And you're Mattie Armstrong, daughter of the town you-know-what."

Even when she said that, the old anger didn't rise to the bait. I looked at Mary Jane Canary, saw what she had become and felt a pity I never would have believed possible. When I finally spoke, it was calmly.

"You're right, I'm Mattie Armstrong from Princeton, Missouri. But that was a long time ago. I've put Princeton behind me."

"Hah!" she snorted. "So have I, I guess. You hate me?"

I sank into the chair near her bed. "No," I said slowly. "Not anymore. I did, once."

"I know. Good thinking on your part. I was worth hating. Maybe still am." She turned away, as though hiding her thoughts.

There were a hundred questions I wanted to ask her, mostly having to do with how she had gotten from that big house with its newly painted picket fence into this condition on the prairie. But I never did ask her anything. And for the first time in a long while, my thoughts went back to Dr. Dinsmore. I wished he could know, could see my reaction and understand how I felt when I was finally confronted with the one person who symbolized all the unpleasantness of my childhood. I felt not anger but a big void, a blank nothing. I had really left Princeton behind, and it had taken a dirty, alcoholic woman to prove it to me.

Mary Jane Canary dried out, as they say, but she was weak, and I kept her in the infirmary two days. Her cowboys came to check on her periodically and let me know they'd take her whenever I said the word, but other than that they stayed away.

Em nearly ordered me to kick her out of the infirmary. "Okay; she's sober now. You've done your job. I don't want scum like her and her friends around Nora. Get rid of her."

I didn't explain to him why I had to keep Mary Jane and maybe bend over backward to take extra care of her. It wasn't as though I owed her, but it was gratitude. She didn't know it, but she had just done me a great service.

After that one time, Mary Jane Canary never again mentioned Princeton to me nor talked as though we knew each other. She was loud, demanding and difficult, and I was relieved when I finally told her friends they could take her out of the infirmary. I never heard from her again, though years later I heard the story about Calamity Jane claiming she was the wife of Wild Bill Hickok and how when she died they finally did bury her next to him. That, I thought, is a fitting end for Mary Jane Canary.

Summer seemed to end before we knew it. Em kept busy

on the claim, where our small herd of cattle was slowly increasing. I occasionally was given a calf or yearling in payment for medical services, and by then we had upward of twenty animals, including calves. Not much, but a start, Em used to tell me, and I thought about starting a cattle fund to increase the herd. But between the cattle and his crop of wheat, Em went to the claim every day and seemed busy. Lord knows, he came home sweaty and hot.

Most days, it was too hot for Sara to take Nora far, let alone out to the claim with Em, but she developed a true genius at keeping that child occupied and happy. Sara never seemed to tire of prancing and acting silly to delight Nora, and Nora would reward her outlandish behavior with chorts and snorts of happiness. Much as I loved Nora, it was the kind of play for which I had neither time nor patience.

My work kept me busy, and I was now trying to write a paper for publication about Jim Weatherby's injury, so I spent long hours in my office. But occasionally I broke free to join Sara and Nora in an early-morning stroll, when there was some cool breeze, and in the evenings all of us sometimes went to the baseball games. Will Henry still played on the Benteen team, and we all wanted to cheer for him. Once the Gelsons rode in and spent the night camped in our backyard. We all had a grand picnic, and I considered it one of the highlights of the summer.

But as summers do, this one ended too quickly, and it was time for Sara to return to Omaha.

"Can't you just write your father and tell him you've decided to stay?" Em was almost pleading with her.

"Em doesn't know Papa, does he, Mattie?" She laughed

as she looked at me, still unaware, I gathered, of the cause of my leaving Omaha and the nature of my final relationship with her father.

"No, he's never met him, Sara, but I've told him a great deal about your father." That was a slight lie, because though I had told Em about Dr. Dinsmore, I had never told the full truth.

"Papa would never understand. He'd be so angry he'd come out here himself to get me." Sara thought it a fine joke, because she never considered staying in Benteen. But Em was not able to see it as funny.

"Why do you have to go back?" he persisted.

"Em," I said, somewhat out of patience, "her father wants her to come back, and it would be purely selfish of us to keep her out here on the prairie when all the opportunities of a major city are open to her."

"Hogwash! I grew up in one of those so-called major cities, and you can give me the prairie any day. Now, we'll just find her some strapping young farmer who stands to be rich one day . . ."

Sara left in late August. I worried some about her taking that long train trip in the hottest time of the year. Railroad cars were like small infernos then, even when the windows were open, and cinders blew in at you and dirtied your clothes, your hair and your face. But Sara decided it was time for her to return, and there was no stopping her.

Nora seemed to know she was leaving, for she was fretful all the day before and clung to Sara, not allowing anyone else near her, much to the distress of Em.

The next day I stood at the front gate, holding a sobbing Nora and waving brightly while Em drove off to take Sara to the train. I felt a slight lump at seeing her go, but it was easy for me to accept that she could not stay, not for her sake nor ours.

Sara wrote immediately to assure us she had arrived safely, and she wrote periodically thereafter. Em and I settled down to raise our child, a family of three, Em with his claim and various other business enterprises that seemed to crop up, me with my growing and satisfactory practice, and Nora with all the business of learning and growing to do. I viewed it as a steady but wonderful period in our lives.

LIFE on the prairie could be harsh and it could be beautiful. Mostly from those days, I remember the beauty. I loved going on house calls alone, much to Em's distress, and would, if the day was pretty, simply set out on horseback across the waving sea of grass. Those were the days I abandoned my buggy and rode for the pure joy of being outside. They say pioneer women—and men, too, I suppose—developed an uncanny sense of direction, so that they could point themselves toward a destination and, without any cattle track or anything, cross the prairie without getting lost. I knew it wasn't an uncanny sense, because Jim Reeves had taught me much about direction and the prairie, but I did develop that feeling of being at home and secure out there in the midst of nowhere. And I loved it, loved the feeling of freedom and space and openness. It was as though the confines of Princeton were finally behind me once and for all.

But the prairie could be cruel, and I saw much of that,

too. I saw a man die of lockjaw because he'd rammed a rusty nail through his foot. I was called too late but we had no tetanus antitoxin then, and I could have done little except clean the wound with strong spirits and pray— sometimes it worked—but by the time I got there I could only comfort the family and try to ease his pain. Still, he died in terrible spasms and suffering, and I suddenly saw everyone around me threatened by every nail in every piece of wood.

And I saw young children die of diphtheria and cholera. Sometimes they would linger days, and sometimes I would think I was winning the battle, only to lose them with heartbreaking suddenness. Prairie children had a diminished chance for survival, and families knew that only too well. Still, I took each defeat personally. And each death made me fiercely protective of Nora.

"What do you mean she can't go outside barefoot? That's the silliest garbage I ever heard of. She's my daughter, and she'll go barefoot in the summer if I say so. What kid ever wore shoes all summer?" Em fairly screamed at me.

"My child," I answered as calmly as I could, "and you can't cross me on this. I won't take a chance that she'll step on a rusty nail, or even a wasp's nest. She wears shoes."

In the end, Nora went barefoot, holding her father's hand and grinning back at me like a victorious conqueror.

She grew more charming with each day added to her age. Dark, curly hair framed a pixielike face dominated by two huge brown eyes that could sparkle with mischief and turn equally expressive with self-pity when she was thwarted. Trouble was, Nora was seldom thwarted when Em was around, and mostly, my efforts at discipline were countermanded. She soon learned to run to Em any time I gave her an order or issued a warning.

"Mattie, you're so busy. You've got to slow down, take time with her, learn some patience. She's only a child."

It was the end of a long day, filled with this one's cough and that one's cold, none of it serious but all of it wearing, and I was out of patience.

"Em, have you ever tried to housebreak a puppy? You can't do it by letting the puppy have its way. You have to be firm. The same is true for Nora."

The look on his face was truly priceless. From understanding sympathy, which had been his opening attitude, he changed rapidly to indignation, his eyes growing wide and his mouth hanging open. When he finally spoke, it was through his nose in a tone calculated to impress.

"You cannot compare our child to a dog. She is a brilliant, unusual little girl."

"I agree, she's brilliant. But she's undisciplined, because you let her have her way over everything. I tell her no, and you say, 'Oh, it's all right, honey.' I tell her to go to bed, and you suggest she sit on your lap a little longer. Nora is learning to get her way by hook or crook, and it's not a good lesson for her."

"Why not?"

Sometimes Em's deliberate disregard of accepted truths had me nearly ready to scream in exasperation. Everyone knew that undisciplined children grew up into undisciplined adults and that while you might spare the actual rod, you couldn't back down and give up. Still, Em acted as though discipline were something that had never existed in the world until I told Nora she had to clear the dinner dishes or clean her room. It was one of those endless, circular arguments which I never won because he threw logic out the window. I gave up, one more time, and felt the anger rising in me.

That anger rose in me a lot in those days. It welled up when Em yelled, "Leave me alone! She's my daughter, and I'll raise her the way I want!" and it simmered when he said, "I think Nora is too smart for the local school. We'll have to send her to boarding school."

But Em gave that child something I never could, a sense of herself as a complete individual. While I was still caught seeing her as an extension of myself, something to be loved, cuddled, disciplined and put to bed, he was sometimes, though not always, able to regard her as a separate individual with wishes, angers and needs. It came out in little ways.

"What did you do today, Nora? I'd like to hear about it."

"Would you? Oh, I . . . well, this morning I worked at my books, and Mama helped me, and we learned to spell letters beginning with *P.* Do you know how many words begin with *P?*"

"No," he said solemnly, "how many?"

"I don't know," she laughed. "Mama said lots and lots, but I have learned some. There's potato and preacher and poor and purple and . . . let me see . . . oh, piano."

"That's right, love," he crowed. "Those are good words. And you know what? We're going to have to get you a piano. Soon, so you can learn to play beautiful music and soothe your father when he's tired and cross."

"Oh, you're never cross. Only Mama is."

I was in the kitchen fixing supper, but I heard those words, and they went through me like a knife.

Late that night, I talked to Em about it, when we lay close together in bed and Nora slept soundly in the next room.

"Em, does she really think I'm the only one in the world who ever gets cross?"

"Shhh. Of course she doesn't." His hands reached up under my nightgown and began exploring the sensitive area inside my thighs. I quivered with delight, but my mind wasn't ready to give up the discussion.

Pushing him away, I said, "But, Em, it's not fair. I'm with her all day and trying to see my patients at the same time. And you come home at night, having been free and outdoors all day, and you're not out of patience. She sees you as wonderful."

"Hush," he said, "she'll realize when she's older. It'll be all right." And his magic hands did their work, and I melted, my complaints lost in the passion that Em had taught me.

Em and I had a wonderful private life, as it's euphemistically called. He was a skilled lover, and I accepted without question that there had been many other women in his life—and his bed—before me. The double standard was stronger than ever in those days, and while I would have been horrified myself not to go to my bridal bed a virgin, I would have been equally terrified if I'd thought Em was virginal. But far from it.

He taught me the joys of passion with patience and

understanding, and after one or two awkward encounters, I responded fully every time we made love. They talk about sex problems a lot today, people who must work at odds instead of with each other, and I don't know what all kinds of things. But for Em and me, sexual passion was the great joining together that you read about in books. Even after all the other aspects of our marriage had begun to tarnish, we were still one in bed. Some days at the most awkward moments, my thoughts would fly back to the night before, and I'd catch myself smiling, wondering what this patient or that would think if they knew what was on my mind and what I'd done the night before. Not that making love isn't something most people do, but Em made it so special that I was always sure that it was better for us than any of the rest of the world.

But you can't spend your lives in bed, and we had a real world to face each day.

My real world began early, even if I'd had no calls during the night. Actually, I didn't get called out that much at night. It's just that each instance made such an impression that it seemed more frequent. Once Nora came along, there was no question of Em going with me if I had to go out at night, because he had to stay home with her. I let it be known far and wide that in all except the most dire emergencies, patients were to be brought to me at night, and so it was only a far, poorly timed newborn infant who called me out. Still, I dreaded those long drives at night as much as I enjoyed them on a warm spring or fall day.

But with a full night's sleep behind me, morning was my time. I'd organize my thoughts for the day, make the breakfast in peace and quiet, and only waken Nora and Em when I had to. Once they were up, the days often seemed to go downhill.

It was no time at all until Nora was off to the schoolhouse every morning, carrying her little sack lunch and waving brightly to us. Those first few mornings, my heart was in my mouth as I watched her trudge down the road. You'd have thought I was sending her five miles through the snow when in truth I could watch her all the way to the schoolhouse.

With Nora at school, I turned my attention to my practice, and if Em went on to the claim as usual, my days were busy but satisfying. I kept office hours in the morning, and generally tried to spend the afternoon reading or working on my books until Nora came home. Then I was free to review her lessons with her and start the dinner. I saw that afternoon period as my attempt to assuage Em's disapproval of my profession, to be the devoted mother that he was convinced Nora needed. In truth, Nora always seemed a little bored going over her lessons with me.

If Em stayed around the house, as he sometimes chose to do, my days went less smoothly. He would pop into my office a dozen times, no matter who was there, with tiny questions, bits of advice or inane comments, none of which I wanted to hear. It was as though Em couldn't stand not to be a part of everything that was going on, even my practice. And if I suggested he was bothering me, he either pouted or became angry.

"No time for your husband, huh? Guess I'm just in the way here."

"Em, you know that's not true. But really, you can't come barging in when I'm talking to a patient."

"Someday you'll have gone too far in putting your patients before me," he threatened, but I didn't even take him seriously.

Outwardly, we were still accepted as the ideal couple, one of the most stable and happy in Benteen and the surrounding area, a fixture at every church social, school supper and meeting of the literary society.

"Do we have to go to the literary guild tonight?" Em would ask plaintively.

"Em, you know they need our support. They count on us."

"Can't they, just once, count on someone else? Just think, Mattie, we could go to bed early and—"

"I know exactly what you have in mind, Em . . . and it sounds wonderful, but it'll just have to wait until later. Think how important it is to Benteen to have community activities that will attract more people."

"But think how important some time together is to us . . ."

"Em, we need to support the town so it will grow."

"All right, all right, but you haven't got an ounce of romance in that straight iron soul of yours, Mattie Jones."

"Ask me later," I said lightly, and turned to get Nora ready for the evening.

Benteen was growing. By the time we had lived in town several years, the population had grown nearly to a thousand, and I was getting more and more patients from in town, with less need to ride the prairie. I liked that part, but I wasn't sure I liked the growth, much as I knew we needed it. With two hundred people in town, we'd known them all, and I'd felt like part of a safe, secure world. With a thousand, I couldn't keep track of them, and I felt like I was losing control of my world.

The town boasted several businesses, a bank, saloons, a newspaper and all the trappings of a growing town rather than just a cluster of houses that happened to be built together. Much of the building was done in anticipation of an extension of the railroad from Fort Sidney, but that never happened. Many prairie towns dried up and blew away when the railhead passed them by, but Benteen for some reason seemed to survive and even grow. In later years, it became a retirement community for farmers, but that's getting ahead of my story.

Meantime, a city council of sorts was formed, and Em was asked to sit on it.

"You know, I could try politics someday." He said it seriously, sitting in my office one night while I worked on my account books. The books were the bane of Em's existence, for my bookkeeping system was as erratic as my schedule of charges. I generally accepted what the family could pay me for whatever services I rendered, and I still often got two chickens for delivering a baby or a basket of fresh-picked grapes in the spring for treating a sick child. Of course, enough families paid in cash to give us an income, but I still hoped Em would settle down to something that would bring in more money. But no, he was always chasing the grand scheme, like his idea about politics.

"Politics? Em, really, what do you know about it?"

"That's the beauty of it, Mattie. Nobody else knows any more than I do. And I'd be in at the start, just like I am in this city council here in Benteen. Who knows, maybe I should start by offering myself as mayor here."

"Ralph Whittaker is already the mayor, Em."

"I know, I know. But maybe he won't want that responsibility for long. It would be good training for me." His face darkened. "What's the matter, Mattie? Don't you think I'd be a good politician?"

I took a deep breath. "Yes, Em, I do think you have the makings of a politician. But I don't think you should do it." How to tell him some sense back in my mind knew that he had the makings just because he could charm anybody out of anything, but he didn't have the perseverance that a career in politics would take? Instead, I said, "There's not much money in that, you know. Maybe you should stick to enlarging the farm and cattle herd."

"Money! That's all you ever think about. If you'd do a better job with those books of yours, and make people pay you, you wouldn't always be worried about pennies."

He left the room abruptly, but I wouldn't have answered anyway. It was an old and futile argument, and we had been through it too many times.

Probably our proudest and happiest moment as a family together was the year Nora had the part of Mary in the annual Christmas pageant. I say annual because it was then in its second year, I believe, and Nora was eight or nine.

We worried about that pageant for weeks, it seemed,

sewing a costume, discussing it with Nora, assuring her she would be fine on center stage, especially since she had no lines to speak.

"But what if I get scared?"

"Look out in the audience. Your father and I will be right in front. Besides, Nora, you won't get scared. You've got too much self-confidence for that."

"You don't understand!" she shot back. "Just because you never get scared of anything doesn't mean I don't. Daddy will know what I mean."

It was a measure of how little my own child understood me that she thought I was never scared. Maybe I wasn't afraid to ride out on the prairie alone or undertake a delicate medical procedure, but I was full of unspoken fears she knew nothing about. Mostly those fears had to do with Em and our future, and I pushed them to the back of my mind, where they remained to gnaw lightly but persistently at my consciousness.

Em acted as though Nora's part in the pageant was but the first step to a major acting career, and Nora relished his attention.

"Always knew she had a lot of talent, didn't you, Mattie? You can just tell by the way she carries herself. It would have been a serious mistake to cast any other child in that part."

"Em, for heaven's sake, it's only a Christmas pageant at the school."

"Well, she has to start somewhere. I'm proud of her, even if you aren't."

"Of course I'm proud of her, Em. She's a beautiful and intelligent child. I just want to keep things in proportion for her sake."

"And I want to be sure she realizes how very special she is," he retorted. "She's not like other children, and she never will be."

Later, I knew that it was Nora's bad luck not to be like other children.

Differences between Em and me were forgotten the night of the pageant, and we sat together, holding hands, in the front row of the small cluster of chairs put up in the church meeting room. The school had arranged to have the pageant in the church rather than asking parents to force their grown-up bodies into those small student desks.

Nora was all the things that Mary should be. She looked humble, virginal, awestruck, totally devoted and absolutely beautiful.

"Isn't she something?" Em whispered, loudly enough for everyone in the room to hear.

"Yes, she is, Em, she really is."

"It's all because you take such good care of her. It's really all because of you." He leaned over and kissed my ear right there in public, and I laughed gently and pushed him away.

"Em, behave," I whispered.

Nora's part required nothing of her except a prolonged period of stillness and silence on the stage. She managed it with grace, never once fidgeting or, as one of the watching angels did, scratching rather obviously. She was a lady through and through.

Afterward, she was filled with a need to be praised. "Was I all right? Did I look like Mary? You couldn't see my missing tooth, could you?"

I tucked her in that night and kissed her, saying, "You were the very best thing about the pageant."

"Do you really think so?"

"Yes, dear, I do. Now, hush, I have work to do. You go to sleep."

I went off to my desk but Em stayed with her, talking and praising until she was fast asleep.

As I write, I realize that even that period I viewed as happy was filled with discord. Em and I were, in truth, rarely pleased with each other and much more likely to bicker, differ, quarrel and resent. When we should have been like a team of horses, pulling together in one direction, we were more often at odds, more like a pair of wild stallions fighting over territory. In retrospect, many memories aren't as happy as they seem.

In 1908, when Nora was eleven, we made a trip to Omaha. I had been in Benteen for nearly eighteen years then and had seen civilization come in a big way. Benteen, as I have said, was a growing town, and the prairie itself was more populated. My patients no longer lived so far apart nor expected me to come to them. Other doctors had moved into the general region, so someone who lived, say, thirty miles from Benteen, might find a closer doctor in another direction. The radius of my practice was then twenty miles at the most, far enough for those times when I did have to go. Em said someday I'd have to have one of the new horseless carriages, but I, who'd never seen one, scoffed at him and told him I'd much prefer to stick with old Betsy and my rather fancy enclosed carriage, built for me years ago by Ed Landman.

But back to our trip to Omaha. Em announced that he had to go on business, and nothing would do but that Nora and I go with him. I had mixed emotions about the whole thing, wanting to see the city again, longing for a visit with Sara, and even feeling that now, so many years later, I wouldn't mind facing Dr. Dinsmore. Once I'd gotten over that early anger and dismay at his advances—and it had taken several years for that feeling to subside—I began to put things in perspective and to remember how much he had meant to me for so many years. We had in recent years corresponded some, mostly impersonal letters dwelling on our medical practices, but I knew that he had never married and that he was still lonely, in spite of an active professional and social life.

In truth, what made me uneasy about a trip to Omaha was Em. I didn't know what kind of "business" he had there, and he was most secretive about it, grinning slyly and saying, "Just wait, Mattie, just wait. This is a big deal, really big." And my uncertainty was complicated by an absolute inability to imagine Em and Dr. Dinsmore meeting.

Nora, however, was so excited about the trip, she made up for my rather lukewarm enthusiasm.

"Mama, what's Omaha like? Tell me everything about it!"

"Lord, Nora, it's been too many years since I was there. I probably won't recognize the place, but it was a wonderful city, with fine big houses and lots of electric lights and a huge stockyards."

"The fine houses sound wonderful, but we have electric

lights now in Benteen, and stockyards don't sound interesting at all. Are there lots of stores?"

"Oh, I'm sure there are. We'll buy you some fancy new clothes while we're there. And we'll stay in a hotel, probably a big one."

She beamed in contented anticipation, and I went on to describe hotel dining rooms, at least the best I could from my meager and faraway experience.

"People will really come bring me my food to the table?"

"Just like I do here," I laughed.

"No, Mama, you know what I mean."

"Yes, I do. And yes, gentlemen in uniforms will bring you whatever you order. You tell them what you want and sit there and wait for them to have it cooked and bring it to the table."

Packing was a major chore, even though we would be gone only a week. Nora wanted to take enough clothes for a year, and I realized I had very few suitable dresses for the city. My life seemed spent in shirtwaists and practical cotton or wool skirts. My one good broadcloth was beginning to look a little shabby.

"You need something with lace," Em said, "something soft and feminine."

"Pooh. I'm not the soft and feminine type."

"You could be, you know. Why don't you have Sally Whittaker make you up a good dress for the trip?"

"There's not time for that."

"Well then, we'll just buy you some clothes in Omaha."

"Em, there's not money for that!"

He looked grim and said nothing. It was that old topic

of money that always came between us.

Dr. Dinsmore and Sara met us at the train, both changed in the years since I'd seen them. Sara, now over thirty, had never married, still lived with her father and filled her days giving music lessons to small children and doing volunteer work at the college's free clinic. I, who had so much to fill my life, felt hers was rather empty, and I pitied her. The bright, happy child I had raised and loved had turned into a fairly mild, colorless woman, and I ached for her lost chances for happiness. I wondered if the weak strain inherited from her mother was showing itself.

Dr. Dinsmore was as commanding as ever, silver-haired now that he was in his late fifties but still a handsome man. My heart did a little flip when I first saw him, and a great tangle of emotions welled up. He was courteous and polite as always, giving me a fatherly hug and shaking hands with Em.

Em, for the moment taken aback by Dr. Dinsmore's dignity, was silent. Then he began talking, too much, in that stilted tone which always signaled me that he was nervous and uncertain.

"Certainly good of you to meet us. Been years since either one of us has been to Omaha, and I'm sure we'd be lost. Course, I'll find my way around pretty quick. Got to take care of some business."

"Of course," Dr. Dinsmore said, and I blessed him for not asking what business.

Nora was staring sideways at Sara, uncertain what to make of her and rather obviously disappointed. We had described a laughing, bright girl, and here was a somber lady who barely smiled.

"Are you sure you stayed with me when I was a baby?" Her voice was skeptical.

"Yes, Nora, I'm sure. You were very tiny, but you were determined."

"And still is," Em laughed. "We certainly have missed you, Sara. Any time you want to come back to Benteen, we'll turn out a royal welcome. Might be we could find you some strapping farmer to marry out there."

Sara and Dr. Dinsmore exchanged the briefest of looks, and I had the strangest sensation of untold stories of sadness and even grief. Dimly, I remember that Sara had almost married right after she was with us in Benteen, but I never heard what had happened to cancel the wedding.

Nothing would do but that we would stay at the Dinsmores' instead of the hotel. Their offers of hospitality were gracious and sincere, and Em leapt at them.

"Certainly nice of you. I'm sure Mattie and Nora will be much happier with you while I'm off on business than they would be in a hotel."

I hesitated. "Are you sure . . . Isn't it too much trouble?"

And Nora was downright rude. "You promised me a hotel, Mama, with men to bring me my meals."

Sara smiled in her shy way again, but Dr. Dinsmore laughed openly. "And a hotel meal you shall have, my princess. I'll see to it. But please stay with us. It will make us feel bad if you don't."

Nora shot him a look that said she didn't care how he felt, but his authority still had sway over me, all these years later, and I quickly answered.

"Of course we'll stay."

"Good. Sara will be delighted to have your company

again, Mattie."

"Yes," she echoed, "I will."

For the most part, the visit went well. Em disappeared each day right after breakfast, two times not returning until nearly midnight but always full of stories about the contacts he'd made, how well his work was going and so on.

"What is your business?" Dr. Dinsmore finally asked politely.

"Well, you know, I raise some cattle on Mattie's old claim and some other land we have, but I'm really interested in politics these days. That's what brings me to Omaha."

"Politics, eh? Unfortunately, I know nothing about it beyond worrying about state funding for our school."

The two had little to talk about, and I was just as glad Em was away so much. Dr. Dinsmore and I had long professional talks twice in the evenings, but no mention was made of the unhappy terms on which we had parted.

The closest he came to bringing the subject up was one evening when he stared long at me and then said slowly, "You're not happy, Mattie."

Pride bristled within me, and I tried to laugh his comment away, my laugh too short and harsh to be convincing. "Of course I am. What more could I want? A flourishing practice, a good husband, and an adorable child. No, I'm very happy. Just tired sometimes."

"I see." And he said no more.

Sara and I spent two whole days shopping, and I did buy myself some dresses that Em would think were feminine.

One was a taffeta in soft gray-green, with a lace collar and cuffs, and the other was a challis print, very straight and plain but somehow classic and elegant because of its simplicity. I wore it to dinner that night, when Dr. Dinsmore took us to the hotel for the promised meal that Nora so looked forward to.

"I told Mattie she needed some more feminine clothes." Em seemed to me to be talking too loudly. "Doesn't she look nice tonight?"

"She certainly does," Dr. Dinsmore agreed. "But I have always thought Mattie dressed attractively."

"Sometimes she ought to loosen up and spend a little money on herself," Em persisted. "Fancy up a bit, like this tonight."

I blushed and wished they would change the subject, feeling rather like they were talking about me as if I weren't there. But Em went right on.

"Sara, I think I have you to thank for a good influence on today's shopping trip. You always look so feminine, like you've really taken care to choose your clothes attractively."

Sara said a soft "Thank you, Em," and I burned inwardly at the comparison, though I guess I had it coming. Sara did look lovely, as always, but I wished for that spark of life that I had once seen in her.

We had one long, private talk, when Em had taken Nora on a tour of the city, hoping to run across a horseless carriage to show her.

"Father doesn't think you're happy, Mattie."

"I know, Sara, but I am. At least as happy as I expect to be. I think true happiness is something you have only moments of, like genuine sadness, and most of life is lived somewhere in the middle. So yes, Sara, I'm happy. And you?"

"I guess according to your definition, I'm happy, too, but I still want to live my life at the peak levels of happiness. Sometimes I think if only . . ."

Her voice trailed away, and, uncharacteristically, I prodded. "If only what, dear?"

Tears rolled down her face as she spoke. "There was a man I . . . I loved very much and wanted to marry. Father, well, he didn't think the man was good enough for me, and he forbad the marriage. And now, why, I think I'll just live here forever with Father." She was sobbing openly when she finished, and I reached to take her in my arms. There was nothing I could say, and I knew that I was seeing the other side of that self-confidence and authority. Even if Em was flawed, and I knew then for certain that his flaws were major, I had done the right thing to flee Dr. Dinsmore. I wished I could also loosen Sara's bonds, but that seemed impossible.

The visit ended badly. At the time, I didn't know why. One morning Em announced suddenly that we were to leave that day, two days earlier than we had planned.

"Why, Em?" I protested sleepily, for it was early morning, and he had woken me with his announcement.

"I just have to get back to Benteen. Don't ask questions. I'll wake Nora while you get our things together. The train's at eleven, you know."

"Yes, I know, and two days from now I'll be ready and on it, but not today."

"Mattie, we are going today." He said it with more iron and steel in his voice than I had ever heard from Em in all our years together, and I decided to argue no more. We would go.

We were packed and ready with a cab waiting in a remarkably short time.

"Em, I have to say goodbye to Dr. Dinsmore and Sara. I can't just leave. Where are they?"

"He's gone to the college, and she's in her room with a sick headache."

"Well, I won't just leave," I said determinedly, and headed for Sara's room.

"Mattie, ah, don't disturb her. Dr. Dinsmore said she's really feeling badly this morning."

"Well, sickness is something I know about. Don't worry, I won't disturb her."

I knocked softly but entered without waiting for an answer. Sara was buried in her bed, but she turned toward me and I knew instantly that her sick headache had come from long and hard crying.

"Sara, Sara, what's the matter?"

"Nothing, Mattie, nothing. I'm . . . I'm sorry you have to leave early. I . . . I'll miss you all over again." And she collapsed in tears, burying her face in the bright quilt that contrasted so sharply with her own paleness.

I tried to comfort her and stroke her hair as best as I could, but I didn't want to force her to talk about whatever had made her so unhappy. Still, as I left the room, my head was spinning with questions.

I got them answered on the train, and even I was indignant. Nora had been seated by a window some little distance from us, which gave Em and me a chance to talk.

"Your Dr. Dinsmore is some fellow," Em said bitterly.

"Em, tell the truth about what happened, why we're leaving early. What does it have to do with Sara?"

He stared at the passing landscape and never looked at me as he spoke. "He accused me of making improper advances to her and ordered me out of the house. Said you and Nora could stay as long as you wanted, but I was to be gone before noon."

The words filtered into my consciousness slowly, but when they did, I was filled with naive disbelief. "Improper advances! Em, that's ridiculous! You loved Sara like you do Nora. How could he ever get that idea?"

Wearily, Em recited the story. He'd been unable to sleep and had gotten up to prowl about the house. As he stumbled through the dark, he heard crying from Sara's room and had gone in to comfort her. Dr. Dinsmore found him sitting on the edge of Sara's bed, his arms around her.

"Didn't Sara try to tell him it was innocent?"

"Of course she did, Mattie, but the man's obsessed with his daughter. He wouldn't listen to either of us. Jumped to his own conclusions and stayed with them. It was an ugly scene, I tell you, truly ugly. And that's where Sara's sick headache comes from. He reduced her to tears and me to frustrated rage."

I was silent, trying to piece it all together. I knew Em had a lot of faults, but lust, I was convinced, was not one of them, especially not for a girl he had regarded as a daughter. And Dr. Dinsmore. Was he accusing because he had been guilty of the same sin? I had never dared tell Em the real reason I left Omaha, and now, certainly, it would remain forever my secret. Yet it was a secret I bore as a gigantic burden, because I wasn't sure what it meant for me, for Em and even for poor Sara.

The trip home was not pleasant. Em and I were silent, thinking, and Nora was angry. "I wasn't ready to leave," she informed us loftily. "You promised we wouldn't leave for two more days."

Poor Nora. There was never any room in her life for compromise or understanding the problems of others. Telling her we were sorry but that an emergency dictated we return meant nothing to her. Her wishes had been thwarted, and Nora stood frustration even less well than her father.

Over the years, Em had become increasingly angry and jealous, not of me but of men who had achieved the success that eluded him. We saw little of the Gelsons, in spite of my close friendship with Lucy, because Em resented Jed and the success he'd made of their ranching operation. Their cattle had increased, their crops prospered, their boys, grown strong and tall, helped on the farm, and their whole operation made Em's look like small potatoes. Jed was active in the newly formed farmers' group and was one of the most respected men in our region. Em hated him, though he professed to value the long-standing relationship. I suspect Lucy never liked Em, and so the separation was all right from both sides, except for me. I was caught in the middle.

I never knew when Em's anger would erupt, or over what. He would come home, happy and charming, and we'd have a wonderful evening of companionship, often followed by passionate love. But other evenings he'd come home angry.

"What's in this soup? Last week's garbage?"

Nora would giggle appreciatively and echo, "I don't like it either, Daddy."

I would say mildly, "Em, please, in front of Nora . . ."

"She's my daughter, and I can say whatever I want in front of her. She wouldn't want me to lie to her, would you, baby?"

And Nora would preen and assure him he was right. His anger, so frequently turned at me, never was directed at Nora, and she lived in a state of false security.

I found out about the other woman by accident, or almost. Em had sold some cattle to a widow named Fisher, Lucinda Fisher, who lived about thirty-five miles from Benteen. He showed me the sales slip for three heifers. I was a little curious why a new widow, living alone, would want to increase her herd rather than sell it off and return to town or home, wherever that may be. But Em convinced me that this was a spunky lady who was determined to carry on with her husband's dreams for their land. He felt sorry for her and wanted to help. I thought he was magnanimous, and as long as he was generous with his help but not our money, nothing troubled me. I even asked if he didn't want to bring Lucinda to town to visit, but he said she really worked so hard she wouldn't leave her claim, even briefly. So I sent an occasional gift, like a piece of the cheese given by a patient or oranges when in season and even a shiny new kitchen pot that caught my eye in Whittaker's store. We were long distances apart, but I felt we shared, and I wanted to be Mrs. Fisher's friend.

Lucinda Fisher was far from central in my thoughts. I had other things on my mind, like the deteriorating relationship between Em and me.

"People coming in all hours of the day and night. Man can't have any privacy in his home." He slammed a chest drawer so hard that a bottle of perfume on top fell to the floor.

I picked it up, stood holding it and stared at Em, all kinds of retorts going through my mind.

"Well, what are you staring at me for?"

"Trying to understand your anger. What have I done to you?"

It was his turn to be thoughtful and quiet for a moment, and when he answered, he surprised me. "Probably nothing I haven't allowed you to do, maybe even forced you into."

His anger rarely was that rational, though, and other times he would yell, "If you'd give up that damn practice of yours, we could live like decent human beings, the way other families do."

"If I give up that practice, we could starve, Em Jones. Can't you see the truth when it's in front of you? My practice allows you to run all over the state doing heaven-knows-what and to keep that so-called farm going even though it never produces a penny of income for us."

"Running all over the state? Is that what you think of my career? You know darn well what I'm doing, and someday when I'm elected to high office in this state, you'll have to eat those words."

Em's theory was that he was testing the waters of his political career. When he would be ready to dive in never really came into the conversation.

Once or twice, Em was physically abusive. The first time was one of those small incidents that can escalate before you know it. I had learned the hard way not to argue with him when he was mad, for it never got me any-place. So usually I just bottled my feelings up inside. One evening at the dinner table, my feelings got the better of me.

"I'm tired," I commented to no one in particular.

"I can tell. Dinner tastes like last year's leftovers."

Nora giggled a little and played with the food on her plate.

"Em, I'm sorry if you don't like the dinner, but I'd appreciate it if you'd set a better example of manners for Nora."

"Example, huh? If we're going to talk about examples, why don't you set her a better example of woman's work?"

"Em, please . . ." My tone was pleading. I didn't want to get into that kind of a scene. In truth, I was tired, exhausted, from a steady stream of patients and a restless night of my own the night before.

"Don't 'Em, please' me. I'll speak when I want to. If you'd pay half the attention to cooking and cleaning and raising Nora that you do to other people's problems, we'd all be a lot better off."

It was too much for me, and I wanted to be away from them before the tears came. I jumped from the table, ran into the bedroom, closing and locking the door behind me. Em was at the door in a minute, demanding that I open it. Sobbing on the bed, I ignored him.

When he was silent, I assumed he had left. But I underestimated Em. A foot came crashing through the door, splintering wood all over the floor. A second crash and the door came off the hinges. Em strode into the room to stand over me and yell, "Nobody ever locks me out of my own bedroom." Before I could duck or protect myself, he raised one hand and slapped me hard across the face. Then he left.

Em was gone four days that time. For two days, I had a red mark on my cheek and had to lie to my patients about having fallen in the night and struck my face against the door frame.

When Em came back, neither of us mentioned the incident. But neither did we make up with passionate love as we had earlier in our marriage. Those days, too, were long gone, and there was almost no physical contact between us. I tried occasionally to talk to Em about that, but he dismissed it as my imagination, though he once hinted I should make myself more alluring.

The second time Em ever hurt me, he had been drinking heavily, and for some reason, he took it into his head to harangue me about Jed Gelson.

"Son of a bitch never liked me, never gave me a chance."

I wandered innocently into trouble. "A chance at what?"

"Developing that farm. He's got all the luck, and our claim never gets anywhere."

"Em, it has nothing to do with luck. Jed is a hardworking man."

"Got three sons to help him. And a wife who works. What have I got? A daughter, wild as a March hare because her mother is too busy taking care of other people. No, Gelson could have helped me." He took a large drink from the glass in his hand, and I turned away in disgust.

"Don't turn your back on me. You're just as bad as Gelson. Turned me down when I asked him a favor."

"You asked him a favor?" I whirled to face him.

"Needed help," Em muttered.

"What kind of help, Em?"

"What kind of help, Em?" he mimicked me. "What the hell kind of help do you think I needed? I needed some money, and I was damned if I was going to come to you again."

Em had gone to the Gelsons for money! "Em, you disgust me sometimes." I turned to walk away.

Drunk as he was, Em was fast. He grabbed me, both hands around my throat, and began shaking me so hard that for a moment, I was truly afraid for my life. Yelling, "Nobody looks down on me, nobody!" he held on to me for a moment, then seemed to come to his senses. Slowly he released his hold and stared at me.

It was the next day before he apologized. I was wearing a shirt buttoned high at the neck, and my voice was hoarse.

Such violence stands out in my mind, but it was rare. There were, however, lots of loud arguments and lots of long, stony silences. I never could predict Em's reaction, whether it would be wild anger or childish pouting or, once in a while, rational discussion about what was happening to us, as though it were a phenomenon neither of us understood. I worried, of course, about the effect of all this on Nora, but she seemed unscathed. Surely she was aware, for I would see her creep into her room if we argued or become truly absorbed in a book to avoid our voices. But if Em went into a pout, Nora always went to his side and sat silently. When Em slapped me, she never came near me. I felt as though I was losing both a husband and a child.

I needed an infirmary. Too often patients required more extended care, and my one room with its extra bed wasn't enough. There was young Belinda Atkins, desperately ill with cholera. I recommended to the mother wrapping the girl in wet sheets to control the fever, and she took her home and, best as I know, followed the directions. But it was nip and tuck for several days, and there was more than once that I thought we'd lost that fifteen-year-old girl when we shouldn't have. I'd run out to their house, about four miles out of town, two times a day, and it cut into my day. Wore me out, too. If I'd just been able to have the girl right under my eyes, it would have been better for her and easier on me. There were others, too, new mothers who couldn't care for their infants at first, old people too weak to follow my directions, once in a while a widower who would have been all right if he'd had someone at home to look after him.

I really thought the infirmary was what was wrong between Em and me, that and the whole idea of my practicing medicine. But none of that made sense to me, for Em knew I was a doctor when he started courting me, and he of all people should have known the importance of constant care of the sick. After all, as I'd thought a thousand times, if I hadn't nursed him in my soddie, we probably never would have gotten acquainted. But he was outraged at the mention of an infirmary.

"It's bad enough you run all over, have all kinds of people bringing sickness into this house. I'm not going to spend a penny to build a pesthouse!"

"Em, be reasonable. We'll spend what I have earned."

"You haven't earned that much!"

"No," I admitted, "I'll have to borrow from the bank, but I truly think an infirmary would eventually pay for itself."

"With you taking chickens for pay instead of money?"

"I won't do that. The infirmary will be on a paying basis."

"If you do this, Mattie, I'll walk out of this house forever."

I believed him and dropped the subject for the time being, but in my mind I began to build an infirmary. Not a hospital, nothing so grand, but a place where the sick could be cared for when need be. I could hire someone to help me, to tend to people during the day when I was busy and, of course, to do the cooking. Lord knows I didn't want to have to cook and clean up for a bunch of sick people. I just wanted to make them healthy again.

Life seemed to go on. Nora was twelve, in the fifth form at the little Benteen school and doing well. Already Em was talking about sending her east to school, and I was silently indignant. Omaha had been good enough for me, and it would be good enough for my daughter.

She had grown into a lovely weed of a girl by then, tall for her age and slim but not skinny. Not for her those knobby knees and elbows most kids get at that age. She was graceful and proportioned, as though the Lord knew exactly what he was doing when he put her together. Em had taught her to ride, and she was as at home on the prairie as I was by then. Some days she'd just disappear for hours, and I rarely worried about her. She had that same unerring sense of direction and self-protection that came from living close to the land. But Nora could also sew a fine seam, more like Mama than me, and she was beginning to show an interest in the kitchen.

We had a live-in housekeeper by then, for my practice kept me far too busy to take care of the house and meals. Em had reluctantly built a lean-to onto the house to provide a room for Margaret, a hearty Irish girl who had come off a farm some twenty miles away, where she'd been the oldest of eight children. When it became apparent that Margaret was grown and no husband was in sight for her, her family determined she needed to find work. Keeping house was all she knew, and they approached me. To me, the idea was a godsend, and Margaret was installed in our family as soon as I could arrange it.

Margaret had red hair and the proverbial map of Ireland on her round cheerful face. Her conversation generally kept pace with her disposition, and she was prone to talk constantly. If no one was handy, she talked to herself or, sometimes, burst into song. It drove Em wild, but in another of those combinations that defied explanation, Nora took to Margaret as she did to few people.

Under Margaret's tutelage, Nora developed some very practical, womanly skills, like baking biscuits.

"You like the biscuits, Papa?"

"What? Oh, yes, Nora. They're all right. Margaret is a good cook, even if she does talk all the time."

"I made them. Margaret taught me."

"You made them? My Nora? They're wonderful, sweetheart, best biscuits I ever tasted. Did you hear that, Mattie? She made the biscuits!"

That was how Em always was about Nora. Anything she did was the best, most remarkable, most wonderful ever, and Nora learned early to seek that praise. Em never disciplined but left it to me to scold about a messy bedroom or an uncared-for horse, a lesson undone or a sharp word spoken in anger. His responsibility in parenting seemed to be to provide the fun, and he was great at taking her for long rides, teaching her to judge cattle, throwing the ball so she wouldn't catch like a girl. A lot of the time, I felt left out of their horseplay and laughter, and yet I was never sure how to join in.

I tried to tell myself that life was good and going on as it should, and to some extent I accepted the level at which we were living. But inside, I knew it wasn't what it should be, and I could see no way of changing it. I existed.

That's where we were when Lucinda Fisher finally came to town. Literally, she was dragged to town by Em, who pulled her into my office one day.

"Mattie, this is Lucinda. She needs a tooth pulled."

I looked up to see him holding by the arm a large, tall woman of about my own age, but honestly, less attractive than I was. And you had to go some to beat me! She had dark hair, carelessly put up in a bun behind her head so that strings of hair escaped and hung around her face, which was round and of high color, like she worked in the sun all the time. Her clothes were clean, but I noticed a rip near the hem of her skirt and a button missing on one sleeve. Truthfully, I was disappointed. I'd built up a picture of this plucky widow who lived alone on the land, and in my mind I'd made it a romantic picture. Reality was a disappointment.

"How do you do, Lucinda? It's a pleasure to finally meet you in person."

She murmured, "Thank you," and tried to smile, but it was obvious she was in pain. I had her sit in the chair and got right to work looking at the tooth.

Pulling teeth was not my specialty, but I had done it before. Once in a while a traveling dentist came through Benteen—the kind whose idea of dentistry was to pull teeth, not fix them like they do today—but most of the time I was the only dentist available, just as on occasions I was the preacher and nearly the undertaker.

Once I pulled a tooth from a cowboy who was petrified. He grabbed the arms of the chair like it was going to take off with him and he had to hold on for dear life, and then he stiffened up like a board, absolutely motionless except for his feet, which were busy acting like they were spurring a horse. Every time I'd pull on that tooth, he'd drag his feet backward and rake a spur across my feet. He'd holler about the tooth, and I'd holler about my foot. The friend who had brought him in thought we had both gone crazy, and I thought we never would get that tooth out. Drew blood on my foot, he did.

Lucinda was a more tractable patient, stoic almost. I did the best job of it I could, but pulling a tooth without anesthesia is never easy for the doctor nor the patient. I tried to give her a sip of whisky but she refused, and we just went ahead. Em left the room, claiming he had business outside, and didn't come back until Lucinda's tooth was out, her jaw packed with wet cloths.

"She'll need to stay here a while, Em. I wouldn't want that socket to start bleeding."

"Stay here?" He looked almost alarmed for a moment, then he relaxed. "Where can she stay?"

"Well, for the time being, she can sit right there. If I had an infirmary, with a bed for her to lie down . . ." I let my voice trail off.

"She'll be fine, Mattie. I've got to get her back out to her place and still have time to come home, you know."

Lucinda sat silently while Em and I wrangled over her immediate future.

"Em, I cannot let you take her anywhere for a couple of hours."

In the end, Lucinda stayed silently in that chair for an hour or more, and then I sent them on their way with instructions for her care. Em seemed less concerned now about her welfare than annoyed with both Lucinda and me. I couldn't figure out what was bothering him, but I guess I was too dumb to see the handwriting on the wall. Or recognize a guilty conscience when it presented itself to me.

He did not come home that night, of course, but I was used to his absences now and barely thought to question him. I did ask, though, about his continued relationship with Lucinda, but I asked out of curiosity rather than jealousy.

"Why, Mattie, my love, are you jealous?"

I laughed. "No, Em, curious as to why you would keep up a friendship with someone like that. She . . . she's not your style."

It was his turn to laugh. "You're right. She's not. If I ever cheat on you, Mattie, it won't be with someone like Lucinda Fisher."

I believed him.

In the end, I sent Em away. Or at least, I forced him to make the decision. I guess I stopped fooling myself that life was going on normally. Things had deteriorated to the point that Em barely talked to me, and flinched if I touched him. My efforts to get him to discuss our situation were futile. One day I surprised myself by saying, "Em, within one week, I want you to decide either to do something about our relationship or leave. I won't live this way."

He looked long and hard at me and then nodded his head, but he said nothing.

Two days later he left, saying little except that this was what he had to do and that he really didn't blame me. I blamed him, though, with a rage that frightened me with its intensity. After the first shock and numbness wore off, I would spend hours wondering how this had happened to me, how someone I had loved so much had separated himself from me, how Em who had loved me had become Em who despised me.

If I was distraught, Nora was destroyed by his leaving.

Em had gone to her and told her he had to leave, that Mommy and Daddy could not live together anymore, that he still loved her and all those trite things. But to Nora, the bottom line was that her beloved father had walked out of her life.

She never mentioned it to me. Instead, she went on with her life just as it had always been, pretending there was not a great empty space there.

"Nora, have you heard from your father?"

"No. He's probably busy. Where's the book I was reading?"

"I don't know. Nora, don't you want to talk about your father?"

"No." And she was gone.

It was fall when Em left, and Nora was busy with school and piano lessons she took from Sally Whittaker. At dinner, she was generally her same self, prattling endlessly about the small nothings of her day while I pretended great interest. I was too lost in my own despair to realize that at night, alone, she cried into her pillow. In some ways, Em's leaving set the course for Nora's selfish and destructive life, but that's another story.

Two weeks after Em left, I found out that he had gone straight to Lucinda Fisher. Lucy Gelson told me, and she did it kindly, a gesture meant to help a friend, because she knew I wouldn't want to be the only one who didn't know.

"Mattie, did you ever think there was anything between Em and that Fisher woman?"

I shook my head easily, not a doubt flitting through my mind. "No. Em told me once if he ever left me, it wouldn't be for someone like that. She's . . . well, Lucy, she's so unattractive, and she doesn't care for herself."

"Mattie, he's living out there with her."

"Lucy, you must be mistaken. I don't know where he's living, but I'm sure you're wrong."

"Ask him."

I did, the next time Em came to see Nora and to gather up a few of his belongings. He had developed the irritating habit of dropping by whenever he wanted, usually once a day, so that I never knew when I would look up and see him. It made my days difficult, and I suggested he call before he came. We had one of the few phones in Benteen.

"Call from where, Mattie? There aren't that many phones, and I don't generally have a chance to use one."

"Doesn't Lucinda have a phone?" I said it nastily.

"What does that have to do with it? And no, she doesn't."

I watched his face for signs of guilt but saw none. "Em, are you living with her?"

He turned and stared at me, but finally had the grace not to lie. "Yes, Mattie, I am."

It was worse than his leaving. I felt betrayed, the dishonesty of it turning me dirty. I kept my calm until he left, but for days afterward I cried. Then I decided I didn't want to live my life in tears and bitterness, and I started out to build a new life. I never cried for Em Jones again.

⁓✳⁓

I AWOKE each morning, alone in my bed, with a great lump of dread in my throat. Having decided that you won't live your life in unhappiness is a clear and simple intellectual decision. Translating it into emotional terms is something else, and I seemed incapable of it, slipping instead into a depression where my work, the prairie I loved, even my willful daughter became my enemies.

I went through the days mechanically. "Yes, Mrs. Jones, this cathartic will help you. If it doesn't bring results, see me again in three days."

"No, it's not cholera. The child just has a simple cold. Keep him warm and give him lots of fluids. No, he doesn't need any medicines."

It all seemed trivial to me. I was batting my head against the small problems of others while my own life was one huge, insurmountable problem. I could not see ahead enough to give imaginative shape to that bold new future I wanted to build.

Will Henry and Jim were kind, caring and helpless. I had to stop Will Henry from going out to Lucinda Fisher's to thrash Em.

"Will Henry, you know that won't do any good and isn't the right thing to do."

"I don't care," he muttered, clenching a fist even as he sat at my kitchen table. "Nobody treats my sister like that and gets away with it."

Jim was made of more patient stuff. "Son, he won't get away with it. People earn what they get, and someday, someway, he'll get just what he deserves. But you don't have to be the instrument of that. I've taught you better than that, and you know your ma wouldn't like it."

Big as he was, Will Henry was always silenced by a mention of Mama and what she would or wouldn't like, and it worked again this time. He couldn't let it go, though, without muttering, "I better not meet him in town."

"Like as not, he'll start avoiding Benteen," Jim said mildly. "He ain't made himself none too popular around these parts. Mattie, what's happening to the claim? I didn't see any cattle out there."

"Jim, they must be there. What could he have done with our herd?" I tried to say it lightly, dismissing the flash of fear that went through me. Em wouldn't dare sell the cattle—or would he?

"I'll go check around again. Must be these old eyes. Come on, Will Henry, this lady's got a garden we got to see to today."

"With protectors like the two of you, how can I go wrong?" I tried to laugh, but as always, I was close to tears. This time, my tears sprang from gratitude rather than despair.

I never did cry over Em again, but I cried buckets over lost dreams and my fear of the future. I hated myself for being weak and giving in, but I guess it was that future looming large in front of me that created the lump of dread. All my life, someone else had been responsible for me, even if they hadn't always done that good a job. There was Mama, then Dr. Dinsmore, then when I came to Benteen, Will Henry and Jim, and then, of course, Em. But I couldn't go back to being dependent on Will Henry and Jim at this point. I had to go forward, and the only way I could do it was by myself. Me and that willful, stubborn child of mine.

"Nora, please pick up your room."

"I will."

"Now, Nora."

"I don't have to." It was said coldly, calculatingly and bluntly. "There's no reason to do it now."

"There's one very good reason, miss. I told you to."

"You can't make me."

I resorted to pleas. "Nora, for goodness' sake, can't you be some help instead of trying to make things worse? If I pick up your room, I'll throw the things on the floor into the trash."

"You wouldn't dare." The dark eyes flashed in warning. "I'll go live with Papa."

"No, you won't, and you know it."

Neither of us ever won those arguments, though they were hard on both of us. Not that Nora didn't have her sweet moments. She could be adorable, and everyone in Benteen thought her a charming child. She seemed to save her temper and unpleasantness for me, and I was smart enough to figure out that regardless of blame or fault, she blamed me for Em's leaving. In her eyes, I had destroyed her world and robbed her of the one person she held dear, the one who gave her her own way with absolute consistency. There was no way I could explain the truth to her.

If Nora became my enemy, so, too, did the prairie. I, who had loved to ride abroad on it, came to dread even the closest house call. It seemed as though I was most aware of my aloneness out there on the grass, though year by year the patches of uninterrupted prairie were less and less as farmers built solid homes, replacing their soddies with brick and board, adding durable barns and outbuildings. Still, you could ride for an hour without seeing anyone, and sometimes if that happened to me, I would feel a rush of panic, a momentary feeling of having forgotten all I knew about reading signs and finding my way.

"Nora, come go with me out to the Gelsons'. Luther's sick, and I have to go see about him."

"I don't want to go to the Gelsons'. They're nasty boys, always finding snakes and things."

"You like Lucy. Come on and go with me." I couldn't bring myself to say the truth, that I dreaded so deeply the ride out there alone and needed Nora, not merely wanted but needed her for company. In the end, she got her way and stayed home, and I gritted my teeth and made the trip, making every step of it worse for myself simply through my own dread.

"Mattie, you look exhausted." Lucy greeted me as I pulled the buggy up in front of their new house. "I should have brought Luther to you. I don't think he's that sick. I just asked Jed to stop and tell you when he was in town."

"I truly wish you had brought him, Lucy. The ride out was hard on me today."

She looked keenly at me. "Come inside; I'll brew some tea while you check Luther. I think maybe it's just a fall cold, but I'll feel better if you look at him."

Luther had pneumonia. I heard the congestion in his lungs and prayed that he was as tough as he seemed. Lucy took the news calmly and did as I told her, bundling herself and the child for the trip back to town.

"He can't stay here?"

"I want to watch him, Lucy. Send Jake to tell Jed."

Droopy with fever, Luther, then about eight or nine, simply watched us with glazed eyes.

Lucy and I battled the fever in that child for five days, bathing him with cool water, forcing him to drink broth, holding him close and crooning to him. Each of us read the concern in the other's eyes, but we never spoke of it. Instead, we spoke often of my life, of Em and Nora and the future.

"Will you get a divorce, Mattie?"

"Yes. It's . . . well, it may cause more gossip, but I need to be free of him."

Nobody in Benteen had ever gotten a divorce, and I could imagine there would be much talk. I had supportive friends, like the Gelsons and the Whittakers and others in the community, but there would be those who would cluck and flutter about how I should have put my husband and family first and what a shame and disgrace it was for Nora. There was a lawyer in town now, a young man named Bertram who had opened offices after reading law with an older man in Ogallala. I would consult him soon, especially about the nagging business of the cattle that Jim couldn't locate.

"Mattie, what of Nora?" Lucy asked.

"What of her? I can't give her up, and I can't keep her. She's almost fourteen now, and I'm hard put to tell how much of my trouble with her is the result of the divorce and how much is simply the age she is. But I, well, I never talked to my mother the way she does, and Sara Dinsmore never talked to me that way. I worry about how she'll get along in the world."

Lucy laughed, a short, wry little sound. "I have a feeling Miss Nora will get along fine, with everything going just as she wants it."

"But that's not right, either," I said stubbornly. "She learned that from Em, to expect everything to go just as she wants it, and to throw a tantrum if it doesn't."

"Yes, she learned well from a master, and you may just have to accept that it's too late to undo those early lessons, Mattie."

Silently I cursed him for what he had done to both Nora and me.

Luther Gelson died the fifth day after we brought him to Benteen. He slipped away in one night in a coma, no longer able to breathe for the fluid in his lungs. Lucy was a stoic prairie woman, and she knew the odds for survival of children. She seemed to take the death calmly, her eyes wide with tears and her hands clutching the tiny hands that she folded across his chest. There were no wails or screams, and for a moment I wanted to cry out in her place. But I knew that Lucy's hurt was deep and her grief would go on for a long time. I sent word out to Jed, and Lucy and I simply clung to each other until he arrived, red-eyed but equally stoic.

Jed insisted on making the coffin himself, and he would hear of no burial place but their own land. Light frost had touched the prairie by then, but the ground was soft enough to dig, and the next day a small party from town traipsed out to the Gelsons. It was only five days since I had made the earlier trip, so busy worrying about my own fears and dreads that I had scarcely taken Luther's illness seriously. Now he lay in the ground, and the prairie seemed more than ever to me to be an evil thing.

Will Henry and Jim stood by my side at the funeral, each holding on to my arm, and Nora stood next to Will Henry. Even Nora was strangely affected, staring with unseeing eyes as the minister commended Luther's soul to God, and clutching her uncle as we walked away.

They came back to town with us, and we were a solemn foursome as we sat in the kitchen. It seemed almost too much effort to me to make a pot of coffee, but I drew myself up and started the water heating.

"Mattie, are you all right?" Jim asked it with real concern.

"No, Jim, I'm not." Everything seemed to overwhelm me, and I was swept by an awful despair, as though there was no one good thing in my life that I could hold on to. I buried my head in my hands and gave in to great, gulping sobs that sent Nora running from the room in confusion and left the two men who cared most about me staring helplessly. Finally, Jim came and awkwardly put an arm around my shoulders.

"Will Henry and me, we've talked about it, and we, well, we think maybe you should get away from here awhile. Get a new perspective on things."

"Where would I go?" Even as I asked, I knew the question was silly. I would go nowhere.

"How about to Omaha to see the Dinsmores?"

I almost wailed aloud at the suggestion. The memory of my last visit there still burned in my mind. I knew now that I had not heard the full story from Em and that his arm around Sara had not been as casual and comforting as he protested. It was one of many truths to which I had blinded myself over the years of my marriage.

"No. I cannot, will not go to Omaha." I said it with such finality that Jim backed away, muttering, "Whatever you think best, Mattie."

Finally, I gathered myself together enough to make the coffee and to apologize to both of them for having lost control. They were embarrassed and concerned, and they drank their coffee quietly.

The days following Luther Gelson's funeral were the lowest point in my life, lower even than the teasing I took from Mary Jane Canary in Princeton, for now my grief and despair were adult and deep. As I went through the days routinely seeing the few patients who came, fixing meals for Nora and myself only to find I could not eat, lying endlessly awake in the middle of the night, the idea of going away took more and more shape for me. If only I could escape the prairie, I thought, everything would be all right. It was a foolish thought, and perhaps I even knew it then, but it gave me a fantasy to cling to.

Cora's letter came as the answer to a prayer. She wrote from Omaha, saying she had never married Dwight Peterson and never gone to Chicago but had a successful practice in Omaha, independent of the school, treating women's problems, and she was busier than she wanted to be. Would I consider leaving Benteen and joining her in practice? Her letter prattled on about her life in Omaha, and it did sound glamorous. She apparently had a wide circle of friends, including many gentleman escorts. Though she didn't come right out and say it, I gathered that most of these gentlemen wished to be the special man in her life but each took her on her own terms.

I ached with jealousy, plain, old-fashioned green-eyed envy. Omaha, once my escape from Princeton and poverty, now seemed to offer me a way out of despair, a path away from the small town and back to the city I had loved. I could work with Cora, whom I liked, and I could work with women, a practice that would be meaningful for me. I began to build castles in the air, planning the move, deciding what to sell, what to keep.

For two days I allowed myself to believe this fantasy.

"Mama, what makes you grin like that? I haven't seen you grin in so long!" Nora was amused at me and, I suspect, thankful to see my sour face lightened.

"Oh, Nora, I'm just thinking about something."

"What? You have to tell!"

"No, I don't. But it's Omaha. I . . . I'm thinking of going there."

"To visit the Dinsmores?"

"No. To visit a woman I knew in medical school."

"Why would you do that?"

"Nora, she wants me to move to Omaha and practice with her." I reached and hugged the child in my enthusiasm, but she drew away.

"That's the silliest thing I ever heard of. Of course you won't go to Omaha."

I was startled. "Why not?"

"Because you live here in Benteen. It's our home. I wouldn't go with you. And I doubt you'd really go." With that astute judgement, she stalked out of the room and left me thinking, my castle in the air crumbled.

I began to think in other terms. How could I leave Benteen when I had worked so hard here for so long, making it my town? And would I take Nora away from Benteen, where she was known and loved by an entire community? To Omaha, where she would have no friends? And what about the Dinsmores—could I once again live in the same city with Sara and her father? Finally, of course, there was the legal problem. I had done nothing about a divorce from Em. Yet the dream of Omaha remained attractive, and though I now saw it with more clarity, I did not give it up.

Eventually, I left Nora with the Whittakers and asked Jim to drive me to Fort Sidney to the train.

Cora met me, in a handsome carriage driven by a gentleman she introduced as Mr. Albert. He was, she explained, a lawyer and a close friend. Mr. Albert just smiled briefly at me and turned his adoring eyes on Cora. Age had not withered Cora's blond fragility one whit, nor had it shadowed her bright approach to life.

"Mattie, we could have such a good practice here. Women really want to go to women doctors, even if we don't always get the respect from our male colleagues that we should. You know who I mean," she added darkly, and I wondered if she had tangled with Dr. Dinsmore. He had never liked her, though I had always thought that was caused by jealousy of my affection for her.

"Well, Cora, I'm anxious to see your office and hear all about your work." I felt matronly and dumpy next to her and tried to slink in my seat to hide my height, a trick I had thought I was long past resorting to. It was winter, and

I wore my serviceable cowhide coat that I'd had forever. Cora, on the other hand, wore a flowing black wool cape with a smart fur collar and matching hat. She looked fashionable and sophisticated; I felt very much the country bumpkin.

The next few days reinforced that feeling. Cora took me to a round of parties—dinner with this one, tea with that one. I met a dizzying succession of people whose faces and names I could not remember then and cannot now. I saw very little, however, of her office and practice, and it began to dawn on me why Cora wanted a partner.

"Cora, I must get back to Benteen tomorrow. Can we talk about your practice today?"

"Of course, Mattie, dear. You have had a good time, haven't you? I wanted so badly for you to enjoy your visit."

"Cora, I've loved it," I lied. "But I must get home to Nora and to my own patients."

"Well, your own patients will have to find another doctor, soon, because I intend to steal you away."

We talked seriously then about income and numbers of patients and all the things that make up a doctor's life, and I began to see that my impression was wrong. Cora was truly involved in her practice and had been taking a slight vacation to entertain me. With characteristic kindness, she had wanted to show me a whirl in the big city. What she unintentionally proved to me was that I no longer belonged. Benteen was home.

I saw Dr. Dinsmore and Sara once during my stay, an awkward visit which I regretted and yet which I could not have left out of any trip to Omaha.

"Mattie, Mattie, I told you you were unhappy when you were here . . . and with good reason apparently." He said it wryly, looking at me with a question in his eyes, and I wondered if he could possibly think that I might now return to him.

I tried to speak lightly, but a tangle of memories nearly brought tears to my eyes. Sitting in his study, I remembered another encounter there when I had wanted to bolt and run. I felt a little that way again, with his piercing stare that seemed to know all about my life with its failures and disappointments.

"You have often been right about my life," I reminded him, not adding the "but not always" that surfaced to the tip of my tongue.

"I think I'm right now, too. It would be a good thing for you to accept this offer you have, even though it is with a woman for whom I have less respect than I do for you. You need to return to Omaha. And Sara and I would be delighted, wouldn't we, Sara?"

Sara, now well into her thirties, had greeted me shyly, extending a timid hand in place of the exuberant hugs I had once known, and she had sat silently during our entire visit. Now, directly addressed, she smiled only a little and nodded her head, eyes on her father as if seeking his approval. I saw too clearly that the mother's instability had indeed been visited upon the daughter, and my heart broke for both Sara and her father.

Lowering my eyes to hide the sadness, I answered him. "I truly don't think I belong in Omaha anymore. I think Benteen is my home."

"And your husband?"

This time my answer was strong and defiant. Raising my head, I said clearly, "I intend to divorce him."

"Bravo. That's the Mattie I know and remember. It may have taken you a while, but you've got your spunk back."

Later he sent Sara to the kitchen to see about tea, and we talked privately. Remembering our last private talk, I started to shrink into my chair, the old intimidation and fear returning after nearly twenty years. But then I felt again that self-confidence with which I had answered his question about divorce, and I sat straight and firm, looking him in the eye.

It was he who lowered his eyes and seemed to sink in posture. "Mattie, I know now that what I want can never be between us, and I want to say clearly that you must not let that affect your decision about Cora's offer. I will cause you no trouble. I'll even, if you insist, stay out of your life."

"Thank you," I murmured, truly touched. "But that's not the basis for my decision. I have felt out of place here this week . . . and strangely, even to me, I've felt a longing for the prairie. I belong in Benteen."

"So be it. You have nothing but my best wishes."

We talked then of Sara, and he confirmed my suspicions, though he apparently had little insight into the role his own strong domination might have played in developing her weakness. In the years since his wife's death, understanding of such conditions had progressed, and he felt none of the despair he had once felt, though he knew that caring for Sara would be a lifelong burden.

"That's something I've wanted to ask you, Mattie. I'm

not the spring chicken I like to think of myself as, and, well, I have to plan ahead for her. If anything happens to me, will you take Sara?"

"Of course. Nora and I would welcome her, but surely the day is far off."

"I hope so," he smiled. "Come, let's see where that tea is." He held out a hand of friendship, and I accepted it, feeling at last that he and I had made our peace.

On the train going home, I pressed my nose to the window, taking in as much of the scenery as I could and longing to be instantly back in Benteen. Cora had been understanding about my decision and nonchalant about my profuse thanks for her hospitality.

"No, Mattie, dear, I don't believe I will ever let you return the favor. You'll just have to come to Omaha again to see me. I believe I'd wilt in Benteen."

And she would have, too.

But I took something back with me from Omaha, something indefinable but important. Not only had I decided to commit myself to Benteen, to staying where I had worked to build something, but somehow I had regained my view of the world. I was going home to stay not in defeat but in strength. I felt good about my decision and felt I had made it for all the right reasons. If I had once decided to marry Em Jones for all the wrong reasons, I had now righted that decision.

Will Henry and Jim met me at the train with news that filled me with anger. Em had sold the cattle.

"How can he? They weren't his! Most of those cattle

were taken in as payment for my services. He can't sell them."

Jim tried to calm me down. "He sold them. At auction at Ogallala. They're gone, Mattie, gone so far you can't get them back."

"Well then, I'll get the money!"

"If you can, if you can. Knowing Em, it's probably burned a hole clean through his pocket. Besides, I hear he didn't get a good price for them. Took less than he should have."

Right there on that windswept train platform in Fort Sidney, all my old fears of poverty swept back over me, and I knew I had come back to Benteen to secure my future. I stared long and hard at the distant Nebraska horizon, blue sky meeting the gold and white of dead winter grasses frosted with snow, and I resolved once again that I would never be poor.

"Mattie, you okay?" Will Henry looked puzzled as I turned toward him.

"Yes, Will Henry. For just a moment there, I was remembering Princeton. I'll get those cattle back . . . or a bigger and better herd."

He didn't understand the connection between Princeton and the cattle, but it was all right as long as I knew.

I went to see Wayne Bertram as soon as I got back. The news was not good.

"I doubt, Dr. Armstrong, that we can get much from Mr. Jones in the way of alimony or child support. You can't bleed a turnip, you know."

"No, but I want what's mine. I want payment for those

cattle and clear title to the house."

"Well, about those cattle. They were jointly owned, technically, and if he doesn't have your half the money, we can garnishee his wages . . . but he has no wages. I hear, as a matter of fact, that he's in debt to several people."

Em had done it again, worked his way and run off scot free! In the end, I got a simple divorce and clear title to my house and bank account. There was no mention of visitation rights and how often Em could see Nora.

She pretended it didn't bother her. "Aren't you self-conscious, being the only divorced woman in Benteen?"

"Yes, I am, Nora. But I think it's for the best. Are the other children teasing you?"

"No, not at all." She denied it too quickly, and I suspected they were. But I remembered Lucy's words. Nora could take care of herself.

She proved it one spring day that year by riding out to Lucinda Fisher's claim. She did not ask, simply took her horse and went.

Finishing with the last patient of the day, I called into our living quarters for her and got no answer. Not at all alarmed, I put on my apron, began to see about heating a meat pie for dinner and finally stepped to the door to call her in from outside. Still no answer, but I was unconcerned until I stepped into our three-stall barn and saw that Jonesy, her five-year-old mare, was gone.

Nora knows the prairie, I told myself. She's been out there a hundred and one times. It's just that she's always told me before. Deliberately, I went back to the kitchen and tried to make my mind focus on a batch of biscuit dough. But alarming fears kept jumping in front of me. Her horse had stepped in a hole and thrown her. She'd met a drifter—they weren't real common anymore, but we did have them. She'd been bitten by a snake, even though it was too early in the year for snakes. Finally I gave up and walked to Whittaker's store.

Sally greeted me with bustling cheerfulness, a floury apron around her expansive middle and her hair in straggling ends, sure indications she had been baking. But when she looked at my face, she dusted her hands quickly on her apron and reached toward me.

"Land's sake, Mattie, you look like you've seen a ghost. What's wrong?"

"Nora." I said it tersely. "She's gone."

"Gone? Now, calm down, dear, she's probably just gone for a walk somewhere."

"Jonesy is gone, too."

"Well then, she's gone off on a ride. It's most dark now, and she should be home any minute."

"She's gone to Em, Sally."

"Now, Mattie, how could you know that?"

I shook my head. "I don't know how I know, but that's where she's gone."

Ralph was weighing some nails for a late customer over in a corner, but he had begun sending furtive glances toward us. Our whispering carried across the store but not distinctly enough for him to hear what we were talking about. Finally he broke loose to demand, "What's going on over here?"

Sally told him as calmly as she could, still trying to make believe that I was exaggerating, but Ralph, bless him, came to my defense.

"I bet that's just where that stubborn little baggage went," he exclaimed. "Though heaven knows, I hope she can find the way."

"Ralph, can William ride after Will Henry and Jim? They'll go get her."

"Sure he can. Right away." He bustled off in the back to call William Snellson.

The Whittakers came home with me and ate the leftover meat pie, still cold. We left the biscuit dough in the pan and sat silently over the kitchen table for a long while. In all probability, Nora, with her knowledge of the land and her confidence in herself, would be fine. With any other child, one might have agonized over her being alone and afraid on the prairie at night, but no such thought was appropriate if you knew Nora. In all probability, she had left early enough to arrive well before dark. But still I worried about the freak accident, and I was angry at her for having done this to me.

"Would you have let her go if she'd asked?" Sally inquired.

"No. I don't think she should be visiting Lucinda Fisher's house." I said it firmly, without hesitation.

"And Em doesn't come here to see her anymore."

"He could. No one would stop him."

"He'd hardly be welcome," Ralph said wryly.

"He made his own choices," I countered.

"Yes, and they were the best thing that ever happened to you," Sally said tartly. "But the problem now is Nora. What if she wants to stay out there or go visit more often? Will you let her?"

"I don't know. As I said, if she asked me, I'd have said no. But her going puts it differently. I don't know what I'll do."

But the question never came up. A silent and chastened Nora was brought home in the middle of the night by one tired uncle and one exhausted stepgrandfather. She said nothing to the Whittakers nor to me, but uncharacteristically, she came without being asked to hug me fiercely. Then, wordless, she turned and left the room.

The Whittakers, sensing a need for privacy, melted into the night, taking with them my sincere thanks for their moral support. "Mattie, that's what friends are for," Ralph said. "You're high on our list, and you call whenever we can help."

I felt again as I had the night Will Henry wanted to thrash Em. With friends like that, how could I help but have a full and happy life?

As I turned back inside, Jim twisted his hat in his hands. "She was out there, all right. Hadn't been there too long," he paused, then added, "but long enough, I guess."

"Was she unpleasant about being sent after?"

"No, Mattie, she was docile as a lamb, so quiet I thought maybe I had the wrong child. Course, Em, he wasn't pleasant at all."

"He sure wasn't," echoed Will Henry. "Lucky I didn't knock his fool head off, telling us we had no right to take his daughter, how you should take better care than to let her wander away. Made some cracks about you being too busy with medicine to take care of your child . . ."

As I said wearily, "It's an old argument between us, Will Henry," Jim muttered, "Hush, now, Will Henry. He didn't talk with his mind working right, and there ain't no sense upsetting Mattie with what he said."

"Well then, tell her about Nora."

"What about Nora?" I asked anxiously.

"She talked to us some on the ride home," Jim began, "probably more than the sprite has ever talked to me at any one time in all her life."

"And?" Was he going to make me drag it out of him?

"She had a big shock back there. She kind of rambled, but the gist of it was that Lucinda Fisher couldn't hold a candle to her own mother. Nora thought the lady was dirty, ugly, unpleasant, you name it. And she, well, she couldn't puzzle out why her beloved daddy left home— and her—for someone like that. She cried some and told me, 'Grandpa Jim, I don't think I'll ever understand it, if I live to be a hundred.' I tried to tell her someday she might see it different."

"Why should she?" I asked harshly.

"Mattie, you don't want her to sour on all men, do you? Sure, someday she'll see her daddy different, and you, too, and maybe she'll develop some compassion for both of you. But right now she's hurt, and she don't think she can trust anybody. I maybe come as close to being in her good graces as any of us, and I intend to use that."

I was chastened. Sometimes I hated Em with such passion that I wanted Nora to share that feeling, even though I knew it would be destructive to her. It took someone like Jim to knock me back to my senses. And he did. I never, ever talked with Nora about that night, and she seemed content to let it lie. She did not ask to see Em again, and their visits became more and more rare.

Jim, on the other hand, took to seeing more of Nora. They would ride together, searching for wild plums, rounding up Jim's small herd of cattle on his claim or just exploring. He taught her all those lessons he had taught me years earlier, and she seemed to revel in it.

One night when they had returned for a late supper, Jim sat in the kitchen with me after Nora had gone to bed. Will Henry was off courting, having met a young girl who lived about three miles from their claim.

"Makes for a long ride for him," laughed Jim, "but it's time he settled down. I sure hate to lose that boy, but it's his turn."

"Oh, Jim, you've been so good for him, and for me. And now you're doing for Nora what no one else could."

He sobered. "You never needed that much, Mattie. Most of it came from inside you. Will Henry, yeah, I was able to do some for him. But that girl of yours, I don't know." He shook his head.

"But I thought the two of you were getting along so famously."

"We are, we are. But there's a corner of her that won't open up to anyone. Not me, not you, especially, I suspect, not to her daddy. Nora's going to keep Nora safe from all hurts."

I looked intently at him, hearing what was behind his words. From the time Em deserted, Nora would place her faith in no one, especially in no man, and that careful protectiveness would chart the course for her future life.

In the back of my mind, I heard again that bell of warning . . . or was it doom?

I began to work on my sanitarium. I drew rough sketches of what I wanted—a two-story brick building with windows marching evenly across the front and trees sheltering it from the prairie breeze. Inside, there would be wards for male and female patients and living space for Nora and myself, with an office for me and a huge kitchen in which to prepare what I foresaw as endless meals. I asked Jim to look at the plans, and he scratched his head.

"You left me behind, Mattie. I could build you a soddie, or even a pretty simple clapboard house, but this is more than I can tackle. You'll have to get someone who knows more than I do."

I was crushed. "Who's that? Nobody knows more than you do, Jim Reeves."

"You might have to have somebody come down from Scottsbluff or Fort Sidney," he said slowly, "and it'll cost a bundle, this pipe dream of yours."

"It's not a pipe dream," I said fiercely. "I stayed in Benteen to build a sanitarium, and I will build it."

"I know you will, Mattie. I never doubted you'd do anything you set your mind to. But I want you to understand what's involved."

"All right, tell me. What's involved?"

"Well, first you got to get the land. Where is this thing gonna set?"

"On the edge of town, where I can see the prairie all day long."

"Okay. Who owns that land, and how are you going

to buy it?"

"I don't know who owns it, but I've been trading, taking land when people moved on."

"A speculator, are you now?"

"Jim, don't even say it. I've never taken advantage, and sometimes I've helped a family. It was to both our advantages."

"How much land do you have, Mattie, if you don't mind my asking?"

"Seven claims, Jim."

"Ought to be enough to trade for a piece of town property. Have you picked the spot?"

"Of course."

"I should have known. Want to show me?"

So we saddled horses, and Jim and I rode together out about a mile beyond the last house in Benteen to a rising swell in the land where even in midday there was a breeze and the prairie seemed to surround you.

"You love the land, don't you, Mattie, you who I once dismissed as a hopeless city girl?"

"Yes, I do, Jim, and it's partly because of your teaching. Oh, I went through a spell of hating the prairie, wanting to run away. But it was me I wanted to run from, and now I'm glad I didn't. I want to be where I can see and smell the grasses and the air."

He looked long at me. "I knew about that spell. And I guess I had faith you wouldn't stay in Omaha, but I got kind of worried, me being the one who had suggested it and all. I'm glad you came to your senses, girl."

I laughed to hear that graying old man call me "girl" when I was in my forty-fifth year. But it made me feel good, and I was full of the future.

"I'm glad, too, Jim."

Building the sanitarium seems a blur now. It took nearly five years—Nora was gone from home before I moved into it, but that's another story. The first thing was to acquire the land, and that turned out not to be so difficult. The days of homesteading were gone, and land that close to town, of course, did not lie in the public domain, but by trading and selling, I was able to purchase it and keep two of my claims to run some cattle.

Will Henry married his sweetheart, Nellie McCann. She was a good choice for him, stocky and sturdy from hard farm work all her life, plain, not pretty, but cheerful enough to keep Will Henry happy. She would work hard, keep a good home and probably have lots of babies. It didn't matter that she and I had virtually nothing to talk about, and she inevitably seemed tongue-tied around me, though I knew from Jim she could, at times, be talkative. They moved out to my old soddie, still standing though in need of some repair. Will Henry took over the management of my cattle and began to build himself a small herd. I knew that he would be all right for life.

Jim became my consultant on the sanitarium. Age had crept up on Jim, though. I had no idea how old he actually was. Ever since I'd been in Benteen, it seemed that he'd had no life apart from taking care of Will Henry and me. He'd never looked at another woman, never traveled, never done anything just for himself, except maybe to work on the claim, which he loved. He'd made a middling success of that, not remarkable like Jed Gelson but enough to make a man proud. And now he was a little too old to work so hard.

He was lonely, too, without Will Henry. He'd ride into town and sit for hours at my kitchen table, penciling in sketches and what he called elevations. He turned out to be a credible if unschooled draftsman, and by the time we went to Scottsbluff to seek a builder, we had fairly firm plans drawn, though without the architectural details that would lend permanence.

Building in those days was a much more happenstance thing than it is now, but still, as Jim pointed out, my project needed someone who had some knowledge of architectural principles.

We found him in Eli Able, a giant of a man whose name seemed to suit his talents. Ralph Whittaker had sent me to Scottsbluff to see a man named Newman Smith, who had built one or two buildings in Benteen, many more in Scottsbluff. But Smith wasn't interested in taking on another project in Benteen.

"Too far away, ma'am," he said politely. "I got too many things going on here."

I turned away, obviously dejected, for I knew no one else to go to.

"Tell you what," Smith called after me. "There's a fellow might like to help you. Takes on one project at a time; don't seem to care where they are. Likes to travel across the country, footloose and fancy-free. Name's Eli Able."

"Where would I find Mr. Able?"

"No telling. He lives across town in a boardinghouse. Here, I'll give you the address. But he spends a lot of time in O'Brien's saloon just down the street. You might try there first."

"Thank you." I wasn't exactly pleased about finding a man to build my sanitarium in a saloon, but I thought at least I would talk to Mr. Able. When I told Jim the story, he said, "Well, I'll go into the saloon and find him for you."

"You will not, Jim Reeves. This is my business, and I'm perfectly capable of it."

He chuckled and without another word drove the buggy to O'Brien's.

It was dark inside and smelled of stale beer. O'Brien's looked to me like the kind of saloon that had seen its heyday, with gambling and dancing girls, during the latter part of the last century and had simply existed, getting a little seedier each year, ever since. O'Brien himself looked that way, if that was him behind the bar—a shrunken, tired-looking man who paid me little attention as I walked in. He stood staring, as though lost in thought, a dirty towel on the bar in front of him.

I peered around the dark room, making out one or two tables of men silently sipping midday beer but seeing no one who might, I thought, be Eli Able. A tall, dark man hunched over one end of the bar, but I paid him no attention and approached the bartender.

"Pardon me, but I'm looking for a man called Eli Able."

Wordlessly, he jerked his head toward the tall man. Unsure, I looked again at the bartender, but he nodded his head as if to say, "Yes."

I never had been timid since I'd been grown, but Eli Able somehow unnerved me. He never looked up as I approached, and I had to speak his name, with all the directness I could muster, before he turned around. Then he stared, taking me in from head to toe while I stood there, awkward and unsure. He was, I decided, exactly the kind of man I despised, crude, unlettered, lacking the sophistication of either Dr. Dinsmore or Em.

"Yeah? I'm Eli Able."

"I . . . well, I was told you might help me with a project."

"What kind of project?" He never took his eyes off me, yet somehow his expression showed boredom rather than interest.

"I want to build a sanitarium."

"Ain't never built one of those." He turned back to his drink, as though that finished the matter.

Every instinct in me told me to walk away from this man, but I persisted. Maybe it was those steel-gray eyes that had looked so directly at me, or maybe it was his air of absolute self-confidence, bordering on indifference. To this day, I don't know why, but I asked, "Will you at least look at my drawings?"

He showed the first spark of interest. "You got drawings?"

"Yes, I do."

"Let me see 'em." He held out a hand and took the offered rolls of paper, then motioned for me to follow him to a table. It seemed forever that he studied the drawings, turning them this way and that, never saying a word to me. I almost laughed as I remembered Mama's lesson about sitting without fidgeting, but it was all I could do to keep from twisting and turning in my seat, pestering him with questions. Yet, uncomfortable as he made me, I knew Eli Able was not a man to bother until he was ready to answer.

Finally he looked at me, those eyes staring directly again, and asked, "Where are we gonna build it?"

"In Benteen," I told him.

"Okay. You got the land?"

"Yes."

"I need to see it."

"My buggy's outside." It was the most terse conversation I had ever carried on.

"I'll ride alongside." And that's what he did.

Jim seemed to take to Eli Able instantly. They did no more than shake and "howdy" each other, but I sensed they were comfortable with it.

On the long ride to Benteen, I prattled too much, made nervous by this silent, taciturn man riding alongside my side of the buggy. It was a glorious spring day, and we had the isinglass curtains pulled back, so conversation was easy.

I had talked, at far too much length, about my need for an automobile and how reluctant I was to give up my horse rides on the prairie and my buggy. He merely nodded, though I suspect he had nothing but loathing for the horseless carriages.

The only question he ever asked was "What's a sanitarium, and why do you want one?"

Shifting in my seat to look at him, I said, "I'm a doctor. I need a place where I can care for patients."

"A doctor?" He looked appraisingly at me. "A lady doctor?"

"Yes," I said, feeling somewhat defiant. Would I have to fight that old battle again?

"That's good. I think I'll like helping you, lady doctor."

We rode the rest of the way in silence.

I soon learned to accept Eli's silence. He paced off the property for over an hour, never speaking to Jim or me. Jim didn't find this remarkable at all but leaned casually against the buggy and watched.

Finally Eli said, "Good piece of land, but you got the building setting wrong in your drawings."

"Now, just a minute, Mr. Able. I put the building the way I want it, facing the open prairie."

He looked slightly out of patience. "Land isn't made that way. The building won't set right. Here, Reeves, take a look at this." The two of them walked away, Eli gesturing broadly one minute, then pointing to the drawing the next, and Jim nodding in sage agreement. After a while they came back to me, and Jim said, "He's right, Mattie. Can't do it that way."

More than slightly exasperated, I demanded that they explain it to me. Eli chuckled then.

"I won't try to put anything over on you, lady doctor, really I won't." And then he explained the curve of the land and the need to turn my sanitarium on a slight angle.

"You'll still get your view, and I'll build you a wide verandah for sitting out and staring at that prairie, if you love it that much."

I smiled. "I do."

"And so do I." For the first time, his face softened, and he almost smiled at me.

Eli Able made my heart go thump in a way that no one had in many years, not since Em had courted me, and I blushed with embarrassment, inwardly scolding myself not to be ridiculous. I was, I reminded myself, now in my late forties, a divorced woman, a doctor with a career, and he was a rough, apparently unlettered man I had known less than a day.

It did no good. I was delighted when he announced he would spend the night in Benteen, begin to draw up his lists of materials and to talk money with me.

"I . . . well, I don't have a guest room. Perhaps you could stay on with Jim."

"You got a barn?" he asked.

"Yes, of course."

"I'll stay there."

I put my best effort into dinner that night, stewing one of Nora's chickens and making an apple pie with the last of the dried fruit stored for winter.

Nora liked neither the dinner nor Eli Able. She said nothing when we were all gathered in the kitchen, but her stony silence and the dark look on her face were all I needed as signals.

"What's the matter, princess?" Jim asked. "Cat got your tongue?"

"Nothing's the matter." She said it tightly.

"Sure looks like this is a celebration, and you ain't celebrating."

"I'm not."

Eli ignored her, just as she did him, and it set the tone for their relationship. When he went happily off to the barn, he and Jim having celebrated with a mysteriously produced bottle of whisky, Nora turned on me.

"Mother, how could you hire someone like that? He's . . . well, he's nasty."

"I doubt that, Nora," I said as calmly as I could. "But he is supposed to be very capable." What in heaven's name would she think if she knew the thoughts going through my mind?

Eli Able stayed in Benteen four days. We worked out the materials he would need to get started, and we agreed on the terms. I went to the Benteen State Bank and was able to secure financing that would not send me to the poorhouse, so the sanitarium was under way. I was walking on clouds, though I had to ask myself strictly how much of that airy feeling came from the prospect of the sanitarium being a reality and how much came from Eli Able.

We had loosened with each other during the four days, getting to the point of gentle teasing. He was, I sensed, a man's man who had not spent a lot of time around women, and both Nora and I made him slightly uncomfortable. I, on the other hand, found him so attractive in a strongly physical way and yet so increasingly capable at the work which he was about to undertake that I was like a schoolgirl with a crush, afraid at any minute I'd reveal myself through a blush or an inadvertent comment. It was not an easy way to establish a relationship.

"Eli, how long will it take to build the sanitarium?"

"Don't know, ma'am."

"Stop calling me ma'am. My name is Mattie. Jim uses it all the time, and you can, too."

"Yes, ma'am."

I gave up in exasperation. "You must have some idea of how long it will take you."

His eyes actually twinkled. "Take as long as I want to. Depends on how well I like working for a lady doctor."

I did blush that time.

The last night before Eli returned to Scottsbluff, we had a party of sorts, with the Whittakers, Jim, Will Henry and Nellie, his bride. We toasted the sanitarium with home-made wine given me by a patient, though Jim and Eli stuck to their whisky, pronouncing it much finer stuff.

"What will you call it, Mattie?" Sally asked.

"The Benteen Sanitarium, I guess."

"How about the Armstrong Sanitarium?" asked Jim.

"No. It shouldn't have my name on it."

Eli watched me closely, offering no suggestions. But much later that evening as he headed toward the barn, he laid a brief hand on my shoulder and whispered, "I think you should call it Mattie's Place."

Nora refused to join our party, and I was acutely aware of her absence. She was locked in her room. And as I sat there and looked at the faces of those I held dearest, I thought about other faces that weren't there. Em—did he know about the sanitarium? Was he still as resentful? What would the evening have been like if he'd been there? Probably it would never have come to pass, if there were still Em in my life. I counted my blessings.

But I also thought about Lucy and Jed. They had rarely come in from their claim in the four years since Luther had died. We had remained close, for there was never any thought that I hadn't put out every effort to save the child, but Lucy withdrew into herself. It was that long, deep grieving that I knew was ahead when she took the death with such apparent calm. But on this evening, when we celebrated a milestone in my life, I longed for her to be part of it, and I resolved to ride to see her in the next few days.

Eli Able left the next morning. As I stood by the gate, he reached down from his horse to touch my face in a familiar gesture and murmur, "I'll be back, lady doctor."

Blushing, I looked straight at him for a moment, then turned and ran for the house, hoping no one in town had seen either his gesture or my reaction. But I thought I heard him chuckle as he rode away.

I closed the office and rode out to the Gelsons'. Nora, of course, refused to accompany me. At seventeen, she had left childish pursuits behind, like riding out on the prairie with her mother or her stepgrandfather, and had become, I thought, too interested in boys, particularly in young Clint Folsom, son of the banker and current mayor of Benteen. Clint was an attractive lad, even I could see that, but one spoiled to town ways with no appreciation of hard work. His father boasted of his intellectual superiority and apparently paid little other attention to him. Nora, however, paid a lot of attention to him, and he became her constant companion at whatever social event was going on in town. They took long rides together and lately had begun to go out in Banker Folsom's car, a practice I did not condone at all. But nonetheless, this day Nora was working at Whittaker's, where Sally, with more charity than need, I suspected, had put her to work behind the counter.

I reached the Gelsons' just before midday and received a warm welcome from Lucy.

"Mattie! You're just what I needed. Get down off that horse and come in."

"Thanks, Lucy. I've missed you and decided it was time to come for a visit."

"Well, I'd been wondering about you, too. It's just . . . I still don't like to come to town much. Jed reckons I might never get over it, but I think I will." Then she laughed. "Nice to see you can still ride a horse this far."

"Lucy Gelson, middle age is not that bad!"

She laughed again and led me inside. Lucy and I didn't visit often, but when we did we lost no time making up for long silences. Our friendship, now more than twenty years in duration, seemed to pick up the moment we were together.

"I want to tell you the news, Lucy."

"Is it good news? You look radiant, so I expect that it is."

"It is. The sanitarium is about to become a reality."

"Yes, Jed brought the news from town, and I'm so glad for you. Tell me what's happened."

"Well, you knew I'd purchased the land. Now I've hired a man to do the building." And I told her, briefly, about Eli Able, stressing, I thought, his capabilities and his unusual personality.

"Sounds interesting. I gather you think so, too, Mattie."

"Lucy, what do you mean by that?"

"You know very well what I mean. Oh, drat, here come Jed and Jim. You'll just have to tell me more about Eli Able some other time."

The Gelson men came in for their meal, and I happily joined the family. Jake, the oldest, was away at school, and I could tell that Lucy was keenly aware of her diminished family, with one boy miles away and the other lying in the ground at the edge of their claim. Still, they were a happy family, and I almost wished that Nora and I could have some of their closeness.

Nora brought me a new problem, one I had never anticipated, a few days later. Whereas other girls would have hidden their shame for months, Nora talked openly, almost defiantly, to me.

"I think I'm going to have Clint's baby." She simply announced it one night when we were having dinner alone.

"Nora?"

"You heard me, Mother."

"I . . ." Words truly failed me, I who had clung so to the sanctity of the marriage bed and had seen it violated in my immediate family. I never, never anticipated it with Nora, much as I knew that she was unhappy with her lot in life.

"Are you sure?"

"Yes, Doctor, fairly sure." Her description of her symptoms convinced me.

"Well, I'll have to talk to Mr. Folsom immediately."

"Clint already has."

"What do you mean, he already has?"

"We've worked it all out, Mother. We'll marry very soon, and Clint and I will move to Omaha."

"Is that what you want, Nora?"

"It's a way out of Benteen, isn't it?" She said it fiercely.

I sat stunned, remembering my own desperation to get out of Princeton. It had never occurred to me that she could feel the same way about Benteen, the town I loved and considered home. "Yes, I guess it is. But it could be a painful way out."

"I know that." She was defiant again. "I don't love Clint, and he doesn't really love me. He just thinks he does. But this will work out for both of us."

"How will you live?"

"Mr. Folsom will send us money. You can, too, you know. And Clint will work. He's smart enough to be a bank teller or something, and his father has connections in Omaha."

Such cynicism from one so young, even from my own daughter, where I knew to expect it, shocked and sad- dened me, and I fought an urge to run from the room. Em, I cried silently, look now what you've done, though in fairness I knew that Nora was not a product of Em alone but of both of us and of the uneasy relationship between us. Psychiatrists today might tell you a girl like Nora was seeking love to replace what she lost when her father left, an act she took as personal rejection. That may be nonsense or it may be true in some cases, but that wasn't the case with Nora. She was using poor Clint Folsom.

Stunned, I sat at the table long after Nora had left the room. You usually think that the mother is sought for advice in desperate situations like this, but Nora neither seemed to find it desperate nor to need my advice. It was as though pregnancy outside of marriage was all part of her well-thought-out plan, and she had no need of advice.

At last, I put in a call to Whittaker's, telling them simply that I had urgent business with Jim if they would please put the word out at the store in the morning. Jim still had no phone in his soddie, of course, and word of mouth generally began at the Whittakers' store.

Jim came in the middle of the day. Nora had gone to Whittaker's as though nothing were wrong, leaving me a distraught and blithering idiot. I was so glad to see Jim I literally threw myself into his arms, something I hadn't done in years, and I found comfort from this man who had been such a steady influence in my life.

"Land's sake, Mattie, what in the world has happened?"

"Nora," I blurted out. "She's pregnant."

He was taken aback, but only momentarily. "Lord God in heaven, now there's a pickle if I ever heard of one. Sit down and get me some coffee, so you can tell me about it."

Haltingly, I told the story, all from my point of view, of course, about her cynicism, her using Clint. For the first time, I recognized and voiced my concern for the baby. "She doesn't really want it, Jim. She just sees it as a way out. No baby will be well taken care of by a parent who feels that way."

"You're probably right, Mattie, but it may not be anything you can change. Remember that old Indian saying about changing what you can and accepting what you can't change, and have the smarts to know the difference between?"

I nodded, then had another thought. "Em will have

262

to be told."

"I'll ride out and tell him."

"Thanks, Jim, and try . . . you know, try to . . ."

"I'll just tell him I'll bust every bone in his body if he tries to make trouble."

And that's just what Jim did, from the way he told me the story later. Em had threatened to ride after Clint Folsom immediately, shotgun in hand, until Jim reminded him that a shotgun wedding wasn't necessary. The boy had already agreed eagerly to marry Nora.

"And then I asked him, out plain, I said, 'Em, what makes you think it wasn't more Nora's fault than that boy's? He may be just a pawn in her plan.' Old Em, he got indignant and told me not to talk about his daughter that way, but I reminded him we both knew what kind of child our princess has always been, and that she'd had some experiences as a young child that might have sent her in the what you call calculating direction. He tried to lay all the blame on you, saying yes, if Mattie had paid more attention to the poor child, but I told him to take a good look at himself. Anyway, it all came out all right. Em calmed down, says he wants to come to the wedding, but he won't make any trouble."

I was becoming accustomed to this latest crisis and was able to smile a little at Jim's description of Em's reaction. I could picture for myself those flashing eyes, filled with righteous indignation. Em probably never could be truthful with himself about his part in shaping Nora's character, but Jim had tried. And I was grateful. And could I, I wondered, ever accept my part in having produced this spoiled child turned willful and selfish woman?

Eli Able came back to town in the interval between Nora's announcement and her wedding.

"Morning, lady doctor," he drawled as he came through my office door. "Got a load of supplies out there to put in the barn. Don't want to leave them on the site."

"Oh, Eli, I'm glad you're back. I really am." I paused self-consciously, not able to tell him what had happened but glad for reasons that I couldn't define that he would be around the next days and weeks. "But you don't have to unload in the barn. Nobody will steal anything out there."

"Which one of us is building that damn thing?" He was impatient, but there was a hint of laughter in his voice.

"You are," I murmured.

"Thank you. I'll unload in your barn." And he stalked away.

I almost laughed, though I was not certain which one of us I would have been laughing at.

Eli Able stayed in the kitchen after supper that night. The two of us had eaten alone, Nora being off visiting at the Folsoms, where she apparently had been accepted lovingly as a future daughter-in-law in spite of the situation. I had talked briefly with the Folsoms on one or two occasions and found them neither as horrified as I nor as concerned about the youngsters' future. Mrs. Folsom, having no daughters, wanted to plan the wedding, and I was letting her have her way, barring my adamant refusal to sanction anything more than a small ceremony for the families. So Nora and Mrs. Folsom were planning a wedding that evening, without me.

"Something's bothering you, lady doctor." He said it quietly, staring at me over his coffee.

"It's nothing."

"Yes it is. Tell me what could possibly have happened that bad in the big town of Benteen in the week or so that I was gone."

"How do you know it's bad?"

"The look in your eyes."

I had thought, as always, that I was managing my crisis so well. Strong Mattie, no one had to worry about her. And yet here sat this man, the opposite of everything I had always thought I sought in men, and he pierced right through to the truth. What's more, I sensed that he cared. And it nearly undid me.

With tears that I fought welling up in my eyes, I told him about Nora. He never flickered an eyelash.

"Not surprised. Only met her once, but I'm not surprised."

"Surprise maybe isn't the word for it, Eli. I'm probably not surprised either. I've known for years that Nora had some, uh, traits of which I could not be proud, but I've not known how to deal with it. I guess I just gave up in the face of what I didn't understand, but I never expected this."

"Is it the disgrace that bothers you?"

"I don't think so," I said slowly. "I've always been able to do what I thought was right without worrying too much about what others said or thought. Otherwise I probably wouldn't have divorced Em. No, I think I'm worried about their future and that of the baby."

"Can't control that."

"I know. Jim told me that, too. It's their problem, but—"

"Listen to Jim. He's a good man. But you, you're feeling like a failure at mothering, aren't you?"

He was too perceptive. It took courage for me to answer him. "Yes, I guess I am."

He laughed. "We need to be more like animals. Raise them kids till they can take care of themselves, then forget about them. You've got her to a point she can take care of herself, pretty good care sounds like, so now go on about your sanitarium and whatever else is important to you."

"You can't just wash kids out of your life! Maybe we should be more like dogs and cats, but we aren't! You've just never had kids." I was more than a little indignant that he would sit there spouting advice when he hadn't walked the much-talked-of mile in my moccasins.

"Yes I did. Long time ago. I don't want to talk about it." His face darkened, and in the time I knew him, that's the most I ever heard Eli Able say about his past family life.

Nora was married to Clint Folsom on June 10, 1915. That was also the day Eli broke ground for the sanitarium, and the day when he first did something about the currents that were running between us. Of all the days in my life, perhaps that one deserves the bright red circle.

Nora was a beautiful bride. The ceremony was in the Folsoms' house, before their grand fireplace imported from I don't remember where, but most impressive. Their living room, like ours, still boasted the pineapple-carved walnut furniture of the last century, the muted Aubusson rugs that had been so important to Em. Neither house had caught up with current trends, but the Folsoms' made mine look small and shabby.

The minister asked God's blessing on this couple as they began life's adventure together, and I thought wryly God would need to do more than bless them. I was struck by guilt for my unmotherly attitude toward my own daughter, but I looked with pity on Clint, fresh-faced and eager as he was. I knew he didn't have the stuff it would take to be a success, let alone to live with Nora. Whether he was just naturally weak or his indulgent upbringing was responsible, I didn't know, but Clint Folsom was on the way to being a weak man.

Nora's leave-taking, perhaps because it was public, was effusive. Both Jim and I got large, teary hugs, great protestations about how much she would miss us, promises of daily letters. She did pull me aside briefly to say, with eyes lowered, "I know how you feel, but I want you to know it will be all right. I may not do things your way, but I'll try never to disgrace you."

I reached out to her. "And, Nora, never hurt others, even though you've been hurt." Neither of us had mentioned Em's conspicuous absence from the wedding, but she knew my reference.

"I know." She said it with some sadness.

Jim, Will Henry, Nellie and I stood by Mrs. Folsom as her husband drove the couple off to Fort Sidney and the train. Their luggage would follow, and they would rent furnished quarters, so moving was for them not the chore it had been for me years earlier. Besides, they were going toward civilization, whereas I'd been running from it. In retrospect, the difference in direction suited both Nora and me.

After the ceremony, Jim and I took the buggy to the sanitarium. Eli was there, marking it off with pegs and string, but he stopped work when we approached.

"How was the wedding?"

"Fine. She was pretty."

"I'm sure she was. She's a pretty girl." That was all he said about what had been, to me, such a momentous occasion.

"Okay, lady doctor, you want to turn the first shovel of dirt?"

"Me?"

"Who else? It's your sanitarium."

He handed me a well-used, dirt-encrusted shovel, with a slight "Sorry," and I skimmed off my white gloves to grasp it.

"Where?"

"Don't matter," he laughed. "It's going to be a big building. You just dig anywhere you got a mind to."

Though it was June, and we'd had some rain, the ground was still hard, and I had to struggle more than I thought to get a good full shovel of dirt. Eli and Jim both watched with amusement, though they managed not to laugh. When I threw the dirt high in the air, in what I thought was a gesture of celebration, I showered all of us with it. Then they laughed.

"Reeves, can you do better than that?" Eli demanded.

"If not, you can take me out and shoot me," Jim answered.

In the end, we all shoveled dirt, then declared it time for a celebration and went back to the house.

Eli sat in my kitchen again late that night. "You feel okay about today?"

"I guess."

"Don't sound very positive to me."

"Oh, I think I'm coming to grips with it, but I guess Nora will always be one of my big disappointments . . ."

"More than her daddy?"

"Much more, because I feel like I could have done something different. I don't know what, but . . ."

I fell lost in thought, wondering just what I could have done that might somehow have turned Nora out differently. Maybe it was genetic. I remembered that tiny fist hitting the stuffed bear and wondered if the seeds of Nora's personality might not have been set the night she was conceived, the night Em and I had quarreled so strongly, then made up as violently.

I didn't notice that Eli had risen and come to stand beside me until he gently reached down to take both my elbows and pull me to my feet.

"I know a cure for you, lady doctor." And he leaned to kiss me, a hard and demanding kiss, pressing my body against his. As I started to pull away, he said, "No, don't," and I obeyed automatically.

"Put out the light," he said softly, and again I obeyed.

Without a word he lifted me and carried me to the bedroom, where, with gentleness surprising in view of his huge size, he gently removed my clothes, murmuring soft reassurances all the while. It seemed to me as though a totally new being had occupied Eli Able's body. Gone was that direct, piercing stare, that harsh, terse way of speaking, that impersonal lack of concern over my great tragedies.

A new being must have occupied my body, too, for what I did and what I allowed him to do were totally foreign to me. But each time I started to protest, however feebly, he quieted me with a kiss, sometimes a gentle, enticing one and sometimes hard and urgent. I soon gave myself up to the moment.

Eli was a totally different lover than Em. Whereas Em had taught me the rewards of passion, Eli taught me the joys of slow lovemaking. There was no urgency, no hurry, but rather a deliberate slowness that drew our lovemaking out far into the night and brought me to the brink of pleasure many times. He was a silent lover, with none of Em's verbal seduction, and I was equally silent, as much at a loss for words as I was filled with enjoyment.

At last when we lay fulfilled and content in each other's arms, he spoke. "Feel better, lady doctor?"

I answered truthfully. "I don't know. In lots of ways, yes, but I'm scared, afraid . . . I don't believe I'm here."

This time he laughed softly. "You are, and you will be again."

I couldn't decide if it was a threat or a promise, but I liked the idea.

Toward dawn, I fell into a sound sleep, waking only briefly to be aware that Eli was kissing me and leaving with a gentle "See you at the site in the morning." I reached for him but he was gone.

It was bright daylight, much past my usual hour to get up, when I awoke, and it took me a moment to come to my senses and remember all that had happened. When I did, I was filled with a wild mixture of feelings, ranging from elation to guilt, from delight to fear about how to react when I saw Eli that day.

I needed no fear. He greeted me with his usual "Hey, lady doctor," and went right on working, while I stood awkwardly at the outer wall of the sanitarium-to-be and wondered what to say.

"Ain't got no report this morning," he finally said. "Got off to a kind of slow start today." And then, only then, did he wink at me conspiratorially.

I stood and watched him dig for a while, then left to try to put my whirling mind to the practice of medicine.

Eli came to my kitchen again that night but not to my bedroom. "We need to talk," he said.

Primly, thinking he did not want me to read permanence into a one-night affair, I answered, "There's no need."

Laughing, he reached over to rub my cheek. "Yes, there is, lady doctor. We got to straighten some things out. I ain't gonna eat here anymore, unless, of course, that old Reeves fellow comes along."

"What's he got to do with it?"

"Don't want to compromise your reputation, as the fancy folk say. You're a lady living alone now, and it wouldn't look right for me to take supper with you every night and sleep in your barn."

"I don't care how it looks. I thought we settled that issue when we talked about Nora."

"I care, for you. Don't matter none to me, but you don't want to become the target of town gossip, do you?"

Eli had never heard the story of Ma and Princeton, so he had no way of knowing how close to home he'd hit. Granted, I'd flown in the face of tradition, divorcing Em, and now my daughter had been equally unconcerned for traditional values, but was I ready to become the scarlet lady of Benteen? No, Eli was right. I couldn't bear that reputation, not in a town where I was trying so hard to do right, to do what was needed, to be a substantial citizen. Yet did that mean never having Eli in my bed?

He read my thoughts. "We don't have to give each other up, ma'am." His emphasis on the last word was deliberate and mocking. "But we have to be some careful. I'm moving out to the site, me, my horse and my bedroll. You start sleeping with your door unlocked. You'll be safe enough."

And so began a wonderful but frustrating period of my life. I never knew when and if Eli would come, but I slept with my door unlocked, many nights to be awakened by that amazingly gentle touch, once in a while by a rougher, more demanding need that cried out of what pain I didn't know. Our nights were a mixture of strong need and gentle caring, and I welcomed both. What I came to dread were the nights when I was left wondering whether or not he would come, for Eli was very much his own man and would go a week or more without coming to me in the night. I found myself like the addlepated schoolgirl who can think of nothing more than her love, and it was with effort that I concentrated on my patients and my daily routine.

Outwardly, Eli and I tolerated each other, a great gulf in personalities separating us. On the building site, we appeared to become familiar as co-workers, but the possibility of friendship seemed remote. He persisted in addressing me as "lady doctor," and I tried always to be formally correct with him.

If anybody suspected, it was Jim Reeves with his acute eye for human behavior, his fond but close knowledge of me and his frequent visits to the site. But he said nothing beyond, "It was a good thing when you hired him, Mattie."

"I know," I replied, avoiding Jim's stare. But he gave me an affectionate pat into which I read a sanction of whatever my relationship to Eli might be.

Eli had told me he would work the site alone until he needed help, and then, only then, he would contact some men he knew. It was his way of keeping expenses down and, as he later confessed, of drawing the work out. We broke ground in June 1915, and it was the next spring before he felt compelled to hire help. He meanwhile worked for minimal wages, had some meals at my house and an occasional fling in Scottsbluff, which devastated me. I wondered sometimes if we would be attracted to each other if we were to be public about our affection, but it was a moot point, for Eli had no wish for the world to know his private business.

Eli never talked beyond the present moment, and I, who crossed my bridges miles before I got to them, learned not to anticipate but simply to enjoy.

"What," I asked once, "will you do when the sanitarium is finished?"

"Hush. That's a long way off." He was skilled at silencing me, and I melted in his arms.

He did become accepted in the community, though without any relation to me. Eli would attend church socials, though he shied away from the literary debating society, and he was a regular in the informal discussion group that solved the world's problems regularly in Whittaker's store, by now an expanded and modernized version of the old store that had welcomed me when I moved to Benteen.

Some folks thought he was unusual, to say the least, and mentioned it to me. "Sure is a strange duck you got doing your work for you," Charles Folsom said one day in passing.

"He is different, isn't he?" I agreed. "But he seems to know what he's doing, and he's saving me money."

"That's important," Mr. Folsom agreed. We had hardly strengthened our distant relationship since the marriage of our children, and I found him pompous and overbearing. I had no wish to become close to Nora's in-laws.

Other people were impressed by Eli. Jed Gelson spent a long morning at the site, talking and watching, and came away to tell me, "You got yourself a rare man there, Mattie, a rare man."

I almost blushed, thinking of the other ways in which he was a rare man, beyond his building talents.

In the fall, when Eli had the foundation laid and was ready to frame in the building, he and I both found that most of the townspeople not only had confidence in my project and his building ability, but they saw the sanitarium as a community project. Men turned out to donate half a day here or a day there to help Eli put up the frame of this two-story giant. It was not to be the first two-story building in Benteen, but it surely would be the largest. They helped, though, because they saw it as a building for the town, where people could go for help, not simply as a fulfillment of my dream.

"Lady doctor, you know all this help I'm getting is a way for them to say what they think of you."

"Maybe," I murmured, lost in his arms, "but they wouldn't help if they didn't think you knew what you're doing."

He laughed softly. "We make a heck of a team, don't we?"

I nodded, puzzling, though, at how far the teamship went. I found these days that progress on the sanitarium left me with mixed emotions. I was anxious beyond belief for it to be a completed reality, but the prospect of finishing it brought a turning point in my relationship with Eli. What would happen then?

Outwardly I was the busy physician, treating now mostly the nonacute ills of the townspeople. The days of dire threats such as cholera and diphtheria were gone, though we still had pneumonia, farming accidents and a host of things that could snuff out a life before I knew it. I still occasionally lost a newborn infant, and once, a mother in childbirth, leaving behind a family of four other children and a bewildered, grieving father. But I felt that my skills were pushed to their limit less often, and I was able to form my days into a routine. Without Em, without

Nora, I could at last devote myself to medicine. And during the day, I did wholeheartedly just that.

I did pause several times during my daily routine to recall Eli's words about the town reaction to the sanitarium being a tribute to me. If that was so, the years of riding the prairie and having no life of my own, even the sacrifice of Em and Nora and all I had once held dear, began to be in perspective. Not that the sanitarium was worth losing them for, but that somehow there was a balance to life. I had accomplished what I came to Benteen to do. Years later they gave me an appreciation banquet—filled the high school gymnasium with people who made laudatory speeches until I felt foolish—but it raised nothing in me like the emotion that I felt when I realized the town wanted my sanitarium because they believed in me.

We heard from Nora only occasionally during this period. About two months after she left for Omaha, she wrote to say that her pregnancy had been a false alarm after all, and there would be no early baby. She and Clint, she said, were both relieved and looking forward to building their lives together before the arrival of a child.

I told only Eli about the letter at first, and he echoed my thoughts.

"She really tricked him into that marriage, didn't she? Wasn't even pregnant."

"Probably not," I agreed. "It's the most calculating, well . . . I can't say how I feel about it."

"I know," he said, and I marveled that someone who was supposedly no more than a bed partner could read my mind so closely and be so in touch with what I felt and said. The gulf in our backgrounds and education melted away when we were together, and I found myself thinking in terms of love and permanent relationships. But Eli never spoke of the future.

I finally had to tell Jim about Nora's letter, too, or else he would be waiting impatiently for his first great-grandchild. As usual, he was enigmatic.

"Probably a blessing," he said, never letting on if he suspected the awful trick that Eli and I did.

Jim was old now, though I never did know his age. He had finally consented to move into town, if Eli would build him a room adjacent to the new barn at the sanitarium.

"Build it like a soddie," he instructed Eli.

"Hell, old man, build it yourself," Eli answered, and that's eventually what Jim did. He moved more slowly, but he was still a competent, careful man. I looked forward to having him close, mostly for his companionship but also so that I could watch his health. Not that he ever complained or brought me a problem, but I detected a shortness of breath in him. I could not envision life without Jim Reeves.

The closest Eli came to losing patience with me over the sanitarium was the day I announced that I had called Scottsbluff and ordered a thousand elm trees, all three foot high.

"Good Lord Almighty," he exploded. "What in tarnation are you going to do with a thousand trees?"

"I thought you'd plant them in a big square around the

sanitarium, block it off from the breeze."

"Lady doctor, I ain't no gardener, remember? Besides, you're the one that wanted this darn building where you could see the prairie and feel the breeze, and now you block it off with a bunch of trees." He paused, then grinned. "Course, if they ain't but three foot high, they probably ain't gonna grow anymore, and they won't block anything."

"They'll grow," I said.

Late that night, his arms around me, he suddenly asked, "Are you serious? A thousand trees?"

I collapsed in laughter.

Grumbling all the while, Eli planted the trees, but it was one of the last things he did when the building was completed.

Tom Redbone came into my life during the construction of the sanitarium. And somehow that child walked right into my heart, the child of my soul that Nora had never been, may God forgive an unmotherly thought.

Tom's mother, a pale, tired woman, brought him to the clinic in a buckboard, his arm fixed in a homemade splint of saplings, his face contorted with pain.

"Fell off that big horse of his daddy's, he did. Told him that horse was too big and mean, but you can't tell a boy of twelve nothing. Leastaways, not this one." She said all this in a flat, expressionless tone, a colorless, drab woman without a spark of life in her eyes.

Tom shot her a silent look neither of resentment nor anger, but perhaps resignation, and climbed carefully out of the buckboard. I thought her unfeeling.

"Here, son," I said. "Let me help you hold that arm perfectly still while we get inside."

He was stoic about the pain of setting the arm properly, or at least as stoic as he could be, and I admired him for it.

When I told his mother the fee would be three dollars, she said, "I'll pay what I can when I can. Suppose I have to bring him back all the time, and that will cost me more."

"There will be no charge," I said distantly, "but yes, I would like to check the progress of the arm from time to time, preferably once a week."

Tom, meanwhile, had wandered toward my bookcase and stood transfixed, staring at titles on the shelf.

"Do you like to read, Tom?" I asked.

Before he could answer, his mother broke in. "That fool child would read all the time if'n I'd let him. Wouldn't do a lick of work, just put his nose in a book."

Ignoring her, I went over to the boy, whose eyes told me clearly that he did indeed love to read. "Well, Tom," I said, "you won't be able to do much work for a spell now. Why don't you take a book with you? You can bring it back when I check your arm, and take another one then."

"Could I really?"

"Of course." I was remembering the first time Dr. Dinsmore let me borrow a book, the excitement and pride I had felt, the new world that had opened up to me. At least I had had Mama, who was equally appreciative of fine books. This poor lad had only this complaining shell of a woman to turn to. I wondered about the father but could ask nothing.

When they returned the next week, Tom brought back *The Last of the Mohicans* and traded it for *The Virginian.*

"You like adventure, don't you?" I asked, and he shook his head happily in the affirmative.

"Can't do no work, and I can't be bringing him in here all the time," grumbled his mother. "Got too much work to do out on the place."

Impulsively I suggested that Tom stay with me until his arm healed. "My daughter's room is empty, and surely he can be some help to me," I said.

"How much would it cost?"

Her attitude made me stiffen in anger, and if I hadn't instinctively cared about that boy, I'd have told her to get out. But I managed a polite "There will be no charge. I see a future for your son, and I want to do what I can to help him."

"Why would you want to do that?" Suspicion lurked in her tone.

"Because someone once helped me when I needed it, and if he hadn't, I wouldn't be a physician today. I know how important it is. And this way, I can do something to repay that debt."

"I'll have to talk to his father. If he says it's all right, we'll be back." She left, almost grabbing poor Tom by the broken arm and never giving me a word of appreciation. But as he was hurried out the door, Tom managed to turn and give me a radiant smile that justified my impulsive action.

Cautiously, I told Eli that night what I had done.

"You what? Get rid of your kid, and you take on another one, one you don't even know? Lady doctor, you are impossible!" But he buried his head in my neck as he said it, and I sensed affection and maybe even a little admiration.

Suddenly he sat up. "I guess that means the end of my late-night visits."

"I hadn't thought of that." And it was true, I hadn't.

"Guess you best think," he said dryly.

My heart sank, for giving up Eli was not something I could or would do easily, certainly not for the sake of an unknown youngster and an experiment that might be brief, to say the least.

"Don't you think he'll go to sleep earlier? I intend to be fairly strict with him, just as I was with Nora."

"We'll see, but I don't want that young one to catch me here."

Curious, I asked why not. "Are you afraid the town would find out?"

"No," he said slowly, "I just don't think it would be good for him or your relationship with him. Mind you, I ain't met that kid yet, but I think you got yourself a long-term boarder."

"Maybe so," I muttered.

When Tom did meet Eli, it was a case of instant hero worship. Tom's mother brought him back in three days, and with him, a small sack of shabby clothes.

"His pa says we'll see how this works out. And thanks to you for taking care of him." And she was gone.

Tom stared after her a moment, and I realized he was

virtually being abandoned by a parent. The ease with which his parents gave him to me must have undermined his sense of self-worth, and I briefly condemned myself for not thinking of that sooner.

Putting an arm around him, I said, "I know they'll miss you something awful, Tom."

"Oh, they will and they won't," he said philosophically. "I got two brothers to help them, so they won't have to work harder just because I'm here. And I won't miss them, Dr. Armstrong, I really won't." He didn't elaborate, and I didn't ask why, though I had some strong suspicions.

That very day I took Tom with me to the sanitarium, now a framed-in building slowly being covered with brick. I introduced Tom to Eli.

"Howdy, son," Eli said in his usual terse manner. "Don't know how much help you can be with that arm, but we'll find something for you to do."

"I'd like that," Tom said politely, a shade of uncertainty tinging his voice.

"Eli's teasing you, Tom. You don't have to work on the sanitarium."

"No, I want to," he said deliberately. "I want to do something to help you."

"She's worth helping, ain't she, son?" Eli said with one of his slight smiles, and I saw then that he had made a friend of Tom.

Eli became to Tom what Jim had been to Will Henry. Tom dogged his heels so much that I wondered that Eli, never known for his patience, didn't explode. But he carefully explained things to Tom, told him what he was doing, gave him chores that the boy could manage with his broken arm.

And Tom came back to me at night, exhausted but happy. "Why doesn't Eli ever come here for supper?" he asked one night.

"Oh," I said evasively, "he does sometimes."

"Well, I wish he could come all the time."

So do I, I thought, so do I. "Well, Tom, you just make a point of bringing him home tomorrow night. I'll fix a special supper, maybe stew a hen."

And so, because of Tom, Eli came once again to my house on a regular basis in the daytime. There was no open affection between us, only a bantering kind of play, but with the three of us at the kitchen table in the evenings, I felt again a sense of family. And I felt it stronger than when I really had had a family. There was a comfort and acceptance here that I had never found with Em and Nora.

"Happy, lady doctor?" Eli asked one night as we lay in bed.

"Very. I feel like you and Tom give me a family again, a better family than I had the first time around."

"Don't get too attached to it," he said, almost absently, and I felt a finger of fear.

"Why not?"

"Oh," he answered lightly, "it ain't never good to get attached to something. You never know when fate's gonna zap you."

Fate or a restless builder, I wondered. Eli had been in Benteen almost two years, the sanitarium was nearly finished, and I worried about the future.

Eli had given me a big, shaggy farm collie named

Sheba. Claimed he found her out on the prairie on the way back from one of his flings in Scottsbluff. Sheba was large, enthusiastic and fairly untrained, and inadvertently she led to the lengthening of Tom's visit to me past the time when school began.

His arm had healed nicely, and I took the cast off one day in August.

"Gosh, am I glad to get that off! Sure was hot these days."

"I'll bet," I murmured sympathetically, examining the arm carefully and finding it straight. "All right, you may go outside, but you must remember, Tom, this arm is not as strong yet as it should be. Take care with it."

"Yes, ma'am," he promised obediently, heading for the door.

It wasn't ten minutes before I heard his howl of pain. Rushing to the door, I saw him standing in the yard, holding that arm and fighting back tears. Beside him, Sheba stood whimpering and staring at him.

"Tom! What happened?"

"She knocked me down," he managed to mutter between clenched teeth.

And she had rebroken the arm. I had to set it again, and Tom had to begin the whole healing process over again. I sent word out to his parents, who had been to visit the boy only twice briefly, and they sent back that they would be in to see about him when they could.

I never asked Tom about them, and he talked only infrequently, but I gathered they were not bad people, just like so many other dirt-poor farmers beaten down by poverty and hard work until there was no love and laughter in their lives. They didn't mean to be cruel or uncaring with their children, but they knew no other way. Tom, meanwhile, flourished under my care. Even Eli commented that "the sprout" had grown two inches in as many months, it seemed.

"You know, Mattie," Tom said one evening, "I think I want to be a doctor when I grow up." He had, with my blessing, begun to call me Mattie on the theory that Mother would be inappropriate and Dr. Armstrong was awfully formal.

I was delighted with his statement but tried to hide my enthusiasm. "Are you sure, Tom or is it just that that's the example you see right now?"

He could be a solemn and thoughtful child, and right then he seemed to ponder the question. "You could be right. I like watching you work and helping when I can. But I've never known much about other kinds of work. Maybe I'd like them, too. I'll tell you, though, I won't ever farm like Pa."

Amen, I thought. "Well, that's the whole purpose of going to college, Tom. You learn about a lot of things and find out which one you like best. Then, if you decide to go to medical school, you have to go longer and work pretty hard."

"I know," he said, "but I don't see how I'll ever even get to college. Ma would have a fit."

Yes, I thought, she probably would. But that's one bridge I won't cross until I come to it. "Have you been going to school, Tom?"

"Some. Enough to be able to teach myself reading and stuff."

"Would you like to start school here next month?"

"Ma would never hear of it."

"Would you like it?" I repeated.

"Yes, but—"

"Fine. I'll talk to your mother about it when she comes in."

I suspect the Redbone family was grateful to have one child taken off their hands. They may even have been grateful that he was being given opportunities, but they hesitated not a minute before agreeing that he could attend school in Benteen and stay with me during the school year.

So there I was, a middle-aged doctor with a twelve-year-old protégé, and having an affair with an unlettered builder. I thought my cup runneth over.

The sanitarium was completed in October of 1917, just in time for me to make the move before winter hit. It was a grand building, standing straight and tall, the windows even and regular as I had wanted them, the roof pitched high to shed snow. Upstairs were two large rooms, each with separate private facilities. Downstairs there was the huge kitchen, two small bedrooms, a living area and an office for me. Throughout, it had hardwood floors that gleamed and dark oak baseboards and woodwork, imported with some difficulty. The furniture that had once been Em's pride and joy, now worn and shabby, even seemed to brighten in its new surroundings, and it was a good thing, for I had put every penny I had into that building. New furniture was out of the question beyond the cheap beds with which I filled the upstairs rooms.

"You like it, lady doctor?" Eli and I stood outside, staring at the building early one evening as the sun faded.

"It's what I dreamed of, Eli. It looks just like I thought it should. Are you pleased?"

"Got to say I'm more proud of this than most anything else I've done," he acknowledged.

"Is it finished enough to have a dedication?"

"Dedication? What in the heck do you mean?"

"I want to have a ceremony, ask the new minister to bless the building for the use for which it was intended. Then maybe have punch and cookies and invite people to go through it before I move in."

"You do what you want," he said, obviously disinterested in my dedication ceremony.

"You must be there," I said blindly. "It's your building, too, and you need to share in the celebration."

"Hey, lady doctor, don't you know by now I don't have to do anything? But for you, if it's important, I'll be there."

We set the dedication for the following Sunday afternoon.

Eli was there, awkwardly stuffed into a suit he must have purchased from Whittaker's. I kept referring people to Mr. Able when they wanted to comment on the strength and solidity of the building, and he accepted their congratulations sincerely but solemnly, looking out of place all the while.

When the minister invoked God's blessing on the building and the work that would be done there, Eli bowed his head reverently, then snuck a look at me that nearly caused me to disgrace myself.

The dedication was a success. Everyone in town turned out, and they inspected every inch and corner of the sanitarium, ate almost ten dozen cookies, six batches of brownies and five angel food cakes, and drank gallons of fruit punch.

Tom was ecstatic, running through the crowd, explaining to people how he'd helped with this or that and where his room would be, until, at the end of the day, he drooped visibly. His first night's sleep in our new home began early and was sound.

Eli came to my bed that night. After making love to me gently and long, he said, "I'll leave tomorrow, you know, lady doctor."

I was silent a long time, fighting with my emotions. "I . . . I was afraid that you would soon. You can stay in Benteen, build something else here. I know I heard Ralph Whittaker talking to you about another addition to the store."

"Yeah, he did. But no, I can't stay. Can you leave with me?"

"You know I can't."

"I know. I just said that so you'd see how impossible either one is. If I stayed here, we couldn't go on like this forever. And besides, I'm a wanderer. I can't stay in one place."

"I guess I always knew that, but I hoped it would be different."

"You know what I guess I hoped? That you'd leave with me. It was like a fantasy I had. Once the sanitarium was built, you'd turn it over to someone else and take to the prairie with me."

"I couldn't. I've worked too hard, and Benteen is—"

"I know. I knew when Tom came to live with you. You do what you have to. And I'll do what I have to."

"Will you come to visit?"

"In the middle of the night?" he teased, then became serious. "I don't think so, lady doctor. I think we best just say this was a period in our lives, and now we'll go on to other things. Both of us. Ain't no sense looking back nor clinging to what once was."

I knew he meant it.

Tom and I watched him ride away from the sanitarium the next morning. Tom fretted and complained, saying loudly he didn't see why Eli had to go, until I spoke more harshly than I ever had and he quieted down. Eli gave me no sign of affection beyond a tip of his hat, and then he was gone without looking back. When he had gone a fair distance, I ran into the sanitarium and up to the second floor, where I could follow him until he became a speck on the prairie. Tom found me there, tears running down my face.

"Are you all right, Mattie?"

"Yes, Tom, I am. I'm sad and happy." He looked puzzled, but I knew that once again I had chosen Benteen, and it was the right decision.

EPILOGUE

She sat on the porch, rocking gently and staring beyond the edge of the town toward open farmland. Mid-July heat rose in waves above the crops, like the lines in an imperfect glass window. An occasional white cloud broke the blue of the sky, but the sun was merciless. It was Nebraska at its hottest, and Mattie Armstrong was grateful for the shade of the house, the cool of the tall trees planted near it. She had too often been out on that prairie in the midst of summer, and she knew the ferocity of the summer sun.

Deliberately, she headed for the stairs, carefully reached for the railing and started down the six small steps. Darned steps were too narrow! If she'd known years ago how she was going to age, she'd have had Eli build them wider.

Step by painful step, she proceeded off the porch and down the walk to the road, some fifty yards away. There she turned and looked back at the house and the trees she had planted to break the wind and soften the square construction she had insisted on because it spoke of permanence to her. When it was built, it was the finest building in Benteen, and until 1936, when the town built a hospital, it had been her sanitarium, the place where she could watch over her patients. After that, it had been home to countless young people in need of a little help to finish their education, start their lives in the right direction. Tom Redbone had set a precedent, she reflected. Looking again at the house, she told herself that it was still the finest building in town. She turned then to look at the new houses that had sprung up around her. Ranch-style, they called them, small one-story affairs. At least they hadn't cut her off from the prairie.

She was halfway back to the house when she heard the car. Tom Redbone, come to pay his daily call. He treated her as a duty, she regarded him as a nuisance, and they both depended on these daily visits.

Unfolding his long length from the maroon Pontiac, Tom called. "I suppose I'll have to help you back up those stairs."

"You just try," Mattie replied, grasping the railing and pulling herself up the first step.

Tom reached the foot of the steps before she gained the porch, but he simply stood and watched. At nearly forty years of age, he was tall, thin and a little stooped. A crooked nose, probably the result of a schoolyard battle long ago, kept him from being handsome, but his eyes were intense and blue, and his manner, warm and friendly. His patients generally adored him. His wife, however, was bored by him.

"Well," she said when they were both settled in rockers, "what problem have you brought to worry me today?"

"Let's see." Eyes twinkling, he gazed off into space, touching first one finger and then the next as though counting imaginary problems. "The office caught fire, grasshoppers got my wheat, the head nurse at the clinic quit . . ."

"Very funny."

"I don't feel funny. I came to tell you I'm leaving Benteen." The twinkle disappeared from his eye, and he was instantly sober.

It wasn't unexpected, but the words went through her like a knife, and she knew he heard her draw her breath in sharply.

"Mattie, it's not something you didn't expect."

"I . . . I don't know whether I expected it or not. It's

Susan, isn't it?"

"No!" He stood suddenly and began pacing the length of the porch. "It's partly Susan . . . but it's this town, the way I live, the kind of medicine I practice . . . I'm going back to the university, where I can practice medicine, still have a life for myself and be involved in medicine the way I want to. Not bound . . ."

"Bound by what? Your patients' needs?"

"Mattie, don't try to make me feel guilty. I've stayed here fifteen years. I've paid my dues." He stopped and stared at her. "I know, you stayed fifty, and you don't consider your dues paid yet. But I don't understand that. I don't understand the kind of life you've led. All I know is that I feel like something is going to explode inside me. I've got to do something different."

"And Susan?"

"She'll stay here, keep the farm. She won't be lonely long."

Mattie grunted. "Why don't we send Susan away and let you stay here?" She could not put into words her desperate need. She could not tell him what he should have known, that he was the son she never had, the child her own daughter would never be. Nor could she burden him with responsibility for carrying on the clinic she had established. Yet, selfishly, all these things were what she wanted to say.

"Mattie, don't joke."

"I know. It's a serious matter, and I'm sorry. I was . . . trying to be clever to hide how seriously I feel about it. I . . . It's your decision. I'll support whatever you decide."

He looked down at his toes, like an embarrassed child.

"I know," he muttered.

"I suppose Bella will leave, too." She said it haltingly, fearing to hear the answer. Her granddaughter frustrated her more than half the time, fussing over her as though she had lost her brains with her physical ability, but Mattie was proud of Bella. Somewhere, in five marriages and a final descent into alcoholism, Nora had done something right in raising that girl, something that she herself had failed to do with Nora. Bella made up for all the failures when she came home to Benteen to work in Tom's clinic.

"She'll stay and manage the clinic for someone else, just as she does for me. I've taught her well, if I do say so, and she's bright and capable."

"Bother! I know all that. Will she stay without you?"

"Why shouldn't she? She stays because of the clinic, not because of me."

"Tom Redbone, if you believe that, you're more thick-headed than I thought. The girl's in love with you." There, she had said it.

He looked away, embarrassed. "Don't be silly, Mattie. I'm married, and she's fifteen years younger than I am."

"Makes no difference." Was Bella part of the reason he thought of leaving? She decided to take him off the hook and change the subject. "When do you plan to leave?"

"God, Mattie, I don't know. I'm not planning to leave." He threw his hands in the air in a quick, exasperated gesture. "I haven't really decided to go. I just kind of tried that out on you."

"And what did you think of the reaction?" She asked it with wry bitterness. "Was I a good guinea pig?"

"Disappointing," he replied. "Here, let me take your

blood pressure, and I'll be on my way."

"Fiddlesticks. My blood pressure will be high, and you'll try to tell me I need more medicine than I do. Just go and leave me be."

But he stayed another fifteen minutes, sometimes staring into space, sometimes talking monosyllabically about the weather, the crops, the heat, a new patient or an old one. Mattie responded, letting him set the tone and watching him closely. Then, with another of his sudden, almost nervous gestures, he was gone.

She stayed on the porch long after he had left. It was selfish, she knew, to want him to stay in Benteen. She's raised him to be independent, since the day he came to her as a twelve-year-old, and if that independence took him away now, it was only right. Nor could she expect him to feel bound to Benteen, obligated to care for the health of its citizens as she had felt.

Would he go? She doubted it. If he did, would he be happier? She'd wondered that herself a thousand times, tempted always by practice offers in Omaha, once by a restless love. She had stayed, and now at eighty, she was sure she'd been right. But how could she make Tom understand that? And why did she feel responsible, as though it all came back to her? Tom's unhappiness, the bitterness of Nora, the betrayal of Em, the husband she had loved and then scorned, even the tragic lives of Sara Dinsmore and her father, now both dead and gone . . . Could she, would she have done it differently?

Slowly she got up and limped inside, passing through the living room with its dark walnut furniture and small Oriental rugs that Tom swore would kill her one day. Purposefully, she went to the old rolltop desk in the adjoining room—once it had been her office, but now it was a study, a place where she could pay her bills, write letters, read a little, and think back over a half century as the first woman doctor in Nebraska.

But today she had no time for reverie. Deliberately, she put paper in the typewriter and pulled her chair as close as she could, shifting her weight to ease the pain in her hip.

Arthritis, she thought, doesn't kill you, it just makes you wish it would, and it can kill your spirit. I've seen it happen before. What if, she wondered uncomfortably, I can't finish this . . . or can't finish it as honestly as I want to?

She stared at the blank paper. How did one begin? "I was born" seemed prosaic. So did a statement such as "My earliest memory . . ." Maybe she should explain about her family. How did you explain that tangle, that strange mixture of fierce love and slight shame with which she had grown up and which ultimately had been so central in shaping the course of her life? She began to type.

"My mother was an unmarried mother, fallen woman, they called her . . ."

Center Point Publishing

600 Brooks Road ● PO Box 1
Thorndike ME 04986-0001 USA

(207) 568-3717

US & Canada:
1 800 929-9108